Three of today's hottest writers
invite you to experience…

Sensual nights filled with…
Illicit Dreams by

VICKI LEWIS THOMPSON

The intoxicating thrill of…
Going All the Way by

CARLY PHILLIPS

The supreme satisfaction of being…
His Every Fantasy by

JANELLE DENISON

INVITATIONS TO

Seduction

Some offers are just too good to refuse….

Dear Reader,

Blame it on the bubbly…or in this case, on the sangria. *Invitations to Seduction* owes its creation to a gathering of friends in Chandler, Arizona, a bottle of sweet Spanish wine and an editor who was willing to listen.

It was there in Chandler that the four of us, five counting our editor, entertained the idea for a series based on a book of sexy invitations. You know, the ones you're supposed to share with a lover? The type that are sealed for secrecy, until you and your partner can discover the erotic mystery together? At first we planned just the novella collection, but our editor suggested two related books within the Blaze series introducing readers to a naughty book called *Sexcapades* and the sensual havoc and "happily ever afters" it ultimately causes.

The five of us had great fun linking the stories…and we hope you have equally as much fun reading them!

Happy reading,

Vicki Lewis Thompson
Carly Phillips
Janelle Denison
Julie Elizabeth Leto

VICKI LEWIS THOMPSON

CARLY PHILLIPS

JANELLE DENISON

INVITATIONS TO

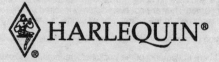

Seduction

HARLEQUIN®

TORONTO • NEW YORK • LONDON
AMSTERDAM • PARIS • SYDNEY • HAMBURG
STOCKHOLM • ATHENS • TOKYO • MILAN • MADRID
PRAGUE • WARSAW • BUDAPEST • AUCKLAND

ISBN 0-373-83574-4

INVITATIONS TO SEDUCTION

Copyright © 2003 by Harlequin Books S.A.

The publisher acknowledges the copyright holders of the individual works as follows:

ILLICIT DREAMS
Copyright © 2003 by Vicki Lewis Thompson

GOING ALL THE WAY
Copyright © 2003 by Karen Drogin

HIS EVERY FANTASY
Copyright © 2003 by Janelle Denison

CONTENTS

Dedication

To us—Vicki, Janelle, Carly and Julie!
All for one and one for all—
these stories are dedicated to good ideas,
good times and, mostly, to good friends.

Don't miss *your* invitation!

June 2003—*Looking for Trouble*
by Julie Elizabeth Leto (Blaze #92)

July 2003—*Invitations to Seduction*
"Illicit Dreams" by Vicki Lewis Thompson
"Going All the Way" by Carly Phillips
"His Every Fantasy" by Janelle Denison

August 2003—*Up to No Good*
by Julie Elizabeth Leto (Blaze #100)

ILLICIT DREAMS
Vicki Lewis Thompson

PROLOGUE

May

HUNTER JORDAN was getting some...again.

Lindsay peered at the lighted dial of her alarm clock. Sheesh. He'd had highly orgasmic sex less than an hour ago. At least that's what Lindsay had concluded from the breathless cries of his girlfriend and his own groan of satisfaction. Now they were starting over. What was with the man?

Or more to the point, *who* was with the man? A very lucky woman, that's who. A blond 38D of a woman, as she'd once seen with her own eyes. Meanwhile Lindsay, a 32B who hadn't had sex—orgasmic or otherwise—since she'd moved here last year, was forced to listen to the steady thump-thump-thump of Hunter's headboard hitting the wall that separated their apartments.

Well, okay, she wasn't exactly forced to listen. She could go into her living room, turn up Sting on the stereo and drown them out, which she'd done during their first go-round. Sort of. Towards the end she'd snuck back into her bedroom to catch the grand finale, pathetic creature that she was. Judging from the way his girlfriend had reacted during their six-month-long relationship, Hunter orchestrated really terrific finales.

Lindsay had to take her kicks where she could find them.

Apparently Hunter was about to create another big fat O for Silicon Sally. She knew because the moaning had commenced. No man had ever made Lindsay moan like that. Well, unless she counted the time that idiot Sherman had mashed her head up against the headboard, repeatedly, and nearly given her a concussion before he realized she was crying for help and not begging him to thrust harder.

Hunter would never make that kind of miscalculation. Anybody could tell he understood women from the way he'd photographed them for this month's swimsuit issue of *Instant Replay*. Lindsay was pretty sure his girlfriend was the one in the purple bikini on the cover. It was hard to tell since she tended not to parade outside Hunter's apartment in a string bikini, but her chest measurements were about right and her face had the high-cheekbone look of a professional model.

Oh, yeah, Hunter understood women, at least according to the cries of feminine pleasure coming through the wall. They escalated in pitch and reached a stirring crescendo. Lindsay was damned stirred, herself. She waited for Hunter to add his deep groans to the mix, but instead the girlfriend started gasping once again, running her words together—*yesohyesohyes*—in a clear indication that Hunter was going for a multi.

Lindsay flung the covers aside and got out of bed, heading for the living room and her stereo. Banging her fist on the wall wasn't an option. She'd been listening to this symphony two or three times a week for six months now, and banging on the wall at this point would let Hunter know she'd been playing voyeur.

She should just buy a vibrator and be done with it, but going down that road was admitting she really wasn't going to have sex with a guy for a very long time. As a perennial optimist, Lindsay kept hoping that wasn't true.

Stomping into the living room, she flipped on her CD player and jacked up the sound, operating by the light from a street lamp outside the window. Then she decided to eat a banana for the oral satisfaction. God, she needed a boyfriend. Hell, she needed a *date*.

Unfortunately, last year's decision to stop catching guys on the rebound had seriously narrowed the field. Her best friend Shauna said it was her nurturing Cancer personality at work. Whatever the reason, she had a real gift for attracting men who'd been recently dumped. Then, after she'd healed their broken hearts, the schmucks moved on. Apparently they didn't like being reminded that once upon a time they'd been extremely vulnerable.

She bit into the banana. Damned poor substitute. Increasingly, the world of men seemed to be divided into the recently dumped and the already involved. Shauna had somehow stumbled upon that rare species, the unattached and unwounded male, and was now engaged to him. Watching Shauna walk around with the satisfied expression of a woman who could have sex whenever she wanted didn't help Lindsay's frustration level any.

As her maid of honor, Lindsay also was required to spend time with Shauna in Divine Events, the wedding shop from hell. Oh, it would be a fabulous place if a girl happened to be having good sex, or even the prospect of good sex. They had this red leather book of sexual fantasies in the reception area, and the pages were meant to be torn out, according to Shauna, who had done her share of tearing. But then Shauna had a guy to act out those fantasies with.

Then there was Lindsay's private torture of living next door to a sex god with bedroom-brown eyes and a body built for loving. Hunter had been part of the already-involved category when he'd moved in, and he was still in that category, damn it. Lindsay couldn't imagine anybody dumping Hunter. He had that killer combo—bad-boy charisma and good-guy charm.

She'd observed the bad-boy charisma from afar, but she'd seen the good-guy charm up close, in the apartment's laundry room. After meeting there by chance one Saturday morning, she and Hunter had discovered they had so much fun talking while the clothes washed that they'd made a habit of it ever since. Therefore she could never, ever let him know that she could hear him having sex through their shared apartment wall. Too embarrassing.

And man-oh-man, did he have sex. Even over Sting at mega-decibels, Lindsay could hear the wild cries, both bass and treble this time, as Hunter and his chesty girlfriend shared their climactic moment. No doubt about it, Lindsay had to get a vibrator…or a genuine, testosterone-laden, certified-to-make-you-come, ready and extremely willing man.

CHAPTER ONE

July

AS HE DID every weeknight, Hunter took the "L" from the *Instant Replay* offices in downtown Chicago to his apartment building. Crammed in with other commuters, he tried to keep cool, but it wasn't easy. The furnace outside set at ninety-five degrees was trying to melt the train, plus, as usual, he was thinking about Lindsay Scott.

He wondered if she'd be home from the bank where she worked, wondered if this was the night he should go over and ask for a cup of sugar, or the current *TV Guide*, or a stamp or a couple of fresh batteries for his remote. Those were the best excuses he'd come up with, and they were all lame. Meanwhile, he was burning up with frustration.

The problem had started when they'd accidentally met in the laundry room. Ever since they'd decided to wash clothes together on Saturday mornings, he'd been having lust-filled dreams about

Lindsay. The first time it had happened, he'd thought it was because Pamela was away on a shoot and he was horny.

But then Pamela had come back from Arizona and they'd returned to their routine of wonderful sex. Yet the dreams about Lindsay hadn't stopped. In fact, they'd become more graphic. In his dream, she'd prance into the laundry room in her normal Saturday style, her brown hair caught up in a ponytail or in one of those butterfly clips, her freckled face without makeup, her shirttails tied at her waist and her ragged cutoffs brushing her smooth thighs.

She'd see him there and pause. Her blue eyes would darken with lust. And they'd do it on top of the washing machine.

Thoughts of Lindsay had started invading his daytime activities, too. The night he'd fantasized about Lindsay while having sex with Pamela, he'd known he had to face the situation like a man. And it wasn't Pamela's fault, so he'd hated like hell to hurt the woman who'd been a terrific bed partner for more than six months.

He'd tried to stroke her ego during the breakup dinner. She'd demanded to know if there was another woman, and he'd told a half truth when he'd said no. After all, he'd only cheated on Pamela in his dreams. Before meeting Lindsay, Hunter had thought maybe Pamela would wind up being his

happily-ever-after. Eventually. When he was ready
for that kind of thing.

Obviously he wasn't ready to be anybody's husband, though, if he could be distracted so easily
while having outstanding sex with a woman he
liked. Still, he had to find out where this obsession
with Lindsay would take him. Unfortunately, Lindsay knew he'd been involved with Pamela. And
although he'd broken off with her three weeks ago,
he couldn't appear at Lindsay's door with, ''Hi, my
girlfriend's been out of the picture for three weeks,
so let's have sex!''

The time just wasn't right for him to be so forward as to ask Lindsay out. Not yet. And he
couldn't use the laundry room as the venue for es-
calating the relationship. No, he'd leave that setup
alone, because it was so tied in with his fantasy
that he didn't trust himself to stay in control. He'd
considered switching banks, just so he'd have an
excuse to visit hers and have her wait on him at
the teller window. But that was way too obvious.

Better to find some reason to knock on her door
in the evening, and see how she reacted to that.
Sooner or later he'd come up with an excuse that
didn't sound stupid. Then he'd have to return whatever he'd borrowed, and maybe he'd bring her a
pizza as a thank-you. He'd take it slow. Eventually

he'd mention that he'd broken up with Pamela, but he'd have to make that reference casual.

If he played this wrong, Lindsay might think he was some callous jerk who discarded one woman and moved quickly onto the next. God, he hoped he wasn't that kind of person. On the surface, he seemed to be acting that way. Well, he'd just have to take the relationship with Lindsay at a snail's pace to prove that he wasn't that shallow.

The walk from the "L" station to the apartment house was filled with the kind of ugly heat and humidity mix that made him wonder how his grandparents had lived in Chicago without central air. They'd owned a brick house not far from here, and as a kid he hadn't noticed the temperature at grandma and grandpa's, probably because he'd spent his time running through the sprinkler or eating homemade peach ice cream. Apparently at the age of thirty-two he'd become a wuss about the weather.

He was still feeling hot and sweaty when he started down the hall toward his fourth-floor apartment. That thermostat was going down to *freeze,* baby. And a shower was definitely in his future. He wondered if Lindsay liked peach ice cream.

Then he noticed activity in front of her door, and suddenly he had no worries about the heat wave. She was talking with a delivery guy who had boxes stacked on a dolly. After a quick assessment of the labels, Hunter decided it was an unassembled entertainment center. A light clicked on in his brain.

"Hey, Lindsay," he called out as he passed. Boy, didn't she look sweet and summery in that white eyelet dress. Maybe he should change banks, no matter how obvious that was. With a teller like Lindsay it was a wonder any guy ever used the ATM.

She glanced up from the delivery slip she'd been signing. "Hey, Hunter."

"Looks like a weekend project."

"Yeah, I decided to be a grown-up and buy something to hold my stuff besides the old blocks and boards." She laughed and tucked her hair behind her ear. She'd left it down today, another tempting change from how she wore it on Saturdays.

"Good luck with it." Hunter decided she looked very much like a grown-up in her heels and nylons. Yowza.

"Thanks, Hunter."

Despite wanting to linger, he forced himself to keep walking toward his apartment door. Then he turned, as if his earlier brainstorm had just come to him. "Listen, putting those things together can be tricky. If you need another pair of hands, I'd be glad to help you." *Another pair of very eager hands.* Oh, jeez. No matter how he tried to beat his libido into submission, it wouldn't behave.

The delivery guy had already started wheeling the boxes into the apartment, but Lindsay poked her head back out to acknowledge his offer. "That's very generous of you. Do you happen to have a screwdriver?"

"Yeah. Sure." Somewhere. He hoped he hadn't made a tactical error. He was a magician with a camera but only barely adequate with hand tools. Well, knock-down furniture came with directions, even if they were usually written by folks with dicey English skills. He'd manage.

"Then I might call on you," Lindsay said.

"Anytime." Hunter waited until he was inside his apartment with the door shut before pumping his fist in triumph. *Yes!*

AN HOUR LATER, Lindsay sat on her living room floor surrounded by packets of nuts and screws, various lengths and widths of pressed wood laminated to look like cherry, her Swiss Army knife and a completely incomprehensible set of instructions. The knife was there for its many screwdriver options, but she had yet to screw anything.

Although she'd never assembled furniture in her life, she'd gambled on her above-average intelligence to get her through. Bad bet. Actually, the entertainment center had been a gamble on more than one front. Such a piece of furniture implied that she'd be staying home to be entertained. But for the past couple of months, she'd focused her attention on going out for that purpose. And she was sick of it.

Yes, she'd deliberately avoided her apartment at night so she wouldn't have to listen to Hunter get it on with his main squeeze. But she'd also tried, really tried, to find a guy of her own. Shauna had chipped in with fix-ups. Her girlfriends at the bank had lined up brothers, cousins, clients. Even the owners of Divine Events had offered a couple of possibilities. They'd obviously noticed how Lindsay eyed their red leather book with longing, noticed how much she wished she had a reason to tear out a page.

None of that concentrated effort had paid off by delivering a guy even a tenth as appealing as Hunter. She'd bought the entertainment center after deciding she'd rather stay home and listen to Hunter having sex in the next apartment than waste her time looking for a Hunter clone. There was only one Hunter Jordan, and he was taken. Sometimes life was like that.

Unfortunately, the first part of her plan, an entertainment center to hold the DVD player and enhanced sound system arriving tomorrow, seemed doomed to sit forever on the launching pad. Throwing the directions across the room, she adjusted one of the butterfly clips holding her hair off her neck and wondered what to do next. If she'd thought Hunter was serious about his offer, she might consider going over there and asking for his help.

Well, damn it, why not ask him? He'd said "anytime," and maybe he'd taken woodworking in high school. It wasn't like she'd planned this caper to lure him over to her apartment. Hopping to her feet, she went into her kitchen and checked to see if she had any beer in the refrigerator.

Good deal. She still had three cans. In her limited experience, when you asked a guy to do a guy thing for you, you needed to have some beer around. She was beginning to feel excited about the prospect of enlisting Hunter and she opened her door to head over to his place.

No sooner had she opened the door than she slammed it shut. His girlfriend was coming down the hall. Damn it to hell.

With a sigh of resignation she walked into her tiny kitchen, opened the refrigerator and took out one of her three beers. This turn of events called for a swig of something stronger than soda. She'd been gone so much she hadn't heard their bedroom symphony in a long time. She didn't want to hear it now, either.

Unfortunately she'd disconnected the speaker wires on her stereo in preparation for putting everything in the entertainment center. She couldn't even use Sting to get her out of this episode. At least one thing was certain—Hunter hadn't meant it when he'd said he'd help her "anytime." He should have added "anytime I'm not having sex with Silicon Sally."

As Lindsay debated whether to tackle the instructions again or put on her shoes and go to the deli for a sandwich, she heard Hunter's girlfriend yelling. Except she wasn't yelling in the way she usually did when she was with Hunter. This sounded a lot more like fighting than fooling around.

Fighting? Thoroughly ashamed of herself, Lindsay ran to the kitchen and grabbed a glass from the cupboard. She didn't know why a glass to the wall worked to make the sound clearer, but for some reason it did. No one would ever know that she'd used a glass a few times back in her pathetic days, when she'd been having vicarious sex with Hunter.

Whoops. Looks like she'd finally admitted to herself what she'd done in the first months of being his neighbor. Putting herself in his girlfriend's place. Ah, self-knowledge could be painful.

She wasn't hearing sexual things tonight, however. Tonight his girlfriend was furious. Lindsay balanced the glass against the bedroom wall, pressed her ear against the bottom and sipped her beer while she listened.

"You thought I cared about you?" the girlfriend bellowed. She had good lungs, that one. "It was about two things—sex and your connections at the magazine. Those are the only reasons I stayed!"

Hunter was harder to hear because he wasn't shouting. Lindsay thought he said something like "I always cared for you," or maybe it was "I'll always care for you." She hoped it was the first and not the second, because this sounded like a really serious fight. If so, she wanted Hunter to walk away with his heart in one piece.

Then she had to admit the chances of that weren't too good. He'd acted as if he really liked this woman, and here she was telling him that he'd been nothing more than a convenient stud service and a good business connection. What a witch.

But if Hunter ended up with a broken heart, then he'd move from the category of already involved to the category of recently dumped, and Lindsay had sworn off that category. Yes, but this was *Hunter* she was talking about. Maybe for him, the star of her forbidden fantasies, she could make an exception. *No,* damn it. No exceptions. She'd been down that road too many times.

"And I'll tell you something else," proclaimed

Hunter's soon-to-be-ex. "It was average sex! On a scale of ten, I'd rate it a five-minus!"

"Ouch." Lindsay's heart ached for Hunter. He was sure to be wounded after this tirade. But if what they'd been doing didn't rate any more than a five-minus, she should win an Oscar.

"Have a nice life!" yelled the woman.

When Hunter's apartment door slammed, Lindsay jumped. It was over. Hunter, the guy she'd never expected to be dumped, had been horribly dumped. She couldn't imagine why. Maybe *Instant Replay* wouldn't promise the model she'd be on the cover of the next swimsuit issue and she'd thought it was Hunter's fault. Or maybe she was just plain crazy.

But poor Hunter. The apartment next door was silent now, and she pictured him slumped in a chair, staring at the wall as he questioned his self-worth and his sexual prowess. Lindsay had listened to plenty of guys tell her how unmanned they'd felt after being dumped. Hunter had been totally emasculated. What guy could handle hearing that he wasn't good in bed? None.

She couldn't stand it. Nobody should have to be alone at a moment like this. She would pretend she hadn't heard them fighting and ask him to help her put the entertainment center together. Demonstrating his manly skill with a screwdriver might bolster his sense of self. He needed a friend, and she would be that friend. It wouldn't go beyond friendship, though. She'd made a resolution, and she was sticking to it.

HUNTER SIGHED and ran a hand through his still-damp hair. Pamela had caught him in the shower, and he'd answered the door in a towel. Yeah, he'd hoped it might be Lindsay asking him to help her with the entertainment center. He was guilty of thinking that the caught-in-the-shower routine might make an impression on her that he could capitalize on later.

He'd probably had a smile on his face when he'd come to the door, too. That's what he got for not checking the peephole first. Pamela's opening move had been to smile back and reach for the knot holding the towel around his hips. When he'd stopped her, all hell had broken loose.

Well, damn. He'd hoped she'd just go away, but apparently she hadn't believed that he didn't want her back in his bed. He doubted very many men, if any, had turned down sex with Pamela. He was a little surprised that he had. Fully clothed, Pamela had the kind of body that made guys forget about being politically correct. Pamela inspired a full-out ogle. Naked, she was centerfold material.

She was also incredibly self-absorbed. At first

he'd been turned on by her willingness to flaunt her body in front of him. She loved to masturbate, and she'd been perfectly happy to let him watch. He'd never met a woman so uninhibited. He had to admit the sex had been amazing.

Funny, but she'd just flung at him the same words he could have said to her. For him, it had been all about the sex. In a way, he owed her, because she'd opened his eyes to inventive games men and women could play in the bedroom. But with Pamela, once they'd moved beyond mutual sexual pleasure, there was nothing left.

So maybe that was the source of his obsession with Lindsay. He longed to take the anything-goes mentality he'd learned from Pamela and apply it to someone he could talk to afterward. Or he had longed to do that, before Pamela had graded him. Five-minus. Damn. He told himself that she'd said that because she was hurt. But she'd had a lot of experience, and maybe he was below average in her book.

Hell, how did a guy ever know what a woman thought of his technique in the sack? Faking was easy for a woman. Now he wondered if all that time she'd been pretending to have multiple orgasms to guarantee that she'd have a good shot at another swimsuit edition cover. He'd sure thought she was really coming, and he'd felt contractions, but maybe a woman with good muscles could fake the contractions, too. He didn't know what to believe.

Standing here wasn't accomplishing anything, though, so he might as well get dressed and figure out what to do about dinner. Lindsay probably had her entertainment center put together by now, so even that supposedly golden opportunity had likely fizzled. With another long sigh, he started back to his bedroom, his hand loosening the knot of the towel.

The doorbell chimed before he could reach the bedroom. As he retraced his steps, he reminded himself of the lesson he'd learned the hard way this afternoon. From now on, he was never, ever opening his front door without looking through the peephole.

Wonder of wonders, Lindsay stood on the other side in a drool-worthy halter top and those cutoffs she liked to wear. She was barefoot. Hunter had never seen her toes because she wore running shoes down to the laundry room. He noticed that her toenails were a bright coral. Sexy.

He opened the door, although by now his hair was too dry for him to look as if he'd just stepped out of the shower. In fact, he might look dorky, as if he was a nudist who couldn't wait to get home and get naked.

Sure enough, Lindsay's smile faltered as her

gaze swept downward. "Uh, I didn't mean to disturb you."

"You didn't. I was in the shower, and then…then I was checking out the Cubs game." *Weak, extremely weak.*

For some reason she seemed to buy it, even though his TV screen was dark. "Oh. Did you, um, want to watch the game?"

"Nah. They're losing."

"Ah. All righty, then." Her smile returned. "Did you mean it when you said you'd help me with the entertainment center? Because I'm in terrible trouble over there. I can't make heads or tails of the instructions."

Shaky confidence or not, he'd be a fool to turn down a chance like this. "I'd be glad to help you. Let me get dressed, and I'll be right over."

"Super. I have beer."

"Beer?"

She paused, looking flustered. "You know, to drink after you help me." She peered at him. "Maybe you don't drink beer."

"I do drink beer." He thought the opportunity was expanding exponentially. "Maybe we can order a pizza, too, once we get the entertainment center built."

"Perfect!" She beamed at him. "Then I'll see you soon."

"Five minutes."

"Great." She started back to her apartment. Then she turned back. "And bring your screwdriver. That's where I'm really gonna need a hand. I don't know how you'll feel about helping once you find out how many screws are involved."

He had no idea how he kept a straight face. "I think I can handle it."

Apparently what she'd said finally registered, because she turned red. "I mean, it looks pretty complicated."

"I knew that's what you meant." He bit the inside of his cheek to keep himself from laughing.

"Bye." Turning, she dashed back inside her apartment.

Hunter closed his door and grinned. How refreshing. A woman who could still blush. Now if he actually managed to help her with the entertainment center, he'd be making progress. And down the line, way down the line, maybe he'd discover what it was like to make love to Lindsay Scott...well, after he'd recovered from Pamela's grading system. Then again, a woman who could blush might not notice that he was only a five-minus.

CHAPTER TWO

OMIGOD, OMIGOD, OMIGOD. Lindsay leaned against her closed door in shock. She'd seen Hunter practically naked. She knew the pattern of his chest hair—little swirls over his pecs and a furry line down to his belly button. She knew the color of his nipples—dark rose. She knew where he had the cutest little mole—to the left of that impressive six-pack.

And under his white towel, he'd been wearing...absolutely nothing. How she'd ever held a normal conversation without drooling right onto his bare feet was a miracle. But she hadn't held a normal conversation. She'd invited him to bring his tool so they could screw.

She put her shaking hands to her still-hot cheeks. How could she have said such a thing? She never slipped up like that. But then she'd never been confronted with the sight of her love god draped in a towel, either. And the big question, the positively *huge* question, was how in heaven's name had that nutcase of a girlfriend walked out on Hunter? Hunter wearing a towel, no less!

Whoever that insane woman was, she must have stopped taking her meds. No mentally healthy female would stand there looking at Hunter in a towel and proceed to break up with him. Incomprehensible. Unless…unless Hunter had a very small…no, not likely. Even though Lindsay hadn't actually seen what was under that towel, God wouldn't create an Adonis like Hunter and give him a tiny tool. No way.

It wouldn't matter to her, of course. Small, large or in-between was of no consequence, because she wouldn't be having anything to do with that part of his anatomy. She only wanted to cheer him up after he'd been slam-dunked by the vicious ex-girlfriend. Even if he was under-endowed—which Lindsay doubted, and it made no difference *anyway*—he didn't deserve that sort of goodbye speech featuring a grade of five-minus.

Sherman, now there was a five-minus for you. Maybe even a three-minus, considering the way her head had hurt for two days. There was no way Hunter, with a body like that and a smile like that and big brown eyes like that, could be in the same league with Sherman. Lindsay trusted her instincts there.

She was still leaning against the door when

Hunter tapped on it, which made her jump about two feet in the air. She glanced at the clock on her living room wall and, sure enough, she'd been sagging against the door, recovering, for five minutes. Hunter was here.

Opening the door, she held onto the knob and cocked one hip, trying to fake total relaxation, as if she hadn't just seen him almost naked. "Hi, there." *I see you're dressed now. Damned shame.*

"Hi."

As she stared at his Cubs T-shirt and khaki shorts, she seemed to develop X-ray vision. His clothes miraculously vanished except for his briefs, or boxers or whatever covered his package. She had no mental picture for that area. Nor would she ever have. Nope. Not ever.

"I found my screwdriver." He held it up, all fourteen inches of it.

"Wow." She stood back and let him into the apartment. "Now that's a screwdriver." She wondered if men bought big screwdrivers as some kind of compensation device. Not that it mattered, of course. Not to her. She wasn't in the market for a guy on the rebound, whether he was packing a big screwdriver or a small screwdriver.

"It's probably too big for this job, though," he said. "It was the only one I could find. I think I used this on the car."

''I wouldn't know if it'll work or not.'' She gestured toward the mess on the floor. ''Obviously, I couldn't even figure out how the parts fit together, let alone which screws go in which holes.'' And that sounded decidedly sexual. She hadn't meant it to. Really, she hadn't. She would not look at the fly of his shorts. Would not.

Hunter glanced at the scattered pieces and tapped the blade of the screwdriver against his palm. ''Did it come with directions?''

Yes, and I'll bet I could come, too, if you directed me to a bed. She had to stop this. Everything reminded her of sex. ''You mean the ones I threw under my sofa bed?'' Now why had she told him it was a sofa bed? Did he care? Did she need to bring the word *bed* into the conversation? *No.* But she was obsessed with the topic of sex right now. She stepped around two boards and picked up the printed booklet lying on the floor.

He cleared his throat. ''Those sofa beds are great for company. That looks like a good one.''

And he qualified as company, so there you go. ''I got it for when my folks visit.'' That was better. Talking about her very conservative parents ought to straighten her up. ''But I let them have my bed and I sleep out here. It's amazingly comfortable. Nice and firm.'' Or maybe she couldn't be straightened up, not with a man like Hunter on the premises.

He eyed the blue plaid cushions. "It looks like it would be comfortable."

"Almost like a real bed." *Want to test it out?*

"And when you get this entertainment center put together," he gestured toward the scattered pieces with the enormous screwdriver, "you'll be all set to watch movies or listen to music in bed."

"Sure will." Oh, baby. She wanted to pull that bed out right now, and let the entertainment center remain in pieces forever. She'd lay money that Hunter was a lot more entertaining than anything she'd stack on those shelves. And she was convinced, despite what his girlfriend had said, that his big ol' tool could do the job just right.

"Then I guess we should get it together." He put out his hand. "Let me take a look at those directions."

As Lindsay gave him the booklet, she reminded herself that her goal was to make him feel better by letting him help her construct the entertainment center. It was not in her job description to mend his ego by having sex with him on the sofa bed and telling him that he was so not a five-minus. She wasn't even supposed to know that he'd been graded and then sent to Dumpsville.

But she did know, and as she sat on the sofa bed

next to him watching him earnestly study the directions, she thought about the cushy mattress folded right underneath them. Hunter looked like such a good guy, such a sweet guy. She could imagine his girlfriend's words running through the back of his mind, even now. They were terrible words, and Lindsay wondered if putting together an entertainment center would be enough comfort.

AN HOUR LATER, Hunter gazed at the wobbly structure he'd leaned up against the wall so it wouldn't fall over. Several pieces hadn't made it into the design. They lay accusingly on the carpet, looking significant. He studied the directions again, wondering where he'd gone wrong.

"Beer?" Lindsay walked out of the kitchen with an icy can in each hand.

She hadn't been much help on the construction, but he'd loved every minute of her hovering over him while he tried to figure out the combination to this entertainment center. "I thought that was for after we finished."

She grinned at him as she handed him the open beer. "That's not finished?"

"Does it look finished to you?" He took a swig of the cold beer.

"Well...." She squinted at the assembly, which had begun to lean to the left. "It's still a little unstable, I guess.'' Then she brightened. ''Maybe once we put the TV on it, that will make it stand better.''

''You put the TV on it, and it'll be goodbye TV, hello Dumpster. This baby needs more work before you put anything on it.''

''If you say so. But I think we should take a break.'' She flopped down on the sofa bed and took a long swallow of her beer.

''I guess you're right.'' He joined her, careful not to get too close. She was awfully damned appealing. They sat there for a while, just drinking their beer and surveying the entertainment center.

''You know, it doesn't look so bad,'' she said finally.

''The more beer you drink, the better it'll look.''

''Good idea.'' She took another sip. ''You hungry?''

''Yeah, as a matter of fact.'' This was fun, exactly how he'd pictured hanging out with Lindsay. No pressure. Easy companionship. They'd muddled through the construction of her furniture without getting into a fight. She didn't seem the least upset that he wasn't a maestro with the screwdriver.

''Then let's have a pizza delivered,'' she said. ''Is veggie okay?''

''I can go with veggie. I figure it's a painless way to get healthy stuff into your diet.''

"Exactly." She popped up, grabbed her cordless phone from the wall next to the kitchen and phoned in their order.

While she did that, he slid off the sofa and sat on the floor next to the extra pieces of wood. Then he picked up the directions again.

"I don't care if we have boards left over." Lindsay sat down next to him and leaned against the sofa bed, stretching her tanned legs in front of her while she continued to sip her beer. "I could use them for shelves under my bathroom vanity."

"But we're not supposed to have boards left over. That's why it's unstable." He leaned back next to her so their shoulders touched, just barely. Cozy. Not too cozy. Just nice. Man, did she have terrific legs. Once more they sat in easy silence, sipping their beer.

"It needs more support," Hunter said at last. The beer was making him very mellow, and he remembered he hadn't had much to eat for lunch, so the alcohol was probably hitting him faster than it normally would.

"Well, I think we should just screw it to the wall and call it good," Lindsay said.

Instantly, cozy went to hot. He now had a picture of Lindsay up against the wall, her raggedy shorts down around her ankles. He tried to put the image out of his mind. "The super would go apeshit if we did that. Besides, you couldn't take it with you when you move." Now there was a depressing thought, Lindsay moving.

"I'm not moving." Her shoulder nudged his and her silky thigh brushed his leg. "Let's screw it to the wall."

He liked the subtle body contact, but he wished she'd quit saying that. He was having a tough time erasing the idea of her bare tush up against the plaster, her legs wrapped around his hips and her halter top untied. "We'd have to find the studs first."

"I know where one is."

He glanced at her, wondering if she meant what he thought she did. "Yeah?" He sounded a little raspy.

"Yeah." She pushed herself to her feet and smiled at him.

If she held out her hand and asked him into the bedroom, he wondered if he could resist.

But she didn't. Carrying her beer can with her, she sashayed over to the wall and knocked on a section of it. "There's a stud right there. I used to have a picture there but I took it down yesterday. The nail hit solid wood when it went in."

"Oh." He didn't know whether to be glad she wasn't coming on to him or sorry. Wait a minute. She didn't know that he'd broken up with his girlfriend. If she started coming on to him, that would be a bad thing. That would mean she was trying to break them up. That wouldn't be nice.

"So here's how we can do it." She stood in front of the lopsided entertainment center and pushed it into position with both hands, which made her cute little bottom stick out. "We nail a board to the back, and use those long screws we have left over to lock this baby right up against the wall. What do you think?"

He thought she was way too sexy, and he could feel an erection coming on. "I think we need to unscrew the top board and put in another shelf. That's what we're missing, is that extra shelf."

"That's too much work. Let's use the stud and a nice long screw." She gazed at him, a challenge in her blue eyes.

He couldn't shake the idea that she was coming on to him. He was debating whether to ask her point-blank whether she was or not when the doorbell rang.

"Pizza's here." She let go of the entertainment center, which sagged even more to the left.

Saved by the pizza. He didn't really want to confront this issue, did he? If she said no, she wasn't coming on to him, he'd feel like an idiot. If she said yes, then he'd have to think less of her for trying to steal another woman's boyfriend. He wasn't another woman's boyfriend anymore, but Lindsay didn't know that.

Setting down his empty beer can, he got to his feet and reached in his back pocket for his wallet. "Let me get it."

"Absolutely not. You're helping me with my entertainment center, so this is my treat." She grabbed her purse from a hook by the door.

"Considering the way that entertainment center is listing to the left, I should be buying."

"Nope." She opened the door, took the pizza box from a kid in a red shirt and thrust a couple of bills at him. "Thanks. Keep the change."

"Okay," Hunter said as she closed the door, "you win. But next time, it's on me."

"Fine." She approached with the pizza box, paper napkins tucked in the side flap. "We could sit in the kitchen, but I'd rather stay out here and study our work in progress."

"Sounds good to me. Want me to get us each another beer?"

She frowned. "Oh. Now that's a wee bit of a problem. I'm out."

"It's absolutely no problem. I have some in my fridge. Be right back."

"I'll leave the door open."

"Just like in *Friends*," he said with a grin.

"I know! And *Seinfeld* was like that too. Nobody

in those shows ever locked a door. Or knocked, for that matter.''

''Want me to knock?''

''No.'' She laughed. ''I'll know it's you, silly. Just go get us some more beer. This project requires more beer.''

''I agree.'' Smiling to himself, he hurried down the short stretch of hall to his door, unlocked it and walked quickly into his kitchen. He couldn't remember the last time he'd had so much fun. This was great, cruising back and forth between his apartment and hers, ordering pizza, sharing their stashes of beer.

He still had to wonder about that *use a stud and a nice long screw* remark, but maybe that was the beer talking. One beer had made him feel pretty damned loose, and she weighed a lot less than he did. The alcohol could have affected her even more, especially if she hadn't had much to eat today, either.

Grabbing a six-pack from the bottom shelf of his refrigerator, he closed the door. For one brief moment he wondered if he should take all six cans over there. If one beer encouraged Lindsay to make suggestive remarks, he wondered what three would accomplish.

He shouldn't want to find out. After all, he'd promised himself this would be a slow, careful campaign. It would take place over weeks, not hours. Getting Lindsay plowed wasn't part of the program.

Ah hell, he doubted they'd drink more than one more apiece, but it was simpler to take the whole thing than to pry a couple out. Then again, if he took the whole six-pack, and matters got out of control, sexually speaking…would he really turn down an opportunity like that?

Being a realist, he had to admit he might not. Under these circumstances, when a woman was throwing out comments about studs and long screws, a guy might be wise to put a couple of condoms in his pocket. He didn't expect to use them—he certainly didn't *plan* to use them. Come to think of it, taking them along might jinx the possibility of sex, just like carrying an umbrella always kept it from raining.

Well, that settled it. He'd take two condoms as a surefire way to keep from having sex with Lindsay.

THE PIZZA soaked up some of the beer in Lindsay's system, which was a good thing. After the half can she'd had before inviting Hunter over and the full can she'd had before the pizza arrived, she was feeling way too frisky and way too willing to bend her rule about avoiding guys on the rebound. Earlier, she'd flirted outrageously with him, but after a couple of warm, cheesy slices of most excellent pizza, she'd regained control of her urges.

"So you're happy with this apartment, then?" Hunter asked, finishing off his fourth slice of pizza.

"Uh, sure." She realized she'd been watching him eat with a little too much rapt attention, but he had such a nice mouth, and watching those even, white teeth bite into the pizza gave her a thrill. "On good days I can walk to work, and on hot days like today, or in the winter, I take the bus." And she lived next door to Hunter, which was really the only perk she cared about.

"I like it, too. It's a good place. Quiet." Hunter drained his beer.

"Pretty quiet." Oops. She should have just agreed with him. "I mean, yes, it's quiet." *Mostly*.

He glanced at her. "What do you mean by *pretty quiet?* Am I making too much—"

"You look like you could use another beer." She jumped up and grabbed the empty can from his hand.

"Well, I—"

"I'm going to have one, too." She quickly swallowed the last of hers. Good grief. The last thing he needed to think about was the wild lovemaking he'd enjoyed with his girlfriend, the she-devil who had just dropped him like a bad habit.

"Are you sure you want another beer?" he called after her.

"Absolutely." She took their empties and escaped into the kitchen. Once there she knocked her forehead softly against the front of the refrigerator. She shouldn't be allowed to drink and talk.

Pretty quiet, indeed. Her tongue was getting looser and looser. She would not drink this beer she was getting out, only pretend to drink it. One more beer and no telling what she'd say. Or do.

As she walked back into the room, she decided to maneuver a change of subject. After handing him his beer, she remained standing, her attention on the entertainment center. "I have a new idea. I can prop my easy chair up against the side that's leaning. In fact, if you'll hold my beer, I'll move the chair."

He waved a hand in protest. "Don't go moving the chair over there yet. That will look dumb." He patted the floor next to him. "C'mon and sit down and we'll talk about other options."

"I think the chair's a great option." But she sat down next to him, anyway, because she really didn't want to drag it over there right this minute. It was a very heavy chair.

"Propping the chair against the entertainment center is not a great option, even if it looked good, which it won't," he said. "Because then you won't be able to see the TV from the chair. Sometime you might have people over and need that chair for watching TV."

"Maybe."

"After we finish this beer, we'll take the top shelf off and put in the middle one. That'll fix the problem."

"Okay." Now she'd done it. He expected her to finish the whole can because she'd made a big deal about wanting it.

"Listen, Lindsay, I've been thinking about something. My apartment's on the end, so you're the only neighbor I could hear, and I don't get any noise from your apartment. From the way you bolted when we started discussing this, I have to believe I'm the one who's been making too much noise. Have I?"

She took a gulp of her beer and thought about what a rotten liar she was. "Oh, not really."

"Have I been disturbing you?"

"Nope, not at all."

"I think I have. Your face is kind of red, like you're embarrassed about something."

She wondered if there was biofeedback training to stop blushing. "Listen, you really haven't bothered me. The thing is, I'm usually here by myself, so naturally you wouldn't hear me." *Yikes, girl, after jamming one foot in your mouth, now you have both of them in there.* "What I meant to say is—"

"Hold it. I'm getting a picture here." He scanned the room. "Your apartment floor plan is flip-flopped from mine, which means that your bedroom...oh, good lord."

She couldn't look at him. Instead she took another healthy swallow of her beer and stared at the sagging entertainment center.

Hunter cleared his throat. "Lindsay, please tell me you can't hear every single thing that goes on in my bedroom."

"Not...really clearly." *Except when I put a glass to the wall.*

He groaned and sank back against the sofa bed. "You heard it all. God, now I'm the one who's embarrassed. If I hadn't had two-plus beers, I'd probably be so embarrassed I'd have to leave right now. But instead I'll just stay here and ask if there's any way in hell you can forget all about what you heard."

Not a snowball's chance in hell. She pressed the cool aluminum can to her hot cheek. "It's no big deal. I think we're too uptight about such things, anyway. I mean, back in frontier days, families had to live in one big room, and don't you suppose that—"

"Lindsay." He put down his beer, caught her

chin and turned her to face him. "I'm sorrier than I can say, and I promise you this—you won't be hearing that anymore."

She looked into his brown eyes, so filled with regret, and she felt like the biggest jerk in the world for reminding him that his girlfriend had walked out on him only hours ago. "She's an idiot."

He smiled gently and stroked his thumb over her chin. "No, she's not," he said softly. "She just—"

"With the way she was moaning, there's no way you're a five-minus!" Then she squeezed her eyes shut. "I didn't mean to say that. I'm sorry, Hunter. I could have gone all night without saying th—"

His mouth covered hers, slicing off her apology.

Considering how she'd bungled things, she thought she'd better put down her beer and kiss him back. It was the neighborly thing to do.

CHAPTER THREE

HUNTER WOULDN'T HAVE KISSED Lindsay if she'd
kept her eyes open. But when she squeezed them
shut as she rattled off her apology, he couldn't resist. And the minute he kissed her, the condoms
started burning a hole in his pocket.

She tasted of pizza and beer, a combo he loved
on their own. Add in the plumpness of her lips, the
warm slide of her tongue against his, the little
whimper that made him immediately hard, and he
was ready to unwrap a raincoat.

No. He wouldn't do that, even though she was
winding her arms around his neck and opening her
mouth for some serious tongue play. The bare skin
of her back was so smooth, so warm. He wanted
to get closer, just a little bit closer. Mouth-to-mouth
was good, but he wanted more body contact. Body
contact was okay if they kept their clothes on.

If he moved his legs this way, and she moved
her legs that way…she followed his lead, shifting
her weight, aligning her torso with his. Oh, excellent. Chest to chest. With only her halter top and

his T-shirt in the way, he could feel her nipples poking against him—a very encouraging sign.

She was as much into this kiss as he was. If her nipples were hard, then he could be reasonably sure other things were happening in that compact little body of hers. Things he'd fantasized about for weeks.

He moaned without meaning to. She wiggled closer. That little wiggle gave him a breast rub that nearly knocked him out. There was something to be said for firm, high breasts that stayed put, bra or no bra.

Although he made his living taking photos of women with extravagant measurements, this was what he really liked—classic proportions, a size that fit his palm when he cupped her breast, when he massaged it, feeling the fullness under his fingers, exactly as he was doing right now....

Whoops. He hadn't meant to do that, either, but she whimpered again when he stroked his thumb over her nipple, so he could hardly stop, could he? And the kiss was getting hotter and wetter by the minute. Lots of heavy breathing going on here. Damn, it felt great to stroke her like this.

Before he could control the urge, he'd pulled at the ties holding the halter top around her neck. It was a mistake to untie them, and he knew it was a mistake, but she broke their intense lip-lock long enough to murmur "yes." That word was enough to make him abandon all thoughts of backpedaling. He was committed to at least this much of a make-out session.

He couldn't have retied that halter, anyway, not with the way he was shaking. The only thing to do was pull that material down and out of the way so he could bring both hands into the equation. Mmm. Perfection. His mouth had been very busy enjoying her mouth, but now his hunger shifted. Breasts that felt this good would taste even better.

He lifted his mouth from hers and dragged in some air. "L-Lindsay…" Damn, he was so worked up he was stuttering. "I want—"

"Me, too, oh, me, too." And with that she shifted her body yet again, pulling him down with her. They knocked over both beer cans.

He didn't care, but it was her carpet. "Lindsay—"

"Leave them." She was panting, which made her chest heave and those perfect breasts quiver. "Just—"

"You bet." Her tight nipples claimed all his attention. And she was incredibly responsive. Every flick of his tongue made her gasp. When he finally settled down to some intense oral stimulation, she dug her fingers into his scalp and arched right up off the floor, moaning his name.

Good thing she did that, because for a moment there he couldn't remember his name. Her cry reminded him of who he was, and what he didn't intend to do tonight. Unfortunately his penis had a whole different take on the matter. Through no conscious decision of his own, he found himself wedged between her thighs.

Worse yet, she'd begun rocking her hips against him. A continuation of that move would have predictable results, and if he was going to come, he damn sure wasn't going to do it like that. With a groan he forced himself to relinquish her breasts and rise to his hands and knees. He wobbled there, breathing hard, and looked down upon his fantasy woman.

They weren't on top of the washing machine, but otherwise all the elements were in place. Her blue eyes had darkened with lust, exactly as he'd imagined they would, and her hair was coming loose from its butterfly clip. Her halter top was pulled down and her round, sweet breasts glistened from all that contact with his mouth.

The only part left was to strip away her panties and cutoffs. He tried to remember why that was a bad idea. Funny, but right now it seemed like a very *good* idea. She looked ready. He was definitely ready.

She struggled for breath. "Why...why did you

stop? Is it because I'm not very..." Her hands went to her breasts in the first self-conscious move she'd made since he'd kissed her.

"No!" He sank back on his heels so he could grasp her hands and gently ease them away, leaving her breasts bare again. "I love to look at you, touch you, taste you. You're wonderful, everything I want."

She searched his expression, as if she didn't believe him.

He could imagine what this was about. She was comparing her endowments with Pamela's. He could tell her that Pamela's generous breasts had never turned him on like this, but he didn't want Pamela's name to be part of what they were sharing. "I stopped because I want you too much. I'm losing control. I didn't intend—"

"Me, either." The anxiety cleared from her eyes, and the lust came back in a rush. Freeing her hand from his grasp, she reached down and unfastened the metal button at the waistband of her cutoffs. "But now, if we don't finish this, I think I'll go crazy."

He swallowed. "Lindsay, are you sure?"

"Yes." She pulled down the zipper. "And while I'm slipping into something more comfortable, like my birthday suit, you can go next door and get condoms. I'm sure you have some over there."

"I, um, don't have to go next door."

Her eyebrows lifted.

"I thought…" Boy, did this sound stupid, but at the time it had made perfect sense. "When I went to get the beer, I—"

"You planned this?" Some of the light went out of her eyes.

"No! I didn't, I swear! I thought by putting a couple of condoms in my pocket, I'd guarantee that we wouldn't have sex. You know, how whenever you take an umbrella, it never rains."

The light returned to her eyes and the corners of her mouth tilted up. "Well, guess what?"

His chest was so tight with anticipation that he could barely breathe. "What?"

"It's raining."

LINDSAY HAD TRIED to behave herself. She'd really tried. But the minute Hunter had kissed her, she'd sensed his desperation. He needed to make love to someone tonight to validate his sexual ability and wipe out the self-doubt caused by his ex and her grading system. When confronted by that kind of need, especially coming from a babelicious guy like Hunter, Lindsay couldn't turn away.

Not to mention that pumping up his sexual confidence would be no hardship. So far, on a scale of ten, she'd rank him a fifty-eight. Fifty-eight and moving up. She wasn't kidding about needing to finish this. *Right now.*

Then there was the other persuader, too. Once he'd worked himself in between her thighs, once she'd felt the impressive bulge representing his package, she was ready to take him on sight unseen.

She'd had a moment of angst when he'd called a halt, though. After all, she didn't have the D-cup banquet Hunter was used to. But the look in his brown eyes when he'd reassured her had been more than convincing. He was still looking at her that way, not taking his eyes off her except for the split second required to yank his T-shirt over his head.

She managed to pull off her halter top, but then the view of Hunter getting naked sidetracked her. She'd been afraid she'd never see that glorious chest again, and here it was, available for touching, kissing, full body contact. Her mouth began to water.

Then he took the condom packets out of his pocket, which reminded her that time was a-wasting. She lifted her hips from the floor and was about to shove her panties and cutoffs down when he stood, unzipped his shorts and got rid of both shorts and briefs in one smooth move.

The sight of his very large, very erect penis immobilized her completely. Slowly she sank back to the carpet, her gaze riveted to that top-of-the-line sexual equipment. No way could a presentation like that result in a five-minus. No way.

"Is something wrong?" His voice was thick, a perfect complement to the part of him that had totally captured her imagination.

"Everything's right," she murmured as a fresh rush of moisture dampened her panties even more. "Extremely right."

"Lindsay, don't think you have to build me up because of that...that comment Pamela made about me."

So that was her name. Pamela. "Was the woman blind?"

His smile was a little off-center. "Size isn't everything. And I—"

"It's a damned fine start!" Galvanized into action, she shimmied out of her now soaked panties and cutoffs.

He caught his breath. "So beautiful," he said softly as he sank back down to his knees and positioned himself exactly where he'd been before. Only this time, nothing was between them... nothing at all.

Making no move to pick up one of the condom packets, he stayed right where he was and looked his fill, his gaze hungry. That surprised her. This was a man used to swimsuit models, after all. The way he was looking at her, she'd think that he hadn't had sex in a year.

She was the one who hadn't had sex in a year. She could imagine the starving expression on *her* face.

Bracing his hands on either side of her shoulders, he leaned down and kissed her. The restrained passion in that gentle kiss made her tremble. His whole body was taut with sexual energy, and yet he kissed her lightly, brushing his lips over hers as if the moment of truth was hours away instead of seconds. She hoped it was seconds.

"I want you," she whispered. "I really, really want you."

"Good." His warm breath tickled her skin as he kissed her jaw and the hollow of her throat. "Because I really, really want you, too."

She believed him because his wounded ego craved a willing partner tonight. But she didn't dare kid herself that he wanted *her* specifically. She'd made that mistake before, only to have her pride trampled after discovering she'd been the Band-Aid for a broken heart and nothing more.

Having sex with Hunter tonight wasn't wise, but she couldn't resist him, not when he needed her so much. And not when she'd gone so many months without the feel of a man's lips on her body. And certainly not when he kissed her and his slightly bristly cheeks rubbed against her skin, a sensation that was extremely sexy and reminded her this was a bona fide stud braced above her.

He started making little circles with his tongue as he moved lower. She read the signal, and the thought of what he intended to do nearly made her climax. But this was a big step to take, considering they'd never been naked together before. Maybe they needed to work up to a maneuver like that.

"Hunter?" Her voice sounded as if she'd recently run a marathon.

He paused, his tongue dipping lightly into her navel. "Yes, Lindsay?"

"Are you planning to, um, keep going in that direction?"

"Uh-huh."

"I'm…I'm not sure you know me well enough yet."

Laughter trembled in his voice. "I will in a minute." He drew circles with his tongue on her tummy.

Her heart beat so fast she felt dizzy. "You don't think we should start…with the basics?"

"Nah. That's for those five-minus guys." With that he closed in on his target.

And Lindsay lost her mind. He had the mouth of a devil, and he used it without hesitation. She'd had no idea oral sex could feel so encompassing, as if he'd made contact with every single one of her pleasure points.

She moaned, she cried out, she even laughed in delirious abandon as he made her come once, then again, then a third time. She bubbled and fizzed like a bottle of champagne opened on a roller coaster.

Then, while she was still gasping from the last orgasm, he slid back up her damp body and gave her a come-flavored kiss. She savored the erotic taste with long, lazy swipes of her tongue over his. She'd never felt so saturated in sex in her life.

"You're amazing," he murmured against her mouth.

"And you…" She kept her eyes closed as she nibbled his full lower lip. "I rate you about six thousand and eight."

He chuckled. "That's all? Not six thousand and nine?"

"Wouldn't want you to get a big head." She felt the press of his erection against her tummy and reached down to wrap her fingers around it. "I see that one part of you is already swelling out of control."

"Careful." He nuzzled her ear, his breath warm. "After the way you just reacted, I'm right on the edge."

"Then slap a body suit on this bad boy and settle in." She let out a little giggle. Then, exploring him with a light touch, she found herself getting excited all over again. "I'm so ready for you." So this was what sex could be like. Who knew?

"Thanks for the invitation. I accept." He shifted his weight and reached for one of the packets lying beside them on the rug.

She opened her eyes. "You would have waited to be invited?" Such chivalry in connection with sex was totally foreign to her.

He smiled as he propped himself on his elbows and tore open the packet. "It's better that way. You might have needed some recovery time."

"And you would have waited for me, even though you're ready to go off like a rocket?"

"Sure." He reached down and rolled the condom on one-handed.

One-handed. This was obviously a man who didn't fumble. "Tell me, have you ever banged a woman's head against the headboard accidentally when you were thrusting?"

He looked at her as if she'd suddenly started speaking in Greek. "No."

"Didn't think so." Bingo. Even if she only had him for tonight, she now had a whole new yardstick for future lovers. She spread her thighs and beckoned to him. "Come here, you patient man. Let Lindsay make you feel really good."

SO MAYBE he wasn't a five-minus. Despite the red haze of lust clouding his brain, Hunter took a moment to congratulate himself on his first move with Lindsay. She hadn't been faking those cries, not considering the way she'd flailed around and gasped for breath. He'd made her a happy woman, three times over.

Still, he could blow it by rushing this next phase. Poised between her thighs, eager to bury his penis in her silken heat, he forced himself to slow down. That wasn't easy with her clutching his butt cheeks in both hands and urging him forward.

Resisting, he smiled at her and shook his head. "Not so fast. I don't want to hurt you."

"Don't worry about a thing." She gave him a gentle massage. "Your treatment a while ago left me more than ready."

Between her massage and his intense anticipation, he was having trouble keeping cool, but he needed to remember she was small-boned. She might have to get adjusted to him. "Let's see." He eased the latex-covered tip just inside and moaned softly. She was very wet. He clenched his jaw and fought the urge to shove deep.

Her eyes widened. "You *are* big."

He struggled for breath. Not coming immediately

was going to be a major challenge. He'd thought about this, dreamed about this for so long, and the reality was threatening to overwhelm him. "That's... why we're...not rushing."

"Slow is one thing." Her breathing quickened as she continued to knead his bottom. "You've come to a dead stop."

"I'm letting you adjust."

"I'm adjusted. I want more."

"Okay." He slid in another inch and almost climaxed. Looking into her eyes, all he could think about was the laundry-room scene he'd replayed a million times in his head. Her expression in his fantasy had been exactly like this—intense, focused and so hot for him she looked ready to explode.

Her breasts quivered with her rapid breath. "I didn't think...I'd come again..."

"I did." He levered himself forward a little more.

"Hunter, I do believe...you've found my... G spot."

"Then let's work it." He hoped he could manage this without losing control. Instead of pushing any deeper, he adjusted his angle and began to stroke back and forth. It was torture for him as he tried to hold back, but judging from the way she was panting, it was heaven for her.

"Ah, yes...right there...oh, my...oh, yes, *yes,* YES!" She arched toward him just as he eased in. Without warning, he was up to the hilt as her contractions milked his penis. He came quickly, loudly, explosively. For the next moment he was blind, deaf and dumb to everything but the incredible pleasure centered in his groin, the shuddering beauty of each spasm that seemed perfectly matched to hers.

Gradually the room stopped spinning and the ringing in his ears let up. He found himself still balanced on his outstretched arms. In his semiconscious state, he could easily have collapsed onto her, but she was too small to take his full weight. He opened his eyes and discovered hers were squeezed shut as she gasped for air.

Then he glanced down to where, sure enough, they were locked together tight. He should pull out, in case he was hurting her. But this felt so good. "Are you...okay?" He prayed she'd say yes and let him stay a little while.

She kept her eyes closed tight. "I...am...spectacular."

He sighed in relief.

"I'm waiting...for the room to stop spinning."

"I understand. Can I do anything?"

"Yes."

He would do anything, anything she asked, especially if she'd let him come back inside again soon. Very soon. He could already feel the urge returning. "What?"

"I want your ex's phone number."

"Her *phone number?* Why?"

"So I can tell her…" She opened her eyes and grinned at him. "…that she's a freaking idiot!"

He laughed. Sex with Lindsay wasn't really about repairing his ego, but if she wanted to pass out a few compliments, he wouldn't mind. Now the rest of him was as happy as his penis. "Thanks for that." He levered himself away from her. "I need to use your bathroom."

"Sure."

When he returned, she was sitting up, her back braced against the sofa, but she hadn't put on any clothes. He appreciated that, considering that he was walking around her apartment naked. He sat down next to her and took her hand in his. Although he wasn't ready to call it a night, she might be. "This has turned into quite an evening," he said.

She smiled at him and nestled closer. "You could say that."

Her warmth reached out to him, teasing his penis back to life. "But we haven't finished the entertainment center."

"No. We sort of *became* the entertainment center."

"Yeah, we did, didn't we?" He hesitated. She could certainly see that he wasn't ready to call it quits, but he should give her a chance to do that if she was tired. "You, um, might be ready to have me go home, though."

"Funny, but you don't look ready to go home."

"But maybe I should, anyway."

"Why, so you can stock up on condoms?"

He grinned at her. "Ah, Lindsay, I like how you think."

"Listen, if you need to go home, get some sleep, whatever, that's fine with me, but—"

"Actually, I had a different idea."

Her blue eyes took on an interested gleam. "Such as?"

"I was thinking we might do some laundry."

CHAPTER FOUR

"LAUNDRY?" Lindsay tried to control her disappointment, but she couldn't imagine a more boring interlude to follow what had been such a mind-blowing experience. "Why, are you out of socks?"

Hunter swallowed. "It's not about the laundry."

"But you just said—"

"It's about this fantasy I haven't been able to get out of my head. But, hey, it's probably a dumb idea, and I suppose we could get arrested if anybody caught us."

She stared at him as heat flooded through her. Whatever he was leading up to, it was getting him excited. The evidence was right there within her reach. Maybe laundry wasn't such a boring subject, after all. "You've had a fantasy about the laundry room?"

"The laundry room...and you."

This just got better and better. "What sort of fantasy?"

His brown eyes began to smolder and his grip on her hand tightened. "You come into the laundry room, dressed in your halter top and cutoffs, and I...I take off your clothes, and we...we do it on top of the machine.''

"You've actually imagined that happening?'' And she thought he hadn't noticed her except as a laundry buddy.

"Yeah. Are you shocked?''

"Flattered.'' Her nipples became rock-hard. "In this fantasy, is the machine going?''

"I don't know. Is it?''

"Yes. It's vibrating.''

"Okay.'' His erect penis twitched. "The washer's going.''

"I know just the spot. The two older washers in the corner do the most shaking.'' She felt like a bungee jumper at the edge of a steep drop. "Let's do this, Hunter. Let's actually do this.''

"You don't have to convince me.'' He stood and pulled her up with him. "Assuming I can zip my pants, I'll meet you down there in five minutes.'' He let go of her hand and started putting on his clothes. "Whoever gets there first can start those machines.''

She grabbed up her own clothes, but she was quivering so much she decided to dress after he left. Or maybe she'd wear a different set, to make the fantasy more interesting. After all, he'd already removed these particular cutoffs.

Then she had another thought. "What if someone else is in the laundry room?"

"At this hour on a Friday night? I don't think
so." He somehow got his shorts fastened over the
considerable bulge in his briefs.

"Is there a lock on the door down there?"

He pulled his T-shirt over his head before meeting her gaze. "No."

"So we take our chances that somebody will
come along?"

He paused in the act of stepping into his deck
shoes. "Lindsay, you don't have to do this."

"Are you kidding? I absolutely have to do this.
Now get going."

"All right, but if you change your mind—"

"I won't."

"Then I'd be a fool to pass up the chance." He
shoved his feet into his shoes and started for the
door.

"Oh, one more thing. Are we actually washing
clothes?"

He turned back to her. "We might as well."

"Then bring extra condoms. No telling what
we'll think of once we're down there and have to
stay awhile."

He groaned. "At this rate, I'll be so hard I won't
be able to walk down the stairs."

"But you'll manage it, won't you?" she asked hopefully.

His gaze was hotter than the cotton setting on the dryer. "I'll manage it. See you soon."

Once he was out the door, she dashed into her bedroom, her heart racing as she yanked open drawers and rummaged around, putting together her outfit. This event called for her low-riding cutoffs, her black lace panties and her red silk halter top.

She hurried getting dressed so she wouldn't have any time to think of what she was doing. A quick redo of her hair, a touch of lip gloss, and she was ready. Thank goodness her laundry ritual was set, because otherwise she'd have forgotten her key and her change purse for sure.

She was headed for her door, a wicker basketful of clothes propped against her hip, when her phone rang. Thinking it might be Hunter with some last-minute fantasy instructions, she snatched up the receiver with a breathless hello.

"I'll bet you're struggling with that entertainment center," Shauna said. "I should have volunteered Tim to come over and put it together. Why don't you leave it until tomorrow when he can help, and come have a drink with us? We're going down to Rush Street to hear some jazz."

"Um, thanks, but I'm…on my way to do laundry."

"Laundry? At this hour? I thought you always did laundry on Saturday morning with what's-his-name, your sexy neighbor. Hunter, the swimsuit photographer."

Lindsay was so bad at making up stuff. "We, uh, decided to do it now."

"Oh, you did? On a Friday night? That's a major date night. I thought he had a girlfriend with very big—"

"They sort of broke up."

"Really? How long ago?"

Lindsay knew what was coming, and she rushed to fend it off. "I know what you're going to say, but you don't have to worry, because I'm totally in control of this situation." Now there was a big, hairy lie.

"He just broke up with her, didn't he? Oh, Lindsay, tell me you're not going to mend his broken heart. Tell me you're not going down that road again, after all you've been through. I know we haven't come up with anybody decent yet, but sooner or later we will. In the meantime, please don't pick up a guy on the rebound. Please don't."

"I won't." One night of crazed lust didn't make for a relationship, she told herself. She'd swear off Hunter tomorrow. After they had laundry-room sex.

"Well, I suppose it can't be too romantic between you guys, if you're spending your Friday night washing clothes. So you can let him pour out his woes during the spin cycle if you have to, but don't get involved, okay?''

"I won't get involved. I'm not that dumb. I realize he'll go back to swimsuit models once he's over this breakup.'' Maybe even the same swimsuit model. Some of her dumpees had made up with their old girlfriends after gaining confidence from her nurturing care.

"That's exactly right. And don't you forget it.''

"I won't. Bye, Shauna.''

"Before you hang up, tell me if you need Tim to come over tomorrow and finish up your entertainment center. He'll be glad to do it.''

Lindsay glanced at the sagging structure that she and Hunter had labored over. She really didn't want Tim to see it and start laughing at their efforts. "That's okay. It's about done. But thanks, anyway.''

"Call if you change your mind. Bye.''

Lindsay put down the phone and stood still for a moment debating whether she should go down without her laundry and tell Hunter this fantasy wouldn't be happening tonight. Maybe she shouldn't get in any deeper with him, knowing that she was only filling a temporary need.

But, damn it, then she'd be cutting short her one night of abandoned sex with him. Surely she could allow herself this one night. The mistake would be in letting things progress beyond that. She absolutely would not become his interim girlfriend, a temporary replacement for his swimsuit model. If she did that, she'd leave herself open to being discarded once he was over being dumped, exactly as Shauna predicted.

Just for tonight, she would salve Hunter's bruised ego and enjoy the thrill of sex with the man of her dreams. After listening to him through the wall for six months, she certainly deserved that much of a reward.

HUNTER HADN'T WORN his watch, but he was pretty sure more than ten minutes had gone by already. He had his whites in one washer and his darks in the other, and both were agitating like crazy. Still Lindsay hadn't shown up. Well, he'd been afraid this night was too good to be true.

Damned shame. The laundry room had been deserted when he'd arrived, as he'd expected for a Friday night. On the way down here he'd tamed his runaway erection, but once he'd put money into the two machines, added soap and clothes and closed them up, he'd started imagining what was about to happen on top of those white enameled lids. Now his penis strained against his briefs again.

But Lindsay wasn't here. She'd probably had a

chance to think of what he'd suggested and come to her senses. A year ago he never would have thought of something like this, but Pamela had put all kinds of wild ideas into his head. She'd coaxed him into doing it in an elevator and out on the beach next to the lake. He'd discovered the thrill of sexual adventure, and now he wanted to share it with Lindsay.

Instead he might have convinced her that he was some sort of weirdo. She'd seemed excited about the idea while he was there, but she'd still been pumped up with adrenaline from their previous session. When that faded, she might have decided against taking this kind of risk. That could mean he'd screwed things up between them, which was extremely depressing to contemplate.

Then he heard footsteps coming toward the laundry room, and his heartbeat kicked up a notch. But wait…Lindsay didn't walk with a loud clump, clump, clump. Her footsteps were quick and light. These sounded like they were being made by at least a size fourteen.

Sure enough, a guy who looked as if he could play for the Bears came through the doorway carrying a laundry bag over his shoulder. A very big laundry bag. "Hi, bro!" He grinned at Hunter. "Looks like neither one of us scored a date tonight, huh?"

"Well, I—"

"Hey, don't think less of yourself. Women these days…they got *attitude,* man." The guy swung his bag to the floor with a thud. "Half the time they'd rather go out with their girlfriends and drink those fancy martinis than hang with a guy, you know? Anyway, once the Cubs game was over, I wasn't sleepy so I decided to get this done." He opened the bag and started throwing clothes in the nearest washer. Then he moved to the next, and the next, filling up all of the remaining three.

Hunter watched him with a sense of doom. Even if Lindsay showed up, which she might not, the laundry-room fantasy would have to be scuttled unless he could think of some way to get rid of this dateless dude. Maybe Dateless would put his clothes in and leave. That would provide at least twenty minutes of privacy.

Dateless glanced up. "You don't look like you brought anything to do, man."

If you only knew.

"Me, I always bring my games." He reached into the depths of his laundry bag and pulled out a Palm Pilot. "We can both play, if you want."

"Thanks." Hunter grasped at the first thing that came to him. "But you know what? It seems dumb for both of us to stay down here. Why don't you—"

"Hey, want me to mind your clothes for you? I'd be glad to do that. I don't really have anything else to occupy my time tonight. Come on back in an hour or so, and I'll bet most of it will be dry. Just leave me some money for the dryer."

"I was thinking the other way around," Hunter said. "That if you want me to take care of yours, I could do that."

Dateless shrugged. "Like I said, I'm not sleepy and I don't have anything else going on right now." He brightened. "I just downloaded this new game. We could have, like, a tournament while we wait for the clothes."

Hunter wondered if he should agree to the tournament. Lindsay didn't seem to be coming, after all, and his clothes were churning away in the washing machine. Funny how an evening could go from outstanding to disastrous in no time. He'd almost decided to play that tournament when Lindsay walked into the laundry room.

She'd changed to a different pair of cutoffs and halter top, which explained her delay in getting down here. He'd also bet she'd put on new, exciting underwear. Women thought about things like that. Hunter wanted to bang his fists on the washing machine in frustration.

Lindsay paused in the doorway, her expression confused.

"Hi, Lindsay." Hunter couldn't let on that this meeting was more than coincidence. He didn't want Dateless getting any ideas that the rendezvous had been planned. "Guess you decided to wash clothes tonight, too."

"I thought about it." She glanced at Hunter before sweeping her gaze around the laundry room at all the machines humming away. "But it looks like all the machines are taken. I'll come back."

"No, wait!" Dateless said. "This guy's machines were already going when I got here. Look, they're almost to the rinse cycle. Those two machines will be freed up in a jiffy." He seemed desperate not to let this other source of Friday-night company get away. "So you two know each other?"

"We're neighbors," Hunter said.

"Oh, that's cool." Dateless smiled. "I'm Paul. From the second floor. Listen, Lindsay, put your clothes right over there on the folding counter, and you can play in the tournament with Hunter and me until his clothes are done."

Lindsay backed up a step and threw another glance at Hunter. "That's okay. Thanks for the offer, but I have tons of stuff to do upstairs."

Hunter felt like howling in agony. *The opportunity had been right in his grasp.* Now it was gone, and he wasn't sure where he stood with Lindsay.

He'd laid everything on the line, probably way too fast. If they'd been able to enact this fantasy, they might have taken off from there, but this roadblock might change everything.

He didn't know what to say, what he could say, with Dateless Paul hanging on their every word. "Sorry about that," he murmured.

She gave him a small smile. "Maybe it's just as well."

He didn't need an interpreter to figure that one out. She was relieved to have the fun and games canceled. He'd made the exact mistake he'd vowed not to make with her—moving so quickly after his breakup that she doubted his sincerity. How ironic. He'd never been more sincere in his life.

After Lindsay walked out of the laundry room, Paul cleared his throat. "Your neighbor, huh?"

"Yeah." Hunter continued to stare at the empty doorway.

"Ever date her?"

"No." *He'd skipped that part and headed straight for the sex. What a class act he was.*

"Boy, I would have by now, that's for sure. I would have asked for her phone number, except with you two knowing each other, I wasn't sure if I'd be trespassing or something."

Hunter glanced up at Paul, who had to be at least

seven feet tall. "Actually, I'm not dating her, but I plan to."

Paul smiled. "I thought so, from the way you were looking at her. She's a little skittish, though, huh?"

"I'll work through it." He hoped he could work through it. He was very afraid that he'd blown his chance to create something wonderful with Lindsay.

"Well, good luck. Just because I'm not getting any doesn't mean you shouldn't. Wanna play this game?"

Hunter sighed. Sometimes life just sucked. "Sure."

LINDSAY CARRIED her laundry back upstairs and tried to tell herself that she'd dodged a bullet. Having Paul show up to spoil the party had been like having a seven-foot-tall guardian angel swoop down to save her. Eventually, like maybe in about fifty years, she might forget the sex she'd had with Hunter in her living room. But she would never have forgotten laundry-room sex.

For Hunter, though, it would have been different. He'd been very recently dumped, so laundry-room sex for him would have been about repairing his ego. One wild session in the laundry room might have done the trick, especially with the way Lindsay had been rating him off the charts. Then he would have had no more need for her, while she'd be desperate for more of him.

Well, she was already desperate for more of him. So that proved that laundry-room sex, added to living-room-floor sex, would have made her life one big ball of misery when Hunter decided he'd rebounded and was ready for more swimsuit models. Yeah, Paul had done her a gigantic favor by getting the urge to wash his duds tonight. Really.

After letting herself back in the apartment, she plopped the laundry basket on the floor. No sense in putting it away, because she still had to do laundry this weekend. She wouldn't be doing it tomorrow morning, though. Saturday-morning laundry encounters with Hunter were over, so she'd find another time slot and shake up her routine.

Unsure what to do next, she sat down on the floor beside the laundry basket. For the moment she couldn't make herself go into the living room, where the overturned beer cans and partly assembled entertainment unit would remind her of glories that would never be again.

Oh, Hunter might want to get it on some more. After all, his fantasy had gone unfulfilled. But Lindsay had promised herself not to drag out the connection beyond tonight, and she would keep that promise.

A soft knock sounded at her door. "Lindsay?" Hunter called softly. "Are you still awake?"

The urge to leap up and fling open the door nearly overpowered her. No, she must not. She wouldn't respect herself in the morning.

He tapped again. "Lindsay?"

Her resolve was slipping. She couldn't get up and move away from the door because he might hear that. But listening to his voice was torture. She grabbed some laundry in each hand and held the bunched clothing against her ears, blocking out the sound of his voice. Then she closed her eyes and pictured all the guys who had come crawling to her, their hearts broken, only to say goodbye once the pain was gone.

After many long moments, she took the wad of laundry away from one ear. Silence. Hunter had left.

With a deep sigh, she tossed the laundry back in the basket and stood. Considering how gorgeous Hunter was, and considering his job as a photographer of swimsuit models, she would give him about two weeks before he replaced Silicon Sally with one of her big-busted friends. Although that thought gave Lindsay physical pain, she had to face reality. Once he started dating someone else, her decision to cut off their interaction would be vindicated. The next two weeks promised to be a living hell.

CHAPTER FIVE

As THE DAYS PASSED, Hunter looked for some sign, any sign, that Lindsay thought kindly of him. But if they happened to pass in the hall, her smile was automatic and fake, the kind of polite smile that you gave to strangers on the street. There was no welcome in her eyes whatsoever.

He was sure that she thought he was slime. He didn't know how to correct the picture, because he *was* slime. Instead of following his game plan of several casual dates leading up to more intense dates and finally culminating in the sleepover date, he'd jumped straight to "hide the salami." He had the restraint of a bunny rabbit.

But he still might have saved the situation if he hadn't suggested the laundry-room sex. They could have stayed right up there in her apartment and enjoyed themselves some more, but no, he'd brought up his fantasy. Dumb, dumb, dumb.

After she'd left the laundry room on that fateful night, he'd thought maybe if he talked to her before she cooled off completely, he'd be able to explain himself. But she hadn't answered her door. She'd already cooled off by that time, apparently. Yep, he was slime.

And the worst of it was, he thought this woman might be the one, his soul mate, his forever-and-ever girl. There she was living right next door, and he'd messed up his chance to create a relationship by suggesting kinky sex. Plus he had no idea whatsoever how to repair the damage.

She'd changed her laundry time. He found that out right away, because the next morning he'd gone down there on the chance that she'd be washing her clothes at ten, the way she always had. No Lindsay.

Desperate and pathetic man that he was, he started checking the laundry room at various times on Saturday and Sunday. The first weekend after their disaster he'd had no luck. He'd wondered if she'd resorted to trundling her clothes to the Laundromat three blocks away.

The second weekend, though, he hit pay dirt. He poked his head in on Sunday afternoon and, sure enough, there she was, sitting on the laundry room's only folding chair reading a book while her clothes whirled in the dryer.

He walked in. "Hi."

She glanced up and, for a second, there was a

spark in her eyes. Then she doused it. "Hi, Hunter. How have you been?"

He wondered what she'd say if he told her the truth, that he had trouble sleeping, and when he did, he dreamed of her constantly. She'd probably think it was a line to get her back into bed. She might not believe that he was so tortured over her that he hadn't been concentrating at work and had screwed up a couple of shoots in the past week alone.

So he told her he'd been fine. "How about you? How've you been?"

"Just great." She smiled that fakey smile again. "Couldn't be better."

"Good." He nodded, wondering how in hell to proceed. "That's good." He glanced at her clothes tumbling in the dryer. The silence was broken only by the thumps and clicks her stuff made as it hit the metal drum.

"Entertainment center working out okay?" he asked, knowing he was treading on dangerous ground mentioning that.

"Sure is."

He sincerely doubted that, unless she'd called in a carpenter to shore the thing up. "It holds every-thing?"

"Yep."

"Good." Somehow he had to prolong this con-versation, because the sight of her was like water to a man dying of thirst. Her halter top was new, but her cutoffs might be the same ones she'd stripped off for him, or else the second pair she'd worn down to the laundry room. He thought they were the original pair that had got left in a heap on her living-room floor.

"You don't have a laundry basket." Apparently she was tired of his dumb questions. "What brings you down to the basement?"

"You." He had no better answer. "I can understand if you'd want to avoid me, but—"

"Hunter, we can hardly pretend nothing happened and go on like before."

He studied her no-nonsense expression and wondered if that's the one she used when one of her customers was overdrawn at the bank. He was way overdrawn at this bank. "I know," he admitted. "But I really miss the talks we used to have every week while the clothes were washing."

"And the fantasies you were having at the same time?"

He groaned. "I should never have suggested we follow up on that. All the problems started because I suggested it."

"As I said at the time, maybe it was for the best." Her expression didn't soften.

"Look, is there any chance that we can be friends?"

Her gaze flickered slightly. ''So that we can do what?''

Start over. ''Well, we can—''

''Sharing laundry day is not happening. And that was pretty much the extent of our friendship. Unless you want to grocery shop together, or we both adopt dogs that we need to walk, I'm not sure what activities we can do as friends.''

He rubbed the back of his neck while he gazed at her. She was tougher than he'd thought. When he'd made love to her, he could have sworn that she'd enjoyed every second, like him. She'd been carried away by the moment the same way he had. But there was no getting carried away now.

The more he thought about how she'd reacted that night, the more he wondered if she shouldn't take some of the blame for moving too fast. She'd tempted him, hadn't she? Yes, come to think of it, she definitely had tempted him.

If she thought he was a jerk for making love to her so quickly after his breakup, why hadn't she said so in the beginning? Why get all high and mighty now that it was too late? Getting mad at her felt good, so he allowed himself to do that.

''I guess you're right.'' He let his irritation show. ''Once the cat's out of the bag, or the genie's out of the bottle, there's no shoving it back in, is there?''

"Not really." She looked a little less sure of herself, though.

"I mean, the river moves on, you know? If you stand in one place, it's a different river going past all the time, right?" He had no idea what that image was supposed to mean, exactly, but it sounded sort of indignant and philosophical at the same time, like he was above any petty concerns like whether he'd ever get to touch her again.

"I guess so."

"Then I'll see you around, Lindsay." He stalked out of the laundry room, wishing the entire time she'd call him back. But she didn't. From all indications, she was glad to get rid of him.

FOUR DAYS AFTER the laundry-room confrontation, Lindsay met Shauna in front of the glass-and-brass entrance doors of Divine Events. They were using their lunch hours to choose favors for the reception. Lindsay was glad they'd set up the appointment, because she needed to talk to Shauna.

Lindsay had ended up having to ask Tim to redo her entertainment center, after all. That had been the Sunday right after the fateful Friday night and, while Tim had been hard at work in the living room, Shauna had dragged Lindsay into the kitchen and pried most of the story out of her, even the near miss with laundry-room sex.

Shauna had praised Lindsay for her fortitude in ending the affair before it could go any further. She'd been just as certain as Lindsay that Hunter only needed a boost to his ego, and then he'd move on like all the other guys. They both knew Lindsay had a talent for healing broken hearts that caused her to be taken advantage of.

Lindsay had managed to hang onto her resolution to keep far away from Hunter, but this past Sunday's encounter had shaken her resolve. She needed to find out what Shauna thought about this latest turn of events. Lindsay didn't feel even slightly objective about it.

But Shauna's job as a paralegal had kept her very busy so far this week, and between that and spending her evenings with Tim, she hadn't had available gal-pal time. Although this noon meeting would be short and rushed, Lindsay hoped for a moment to talk.

Shauna's blond hair was twisted into a casual arrangement on top of her head, and she'd taken off the short jacket that matched her blue linen dress. "Whew, can you believe the temperature?" She tucked her sunglasses in her shoulder bag. "I'm melting."

"It's hot." The continued heat wave hadn't helped Lindsay's mood. Sexual frustration, indecision and humid heat made for a miserable existence. She grabbed the brass door handle. "Let's get inside and bask in the AC."

"I'm right behind you."

The blissfully cool lobby scented with a gigantic vase of flowers should have soothed Lindsay's frayed nerves. The flower vase sat on a large round table in the center of the room, and the multicolored arrangement was spectacular. Unfortunately, right in front of the vase lay that damned red leather book of sexual fantasies, taunting her. She wondered if any of the fantasies included laundry-room sex.

"Hi, Shauna, Lindsay," called Livia Divine from the top of a wrought-iron spiral staircase. All the offices and consultation rooms were on the second level. "Give me a sec to straighten out a pesky detail, and I'll be right with you."

"Okay, but don't forget we're both on our lunch break," Shauna called back.

"I won't. In fact, I have some hors d'oeuvres for you to munch on while we talk. I told Gia I'd have you taste them and make a decision on that today, too. I only need a couple of minutes to deal with a small crisis involving some mismatched table-cloths, and don't panic, because it's not your event." With that, she hurried back into her office.

Lindsay admired how well the three cousins who ran the business interwove their capabilities. Livia

Divine handled all visuals, from decorations to gowns, while Cecily Divine took care of entertainment and Gia Divine was the caterer. If Lindsay ever had a wedding, which at this point was in serious doubt, she would definitely plan it through Divine Events.

"I sure hope she makes it quick." Shauna walked over to a love seat and sat down. "Work is crazy, and I probably shouldn't even be taking lunch." She opened her purse and started searching through it. "I hope I remembered to bring the list of things I wanted to ask Livia."

Lindsay sat beside her. "Yeah, I know you've been busy, which is why I haven't called you."

Shauna must have picked up something from her tone, because she stopped searching for her list and met Lindsay's gaze. "What's up?"

"He doesn't have a new girlfriend yet."

Shauna didn't have to ask who Lindsay was talking about. "So what? It hasn't been that long."

"More than two weeks. I thought a guy with his contacts would have been dating again within two weeks."

Shauna considered that. "He could be dating. You don't know that he's not dating."

"Yes, I do. He's not dating."

"How do you know that for sure?" Shauna

laughed. "Did you sneak over there and bug his apartment?"

"I live right next door. If he was seeing somebody, I'd catch a glimpse of her sooner or later." Although Shauna was her best friend, Lindsay hadn't told her about all the nights she'd eavesdropped on Hunter's nighttime activities. And she would *never* admit to putting a glass against the wall, not even under extreme torture. "But that's not all. He's been trying to find out when I do laundry. And Sunday he came down to the basement while I was there to talk to me."

Shauna's eyebrows lifted. "And? What did he say?"

"That he missed our laundry-room chats, and he shouldn't have asked me to help him enact his fantasy."

Shauna nodded. "And you said…?"

"That we couldn't go back to the way things had been before."

"Excellent. Keep away from that bad boy. He's rebounding, and you're in the line of fire."

Lindsay stared at the huge bouquet of flowers, a riot of reds, purples, pinks and whites. She'd expected that response from Shauna. "But don't you think if he hasn't started dating again, and he's still wishing we could be friends, and he followed me to the laundry room, that—"

"No, I do not. Look at me, girl." Shauna caught Lindsay's chin and forced her to meet her gaze. "I'm the one who's been around to pick up the pieces, remember?"

"Yes, but this time maybe it's diff—"

"Lindsay, Lindsay, Lindsay. You're a caring, nurturing person. A guy pulls a hangdog expression and you're ready to cuddle him and make it better. Hunter might need that now, but once he's over the breakup, you *know* what he'll do. You've seen him at his most vulnerable. A guy can't handle that. He has to split. We've talked about this a gazillion times."

Lindsay sighed. "I'm sure you're right."

"I am right. I'm only thinking of you, honeybunch. Once I get through this rough patch at work, we'll go out trolling again. Your dream guy is out there. We just haven't found him yet."

Yes, I have.

Livia appeared at the top of the wrought-iron stairs. "Come on up, you guys. Let's pig out on Gia's concoctions while we choose some wedding favors!"

THIRTY MINUTES LATER, chock-full of pâté, minced olives, smoked salmon and various kinds of cheese, Lindsay descended the spiral staircase with Shauna. On the way out the door, she glanced longingly at the red leather book sitting in front of the flower vase.

Although she'd tried to keep her attention on wedding favors and hors d'oeuvres, she'd spent most of the time in Livia's office thinking about Hunter. He'd come looking for her on Sunday. Considering his recent breakup, taking a chance on another rejection had required a lot of courage. And, sure enough, she'd rejected him.

He'd reacted with anger, as any man with an ounce of pride would have. She couldn't expect him to approach her again. According to Shauna, that was a good thing, but Lindsay couldn't accept the finality of it. She'd dreamed about Hunter for six months, and then she'd experienced the most wonderful sex of her life with him.

If that night had been nothing but first aid for his wounded ego, then why hadn't he found another woman to pick up the slack? Two weeks later, which was a long time for a highly sexed guy like Hunter, he still wanted to spend time with her. That wasn't rebound behavior, and she was the expert on that. The guys she'd nursed through broken hearts had clung to her like Velcro for the first two or three weeks after they'd been dumped, as if they needed constant reassurance that they were worthy of attention. She'd seen Hunter a single time over the past two weeks.

Maybe Hunter's ego was in better shape than she'd thought. If so, then she'd blown the chance of a lifetime by brushing him off when he'd come looking for her on Sunday. Making up for that would require something spectacular.

On the sidewalk outside Divine Events, Shauna gave her a hug. "Next week we'll have a girls' night out," she said. "I feel terrible for ignoring you when you're going through this Hunter thing." She looked into Lindsay's eyes before she put on her sunglasses. "Be strong. If you find yourself weakening, call me on my cell and I'll talk you down."

Lindsay smiled. "You sound like I'm addicted to rebound guys."

"For a while there, it was beginning to look that way, but it's been a whole year since you got involved with someone like that. Stay away from Hunter and you're home free."

"Right." Lindsay put on her sunglasses, so Shauna couldn't read the doubts in her eyes. "See you next week."

"Tuesday night," Shauna said. "Let's make it then. We'll start with the usual spot and branch out from there."

"Okay, Tuesday night." The thought of hitting jazz clubs looking for available single men next

Tuesday night sounded awful. She simply wasn't interested.

With a wave, Shauna headed down the street toward the law office where she worked.

Lindsay's bus stop was in the opposite direction. She had exactly enough time to make the next bus, which would get her back to the bank before her lunch break was over. She hesitated, battling her indecision.

She knew herself, and if she walked away from Divine Events now, she wouldn't come back until Shauna scheduled another appointment, which could be three or four weeks away. In three or four weeks her opportunity would have disappeared. It was now or never.

Her heart pounded as she grabbed the brass door handle and walked back inside. No one was in the reception area. She had the red book all to herself. She ran two fingers over the supple leather. There was no title embossed on it.

From Shauna's description, she already knew the book was actually a large paperback the size and thickness of one of her bank training manuals. The leather cover was there for propriety's sake, to disguise the racy title from casual observers. She opened it now and read the title page. *Sexcapades: Secret Games and Wild Adventures for Uninhibited Lovers.*

Hunter would love this. If she had the courage to act out one of the suggestions in this book, he would...what? Be her slave forever? Maybe not. That was a lot to ask for. But after hearing about his laundry-room fantasy she knew that sexual games would definitely get his attention. Did she want that?

She heard a sound from upstairs. Flipping open the book, she grabbed one of the perforated pages and ripped it out. The sound echoed in the reception area. She stuffed the page quickly into her purse and headed for the door. Although she had torn out a page, that didn't mean she had to follow through. She could throw it away when she got home.

"Lindsay? Did you need to see me?" Livia called out to her from the second floor.

Lindsay turned and glanced up the stairs, feeling guilty as a bank robber, certain she was blushing as red as the book on the table. "I, um, forgot something."

Livia smiled. "That happens a lot around here."

"I took a page out of the book," she confessed in one breath. She'd never make a decent thief.

"You're welcome to do that. We leave it on the table so that people can help themselves. When it gets too thin, we bring out a new one."

"Still, it's supposed to be for Divine Events clients, and technically I'm not a client."

Livia smile widened. "Then I'd better warn you about something."

"What?"

"That book has the power to turn you into a client."

CHAPTER SIX

WHILE SHE WAS at work, Lindsay didn't dare look at the fantasy she'd torn out, and the afternoon of standing at the teller's window smiling at customers dragged by. Maybe she should have torn out several so that she'd have a choice. This one might be way beyond her comfort zone.

Wait a minute—had she really decided to tempt Hunter with a sexual fantasy? Had she gone from merely considering it as a far-fetched possibility to actually planning the seduction? She'd better find out what sort of adventure she'd chosen before she made that decision. Shauna had said some of the concepts in the book were over the top.

She was so caught up in thinking about her *Sex-capades* page that she almost missed seeing Hunter standing in line waiting for a teller. This wasn't his bank, so there could only be one reason why he was here—to see her. That became crystal clear after he let someone go ahead of him when it was his turn and Lindsay was still busy with Mrs. Detweiler.

He looked wonderful—cool and crisp in a white polo shirt and khaki slacks. She'd actually held this beautiful man in her arms. Then she'd turned away the chance to do it again. She was as crazy as his ex.

Or maybe not. Seeing Hunter ignited a sexual response in her, but that wasn't the only thing going on. Her heart ached with the kind of longing that suggested she'd moved beyond mere lust. Maybe she'd gone beyond mere lust weeks ago. Shauna had told her that she suspected Lindsay was falling in love with Hunter, thus Shauna's fiercely protective stance.

Hunter posed a danger, no doubt about it. And yet he didn't look dangerous standing there. He looked dear, sweet and sexier than should be legal. Most important of all, he'd come to the bank to see her.

Poor Mrs. Detweiler must have thought she was on drugs. A simple deposit of the white-haired woman's Social Security check turned into a three-act play as Lindsay entered the wrong amount twice, dropped the deposit slip on the floor and tore it in half when she pulled it out from under a corner of the counter.

"This isn't like you, Lindsay," Mrs. Detweiler said. "And you look flushed, too. You'd better go for a checkup."

"I'm fine, Mrs. Detweiler." Lindsay finally managed to hand the older woman her deposit slip while she tried to ignore Hunter gesturing yet another person ahead of him in line. "It's been one of those days."

"All the same, it wouldn't hurt to see a doctor. Dealing with people all day, you could have picked up anything, anything at all."

"I suppose that's true."

"Young people today don't take care of themselves. You don't get enough sleep, for one thing."

Lindsay certainly fit in that category. She found it tough to sleep while yearning for Hunter.

"So will you promise to make an appointment for yourself?" Mrs. Detweiler asked.

"Yes, yes, I will. And thank you, Mrs. Detweiler." When Lindsay forced herself to smile, her face felt stiffer than cardboard. Despite that, she wanted to appear as cool and collected as Hunter looked standing there in line. Instead a fire raged inside her and sweat trickled down her back.

"You're welcome. See you next month." Mrs. Detweiler tucked her deposit slip into her purse and left.

Hunter walked toward her window and Lindsay swallowed. "Hello."

"Hello." He slid a check across the granite counter. "I need to cash this."

"Certainly." Her pulse racing, her response on autopilot, Lindsay took the check, which was from *Instant Replay*. When she flipped it over, she saw that he'd forgotten to sign it. Maybe he wasn't as composed as he looked. "You need to endorse this." She pushed a pen toward him along with the check, willing her hands not to shake.

"Oh, right." He scribbled his name across the short end of the check. "I, um, I'm going out of town on assignment."

"Out of town?" The question came out in a squeak of protest. Damn. She cleared her throat. "I, uh, mean...I didn't know you were going somewhere." That could have an impact on several things, including the fantasy she had hidden in her purse in the back room.

She glanced at the address on the front of his check and noticed the *Instant Replay* offices were on Michigan Avenue not far from Divine Events. Lucky she hadn't run into him after tearing out the page. No telling how she might have reacted.

"The editor just told me yesterday. There's a women's tennis program down in Florida that's turning out some awesome players. I'll take a day to shoot some of the stars, and then I'm flying down to Nassau to do a photo spread on snorkeling."

"Sounds like a fairly extensive trip."

"Ten days."

Ten days. If she had to spend ten days stewing in her knowledge of how she felt about him and debating whether to use the fantasy, she'd be ready for the funny farm by the time he got back. She opened her cash drawer. "How did you want this?"

"All hundreds, I guess. No, wait, better give me at least two hundred of it in tens and twenties."

She nodded and concentrated on the money as she counted it out for him. If she'd screwed up Mrs. Detweiler's deposit, she was certainly capable of short-changing Hunter.

When she finished laying the bills on the counter, he scooped them up and stuffed them in his wallet. "Thanks."

"When are you leaving?" She tried her best to make the question sound like idle curiosity.

From the way his head came up and the intensity of his expression, she'd failed. "I'm taking the red-eye out tomorrow night. Why?" He waited expectantly.

She had no idea what to say. "I...wondered if you...wanted me to...water your plants." *Or give you a going away party you'll never forget?*

"Thanks, but I don't have any plants. Although now that you mention it, I could use a favor." He fished in his pocket and came up with a small key. "I'd appreciate it if you'd take in my mail."

Her hopes, raised by his cashing a check here when he could have cashed it at his own bank, died. He needed someone to take in his mail, and he'd thought of a way to cash his check and get the mail question out of the way in one trip.

"I can do that." She took the mailbox key and tucked it in the pocket of her jacket.

"Thanks. I'll see you when I get back, then."

"Have a safe trip." Now wasn't that a boring exchange? He would never guess from this conversation that earlier today she'd ripped a page out of a book full of wild sexual adventures and that she'd been planning to use the page to seduce *him*. Obviously he'd put his laundry-room fantasies behind him and now he only saw her as a convenient neighbor who'd take in his mail. Meanwhile she'd fallen hard for the boy next door. What a depressing turn of events.

HUNTER LEFT the bank and headed for his favorite corner bar and an early dinner. He ordered a beer and a sandwich. Then he ordered another beer, and another. Watching sports he didn't care about and talking with people he barely knew, he proceeded to get thoroughly smashed.

If he'd had some idea that Lindsay would be

sorry to see him leave on this trip, or that she'd suggest they might have dinner together before he went, he'd been dreaming. The mail thing had been his feeble, pathetic excuse to see her again and tell her he was going. He didn't need her to take in his mail. For years he'd had an arrangement with the post office and they held his mail any time he went out of town. All he had to do was notify them.

Now he'd roped Lindsay into collecting his mail, and she would, because she was polite and considerate. She was a helpful person. She'd looked incredible in that turquoise silk suit, although the jacket had hidden her curves. She'd look good wearing a green garbage bag. She was a goddess. And he was a sex-crazed lunatic who wasn't worthy of standing in front of her teller window.

Finally he grew tired of the bar and poured himself into a cab. Back in his apartment, he stumbled around getting ready for bed. Then he tried to be a little quieter. Now that he knew how easily Lindsay could hear him, he didn't want to add to his sins by waking her up.

Yes, he did. He wanted to pound on that wall and beg her to let him come over and make love to her until he had to fly out tomorrow night. He could imagine how she'd react if he started banging on the wall and shouting her name. She'd probably call the cops.

With a heavy sigh, he lay on the bed under the cooling breeze of the AC. It didn't help cool his blood a damn bit. The bed began to revolve, and he grimaced. He'd have a beauty of a hangover at work tomorrow. Fortunately all he had to do was handle a backlog of picture editing he'd been putting off for weeks. He always liked to tie up loose ends before he took off on an assignment.

But there was one loose end he wouldn't be able to do anything about. When he got back, Lindsay would be even farther away, even though she continued to live right next door. He turned over and pounded the pillow in despair.

LINDSAY WAS SITTING UP in bed, the fantasy sheet on her lap, her thoughts scrambled, when she heard Hunter come home. She automatically listened to discover whether he was alone. Judging from the way he was banging around without talking, he was most definitely alone, and he was either upset, drunk or both.

She'd had some time to think after Hunter had left the bank. He'd never asked her to take in his mail in the many months they'd been neighbors, and she knew for a fact he'd gone out of town on assignments before, because he used to tell her when he wouldn't be showing up to do laundry.

Because of all the traveling, he would have set

up a system with the post office a long time ago. It was only logical. That meant the visit to her bank and the mail request had been another attempt to make contact, to break through the barrier she'd thrown up.

She didn't know if it was sexual desire or something more that was driving him. Shauna would say that he was still in rebound mode, and for some reason he was stubbornly counting on her to get him through. Maybe so, but Lindsay had a gut feeling that something else was going on.

Shauna would kill her for even considering that Hunter's attraction to her might be the real deal and not his reaction to being dumped. But Shauna didn't know the whole story, and because of Lindsay's history, she had reason to be skeptical. Lindsay didn't want that history to cause her to make a terrible mistake of a different kind from that which Shauna feared.

Hunter had approached her again, and that was huge. After being rejected by his ex, he'd risked more rejection by coming to the bank today. Sure enough, she'd offered him no encouragement. If he was banging around his apartment because he was upset, she might be the reason.

She could go over there, knock on his door and find out. But if he'd spent the night drinking his cares away, the encounter might not be all she could hope for. Besides, that wouldn't have even the slightest touch of fantasy, and if she and Hunter had a future, she wanted that future to be filled with the kind of sexual excitement they both loved.

Glancing at the page from *Sexcapades* lying in her lap, she took a deep breath. Attempting this sexual fantasy would take courage even if she were completely sure of the man in question. With Hunter, she was sure of nothing. She might embarrass herself and go down in bitter defeat.

But then again, she might win the day. She had very few hours in which to make a decision. Overriding Shauna's warnings that echoed in her head, she read the fantasy one more time.

HUNTER DRAGGED HIMSELF through the next morning with the help of coffee and aspirin. Fortunately nobody at the office needed him for anything, or maybe they sensed he was a bear with a wounded paw. In any case, the rest of the staff left him alone in his little windowless cubicle to work as best he could. By lunchtime he actually felt like eating something and accepted the invitation from some work buddies to go with them to get a sandwich.

His outlook improved considerably after that, and when four o'clock rolled around, he was beginning to think he might live. As he clicked through more digital shots on his computer, he thought about the approaching trip. He'd get some sleep on the plane that night, and by tomorrow he should be in shape to shoot the tennis stars.

The tennis pro running the program had specifically requested him, and Hunter had a good idea why. The pro apparently wanted to put some glamour into his program, and Hunter was known for his ability to take pictures with a certain mystique about them.

Because he'd always had that ability, he'd never questioned it. But after discovering a wilder brand of sex with Pamela's help, he'd concluded that he had a hedonistic streak. Pamela had brought it up to a conscious level, but it had been there all along, running underneath everything he did and influencing the way he photographed women.

He'd spent a good part of the day editing previous work, and when he flipped through his shots, he could see it. He used light to bring out the curve of a breast, the pout of a lower lip, the tilt of a pelvis. He loved the possibilities suggested by the female form. That devotion was the basis of his career.

It was a big part of his attraction to Lindsay, too. She had a classic body, and he was just the guy to appreciate that. He wished they had the closeness that would allow him to photograph her in the nude. With digital photography, it could be a totally private project, produced only for his creative satisfaction.

Yes, Lindsay beckoned to the artist in him, but there was another link, too. As Pamela had recognized the pleasure seeker in him, he recognized the pleasure seeker in Lindsay. She hadn't balked at his laundry-room suggestion. Instinctively he'd known she could be sexually daring.

But she was so much more than that. She was his cheerful companion during their Saturday-morning suds-and-duds fests. She was his spunky neighbor who thought she could put together an entertainment center with a Swiss Army knife. And she was also the caring woman who hadn't wanted him to be alone after getting a sexual rating of five-minus.

No doubt about it, he was hooked on Lindsay Scott. But he couldn't do a damned thing about it. The friendship route was closed to him now, and he'd burned the sexual route to ashes in one ill-advised night.

Maybe while he was on this assignment he'd come up with a way around the difficulties. Maybe ten days without seeing him would make her miss him enough that they could patch things up. Maybe—

"Hunter?"

He glanced up from the screen and blinked.

Lindsay stood in his office wearing a trench coat. In July. In the middle of the hottest summer in recent memory. She looked like a moll in a gangster movie.

He swallowed. "Hi. Aren't you…supposed to be at the bank?" *Wearing normal summer clothes?*

"I left a little early." Her cheeks were flushed, probably from wearing the coat outside. Even in the air-conditioned building that coat had to be uncomfortable.

A possibility whispered through his mind, but he dismissed it. Such things didn't really happen. "So what brings you down to Michigan Avenue?"

She cleared her throat. "I, uh, thought that after all that work helping me put the entertainment center together, you might like to come over and see a movie."

He forgot to breathe. She was issuing an invitation, but he couldn't figure out exactly what kind. And, hell, he was leaving town at midnight. "You mean when I get back from this assignment?"

"I mean before you leave."

Oh, no. She wanted to make up. In the most time-honored way. But he couldn't figure out the trench coat, unless… Surely she wouldn't have some skimpy outfit on under it. Pamela might try something like that, but not Lindsay. At least not this early in the game.

Yet he couldn't imagine why else she'd wear the coat. As his body started heating up, he cursed the magazine for sending him on assignment and wondered how much it would cost him to delay his flight until tomorrow. "I don't have a lot of time."

Uncertainty flickered in her eyes. "Then maybe it's not a good idea. You probably have to pack, and—"

"I'm a fast packer." He'd get on the plane without a suitcase and improvise when he arrived if it meant quality time with Lindsay. "I didn't say I couldn't see a movie tonight. I was only warning you that I have to catch a plane."

"So you would like to do the movie thing?"

He looked directly into her eyes. "Very much."

"Would you like to help me pick it out? There's a video place not far from here, and then we could ride the 'L' home together."

Something was going on. He wasn't sure what, but he had a feeling he was going to like it a lot. "Sure. Let me close up shop here."

"Take your time." She loosened the belt of her trench coat.

He stared at the belt, wondering... No, his imagination was getting the best of him. "Have a seat, if you want."

"I'd rather look around your office. You have some great pictures on the walls. Although I have to say it's a little warm in here.'' Then she opened her coat.

He gasped. Under the coat she wore stockings, a black lace garter belt...and nothing else.

CHAPTER SEVEN

"WHOOPS." Lindsay pulled her coat together and retied the belt. She was *way* out of her comfort zone. Her heart pounded and her palms were slippery with sweat, but Hunter's expression was worth it all.

He looked as if someone had set off a strobe light two inches from his face. "Wh-what…are you…" His voice trailed off, as if he'd forgotten how to string words together.

She smiled and wandered over to the pictures lining the wall near his desk, so he'd get a look at her four-inch heels and the seam going up the back of her stockings. "You're very talented, Hunter. I particularly like this one." She reached up and pointed to a framed photo of a couple silhouetted on a beach at sunset. Her coat rose to mid-thigh.

"Let's get the hell out of here." Hunter sounded like a man with a bad cold.

She glanced over her shoulder. "To the video store?"

His breathing was labored. "Forget the video store. I'll call a cab."

"Oh, no, Hunter." She turned and prowled back to his desk. She was loving this, absolutely loving it. Excitement rushed through her, making her wet and achy. One look at Hunter's lap told her of his condition.

She perched on the edge of his desk and let her coat fall away from one silk-covered thigh. "You wouldn't want to ruin my fantasy, now would you?"

A muscle in his jaw twitched as he stared at her smooth thigh. When he glanced up, his eyes were nearly all pupil, no iris. "Lindsay, you're *naked.*"

"I know. Isn't it amazing?"

"It sure as hell is. And I'm—"

"Going crazy, I hope." She leaned toward him. "You and I know what's happening, but no one else will."

"That's what you think. Don't forget, I don't have a trench coat."

She laughed and gazed deliberately at his crotch. "So you have a slightly *bigger* challenge, so to speak. But you're not running nearly the same risk, so don't complain to me."

He quivered. "I can't believe you're doing this."

"But I am." She slid off the desk and walked

deliberately toward the door of his office. "Next stop, the video store."

"Wait!"

"Sorry, I have to get a move on. You said something about needing to catch a plane." As she left his office, she heard his soft curse and the sound of rapidly clicking keys on his computer.

Then he was beside her, his camera bag slung over one shoulder. "Okay, let's go."

"Glad you could make it." She smiled at his curious co-workers as she and Hunter headed down the hall and through the *Instant Replay* reception area. She was prepared to stroll, but Hunter took her elbow and propelled her as fast as her four-inch heels would allow. "In a hurry?" she asked.

"You have no idea." He called out a few quick goodbyes along the way before hustling her out into the hall and shoving her into the first available elevator.

When the elevator turned out to be empty, she flashed him again, quickly opening her coat and then closing it just as fast.

He groaned.

"It's all part of the fantasy." She retied the belt as the elevator stopped to take on more passengers. Desire was so thick in the small enclosure she wondered if the two businessmen who got on would sense it.

They both eyed her with interest, glanced at the grip Hunter had on her elbow and looked away, as if understanding a territorial signal.

Out on the street, people were too busy with their own concerns to pay much attention to a woman wearing a trench coat in July. The sun had disappeared behind the tall buildings, so she no longer needed sunglasses. She left them in her coat pocket.

On the way to Hunter's office she'd worn them for disguise more than anything. She'd been self-conscious about appearing in public like this, but now with Hunter striding along beside her in a state of sexual arousal, she didn't care what anyone else might think. She didn't imagine he'd easily forget escorting a nearly naked woman down Michigan Avenue. The memory should carry him way beyond the ten days he'd be gone.

"What changed?" he asked as they dodged pedestrians on their rapid course toward the video store. He concentrated on keeping them moving and didn't look at her.

"What do you mean?"

"Yesterday you wouldn't give me the time of day. Today you seem determined to turn me inside out." He steered her around a pair of teenagers wearing earphones. "What changed?"

"I had a chance to think about you asking me to get your mail. Did you really have to do that?"

"No."

Warmth flooded through her. What a great feeling to know that Hunter had actively pursued her. "That's what I thought." Or at least what she'd hoped.

"But why—oh, never mind why. I'm not going to louse this up with questions. Here's the video place." He held the door open for her. "Do I have to even ask what section you're going to look through?"

She paused to smile at him. "Probably not. Follow me."

"Don't worry. I'm right behind you."

She located the adult video section and sauntered toward it. She could almost feel Hunter's hot breath on her neck as he followed her. At four-thirty in the afternoon the store was almost empty of customers. She and Hunter were the only ones in the adult aisle, which played right into her hands. Slowly she scanned the shelves.

"I suppose this is going to take a while." Although he was obviously trying to appear blasé, the tremor in his voice betrayed him.

"Naturally." She tapped her finger against her mouth. "Maybe this one." She stretched to the top shelf for a video titled *Caution: Hot When Turned On.* "This could be a sign posted on a clothes dryer, don't you think?"

"I can't think."

"Brain fried?"

"Uh-huh."

"Poor baby." She handed him the video. "Hold this."

"Can we take this one and leave?"

"No." She glanced around to make sure they were still alone. "I just wanted you to hold it so I could do this." She pulled the lapels of her coat apart and gave him a quick peek at her breasts.

"Lindsay!"

She covered up again and batted her eyelashes at him. "Goodness, but you're jumpy."

He lowered his voice. "I'm about to jump *you*, right here in the aisle. How would you like that, if I backed you up against a shelf and did you, right here and now? I could be inside you in three seconds."

A shiver, part excitement, part apprehension, ran from the base of her spine to her neck, making the tiny hairs stand on end. "You wouldn't do that."

"An hour ago I would have agreed with you." His eyes glittered. "But you're pushing me. No telling what I might do if you push far enough."

"That sounds like a threat." She ran her tongue over her lips. The *Sexcapades* book hadn't anticipated a man out of control. As the seducer, she was supposed to have him at her mercy, ready to obey her command, following her around like a puppy. At the moment, Hunter looked more like a full-grown Doberman.

"I don't make threats." He held up the video. "You might want to get this one."

She backed up a step. "The video store part was supposed to take longer."

"Who says?" He advanced, the video in his hand. "Did somebody script this fantasy?"

She wasn't prepared to tell him about the *Sexcapades* book, at least not yet. "Uh, well—"

"Never mind. I don't care where you got the idea, but I strongly suggest you rent this video while I go outside and hail us a cab."

"But the 'L' would take longer and build the excitement."

"A trainload of commuters would get quite a show if we take the 'L'."

"It's also cheaper than a cab."

"As if I care at a moment like this." He handed her the video. "See you outside in five minutes."

HUNTER CHARGED for the front door of the video store, afraid if he stood in that aisle another nanosecond he would grab Lindsay and shove her coat open. No woman, not even a wild one like Pamela, had driven him past reason. But as he'd watched Lindsay sashaying along beside the shelves of adult videos, he'd felt reason slipping away and animal instinct taking over.

He stood outside on the sidewalk gulping in the sultry air. His blood pumped frantically, and he had to use his camera case to disguise his erection. Lindsay had no idea the power she had, and she'd used it with reckless abandon. Her stunt was incredible overkill. If she'd suggested dinner yesterday, he would have been her slave. Instead she'd appeared today wearing only a trench coat.

A cab. He was out here to get a cab. With tremendous effort, he shoved the picture of Lindsay flashing him out of his fevered brain long enough to whistle for a taxi. Fortunately one swerved to the curb exactly as Lindsay came out of the store, a small bag in one hand. The video. As if they'd need to watch it.

He used some care getting her into the cab, because he didn't want that trench coat to shift and expose anything illegal. Then he climbed in after her and gave the cabbie the address. As the taxi veered back into traffic, Hunter gripped his camera bag with both hands. Now he had to ride through the streets of downtown Chicago at rush hour with a naked woman next to him.

Lindsay pulled the video out of the bag. "Have you seen this one?"

Hunter gritted his teeth. "No."

"Me, either. That's good, that it'll be a new movie for both of us." She sounded as if she were discussing the latest James Bond flick.

Condoms. He wondered if she'd thought of that, because they wouldn't get beyond the front entryway of her apartment, and he wasn't packing any. Hadn't thought there was a reason to. Hadn't counted on a naked Lindsay waltzing into his office this afternoon.

He cleared his throat. "Do you, uh, have the necessary, uh…" He was afraid the cabbie might be listening. After all, he'd picked them up outside of a video store and one of them was wearing a trench coat in July. He might think Lindsay was a hooker. "I mean, I'm not prepared for…"

She lowered her voice to a silky, seductive level. "I'm prepared. Extremely prepared."

He didn't dare look at her. Instead he faced forward, his back straight and his fingers clutching the camera bag in a death grip. "Good."

She leaned closer and whispered in his ear. "It will be. Very."

"Watch it." His erection strained against his briefs. "We're only halfway home."

"I'm surprised at you," she said softly. "You've had so much experience, that I thought you'd be more calm about this."

"Experience?" Nothing had prepared him for an event like this.

"I'm only judging from what went on in your apartment for six months. From what I heard through the wall, I would assume that you've had lots of—"

"Lindsay."

"What?"

"Don't talk."

"That bad, huh?" She sounded pleased with herself.

"That bad." He wasn't ashamed to admit it. He prayed for an opening in traffic as their journey turned into an endless taxi ride. Every sway of the cab and every jolt when the driver hit the brakes tortured his aching penis. He focused on baseball stats, counted up his frequent flyer miles, silently recited his Social Security number a dozen times and tried to remember the phone numbers of all the people he knew.

Finally. The cab pulled up in front of the apartment building and by some miracle Hunter remembered to pay the guy. Somehow he stumbled up the four flights of stairs without grabbing Lindsay on one of the landings. She seemed to be having a high old time, giggling at his haste. Yeah, well, he'd see how she felt in a few minutes, when he ripped off that trench coat and… No, he'd better not think of that until they were inside her door.

He was glad that she was fast with the key, and he nearly pushed her through the door once she opened it.

"Okay." He plopped the camera bag on the floor. "Forget the video." He turned to her. "I want…" He halted. She still had on that maddening trench coat, but now she was holding her laundry basket.

Her eyes glowed with blue flame and her chest heaved as she struggled for breath. Her calmness seemed to have disappeared. "As you might have noticed, I have…nothing to wear. I need to wash…a few things. Do you mind?"

And he'd thought this couldn't get more intense. He took a shaky breath. "You're gonna kill me, you know that?"

"Yes, but you'll die a happy man." She reached into the basket and tossed him a condom.

His reflexes must not have been totally shot, because he caught it and put it in his pocket.

"Come on, Hunter." She gave him a long once-over. "Let's combine fantasies."

He nodded, his brain spinning, his body straining with almost unbearable tension. Once again, he followed her, this time down to the basement. If somebody was in there washing clothes, he'd throw them out. He didn't care what the consequences would be.

Instead, the door to the laundry room was closed, and a sign was tacked on it that read Laundry Room Temporarily Closed Due to Electrical Problems.

"Damn it!" Hunter's frustration reached the boiling point. No way could he make it back up those stairs without some kind of relief. No way.

Lindsay laughed, turned the knob and walked inside. "Like my sign?"

Her sign. Hunter dashed inside the laundry room and slammed the door shut. "I love your sign. Lindsay, we don't have to start the washers. We can just do it right here. On the floor. Anywhere. Let me take off that damned coat." He reached for her.

"Nope." She danced out of reach. "These clothes are going in those two old washers."

"I don't care about the fantasy! I need—"

"Hands off." She laughed again, the sound bubbling with excitement as she threw clothes into the washers. "We're doing this, Hunter. Don't chicken out on me now."

That brought him up short, even if didn't do anything for his condition. Pamela used to warn him not to chicken out, and he'd moved beyond his normal limits because of her taunts. He wasn't about to backtrack now just because Lindsay happened to

be the hottest woman he'd ever known. No, by
damn, he'd prove he was up to the challenge.

So he stood, his fists clenched, all of him
clenched, while Lindsay put in soap, *fabric soft-
ener,* for God's sake, and money to start the machine.

After eons had gone by, she glanced over her
shoulder again. "Hunter, would you please take my
coat?"

Oh, yes, he most certainly would. Hands trembling, he reached for the collar and drew the coat
down, down, until it cleared her arms. Then he
tossed it across the top of the two machines.

Slowly she rotated on those impossibly high
heels. "This is it."

And he knew he had to take the time to burn this
picture into his mind—Lindsay standing before
him, her gaze hot, her breasts lifted, her hips circled
with a black lace garter belt. And below that, her
downy triangle of curls guided him to everything
he desired in the world at this moment.

"You're magnificent," he said, his voice a low
growl of appreciation.

"Just call me Laundry-Room Girl."

"I call you amazing." He couldn't wait any
longer. Grasping her waist, he lifted her up onto
the nearest machine. And didn't that put her in the
perfect position for him to drive her crazy for a

change? Before she could react, he was on his knees, his shoulders slipping under her silk-clad thighs.

Her gasp as he zeroed in on his target was more than enough reward, but he had more rewards in mind. Loving her this way tested his endurance even more, but finally he had a chance to level the playing field and make her as wild as he was.

"Oh, Hunter…the vibration is…oh…oh, *my*."

About damn time, he thought. She'd been in control way too long. Her heels dug into his back as he took her higher and higher.

Gasping and crying out his name, she came in a rush of moisture that made him dizzy with triumph. He eased slowly away from her, stood on shaky legs and reached for the zipper of his fly. Then he took out the condom. He could barely manage the necessary movements as he trembled with the need to be inside her, sliding back and forth in that slick, warm chamber.

He gazed at her flushed, responsive body. His voice was thick with unreleased tension. "Lie down."

With a moan of surrender, she turned and lay back, bending her knees. Her upper body rested on one washer and her hips on the other. Hunter had just enough room to climb up between her thighs. "Scoot…scoot up."

She was breathing as hard as he was. "My head will be off the edge."

He grinned at her, feeling wilder and more reckless than at any time in his sexual life. "This is insane."

"Yeah, it is."

He grabbed the control panel at the back of the washer and slipped his other hand under her head. "Scoot up. I'll hold your head."

She did, which put her in range of his very stiff penis.

"Now lift your hips."

Clutching the control panel in imitation of his move, she lifted her hips. "Like that?"

"Like that." And he pushed deep inside her. He closed his eyes, his head swimming with pleasure.

"Good?"

"You have no idea." He opened his eyes and gazed down at her. At this moment she owned him, body and soul.

She smiled at him. "Better do me quick before I collapse."

"Trust me, this won't take long." He began a rapid, yet controlled rhythm, and the agitating machines beneath him sent vibrations up through his knees to his groin, creating an unreal sensation that would bring him to a climax in no time at all.

"Mmm." She gripped his bottom with her free hand.

He slowed, forced his body back a few notches, and looked into her eyes. "Gonna come again, Laundry-Room Girl?"

"Could be." She rotated her hips. "Maybe I can hang out in this position longer than I thought."

"Then you set the pace." Somehow he'd hold back the climax shouldering its way toward the front of the line. "Tell me what you want."

"Slower. A little deeper."

He shifted and thrust home, once, twice, three times.

"Like that." She began to pant as he maintained a steady pace. "Oh, yes, like that."

Each time he pushed into her, his heart opened a little wider. They belonged together. Forever.

"There…that's it…yes, *yes!*" She arched against him as spasms rippled through her.

That tipped him over the edge and, with a groan of pure satisfaction, he let go, erupting in a burst that took his breath away. As he shuddered against her, he lost what remained of his heart. She had all of him, to do with whatever she wanted.

CHAPTER EIGHT

LINDSAY FELT like a million bucks. Her *Sexcapades* fantasy had worked even better than she'd imagined it would, and Hunter seemed totally blown away by her sense of sexual adventure. But they both agreed that they'd had enough risky business for one night and decided to continue what was left of the evening upstairs, in an actual bed. They took out her soggy clothes—sweatshirts and all her old jeans—and tossed them in the dryer.

Then they crept upstairs and into her apartment, where they ate whatever food they could scrounge from her refrigerator. After that they made love until Hunter finally ran out of time.

"I don't want to leave," he said as he pulled on his clothes so he could go back to his apartment and pack. "I feel like canceling the trip."

"Don't do that." She dressed quickly in cutoffs and a T-shirt. "Too many people are counting on you. The time will go by fast." She didn't believe that, but it was the sort of thing lovers said to each other when they had to part.

"It will drag by, and you know it." He paused to gaze at her. "Lindsay, we need to talk. About us, about—"

She put a finger to his lips. "We will. When you get back. Tonight has been wild and crazy. Let it all settle in your mind a bit. Then we'll talk."

"You do realize this is serious, what we have going on."

She nodded, happier than she'd ever been in her life. "Yes." But she wanted him to go away for ten days and come back just as sure as he was now. Then she could fully trust the words that came out of his mouth. Right now, they could be a product of all those excellent climaxes.

"Just so you realize that." He kissed her quickly. "My flight home leaves Nassau in the morning, so I'll be back here at a civilized time— before you get off work. Then we'll talk."

"Fine." She could imagine what kind of homecoming that would be. They might have to use his apartment so they wouldn't alarm the neighbors next to her.

"Come over and talk to me while I throw a few things in my suitcase, okay?"

"Sure." She followed him out of the bedroom.

Before he reached her front door, he turned back. "Would you give me a picture to take with me? Have you got one I can have?"

Now there was a very good sign. Hunter wanted to carry her picture with him on this trip. "I think I have one around here. Let me take a look, and I'll bring it over in a couple of minutes. You go get started on your packing."

"Okay." He kissed her again. "See you in a minute. I'll leave the door open."

She grinned. "Like in *Friends*."

"Yeah. Like that." With a smile, he left.

Once he was gone, she returned to her bedroom and rummaged through the photo box where she kept her snapshots. Finding one she wanted to give him turned out to be harder than she'd thought. He was a professional photographer, and he'd dated extremely photogenic women. All she had was a box of candid pictures, most of them including family and friends. In each of them she looked ordinary.

Finally she settled on one that Shauna had taken during a weekend trip to Wisconsin last fall. Lindsay was standing in a pile of autumn leaves, laughing. She didn't look like a model, but at least she looked happy.

Leaving the box open on her bed, she took the picture and headed over to Hunter's apartment. Opening his door without knocking felt very good, as if they definitely had something solid going on. She wanted to believe that.

The minute she stepped inside the door, she heard Hunter's voice coming from the bedroom. Apparently he was on the phone.

"I think it's great that you'll be down there, too," he said.

Lindsay's instincts went on alert. She paused, shamelessly eavesdropping on the conversation. It wasn't like she hadn't done that for months with Hunter.

"Of course we're still on speaking terms, Pamela. I don't hold grudges. You should know that. Yeah, it'll be good to see you, too. Well, I gotta finish packing. See you in Nassau. Bye."

He would be seeing his ex in the Bahamas, photographing her for the snorkeling feature, no doubt. He'd said he was looking forward to it. They'd be together in a place known for romance, the perfect place to make up.

And, as always, Lindsay was the rebound girl, set up to take the fall. It was the umpteenth rerun of a very bad movie, and she'd seen it way too many times.

Ice water running through her veins, she backed quietly toward the door. Then she opened it silently and closed it with a bang. Stuffing the picture she'd brought in the pocket of her cutoffs, she called out to Hunter. "Anybody home?"

"Hey!" Hunter came out of the bedroom, his

suitcase in one hand. "I wondered what had happened to you. Did you find a picture for me?"

Lindsay shook her head. "Nothing good."

"Oh, for heaven's sake." Hunter put down the suitcase and came over to pull her into his arms. "I'll bet you have tons of pictures. You just didn't like any of them."

She wondered how she could continue to smile and talk when her heart had been through the shredder. Somehow she managed it. "You caught me. I'm as photogenic as a hedgehog."

"Bullshit." He framed her face in both hands. "When I come back, I want to take about a million pictures of you."

"And risk breaking that expensive camera?"

"Silly woman. You'll be gorgeous." He leaned down and feathered a kiss over her lips. "Stunning."

She fought the tears, but a couple dribbled out and slipped over his fingers.

"Aw, Lindsay, don't cry." He kissed her closed eyelids. "I'll call you while I'm gone."

"That's okay." She sounded choked up, but he probably thought it was because he was leaving. She blinked away the tears. Time to get strong. "You don't have to do that."

"I know I don't *have* to, but I want to."

"I'll bet you don't even know my number."

He looked surprised. "That's a fact. Amazing. Tell it to me."

She recited her phone number, never believing for a minute that he'd remember it.

"Got it." He gazed into her eyes. "I'm going to miss you something terrible, Laundry-Room Girl."

She didn't think so, but he might think he would miss her, at least until he made up with Pamela. "I'll miss you, too," she said.

"I have to go."

"I know."

"Take care of yourself while I'm gone. When I get back, we'll talk."

She nodded. Yes, they probably would. He'd have to tell her that he was back with Pamela, but he'd always cherish the fact that Lindsay had been there when he needed someone. Lindsay had heard it all many times.

Hunter kissed her again, and then, too quickly, they were walking out the door of his apartment. He dropped one last kiss on her lips, squeezed her hand and walked down the hall. At the stairwell he turned and waved. She waved back. And then he was gone.

If this had been the first time she'd ever fallen for a guy after his breakup, she might have been able to convince herself that he wouldn't get back with Pamela during their stay in the Bahamas. She might have been able to explain his conversation on the phone as Hunter merely being polite to someone he still had to work with. Unfortunately, this wasn't the first time. But, by damn, it would be the last.

TEN DAYS LATER, Hunter took a cab from the airport to the apartment. He was going crazy from lack of contact with Lindsay. The trip had been a disaster, with tropical storms screwing up all the plans. Worse yet, the storms had made communication with Chicago dicey. Between the weather and the way it had compressed the shooting schedule, he'd either been without a phone connection or out of time to make the call.

Twice he'd had a brief moment to call when Lindsay was at work, but he didn't have that number. The 800 number for the bank got him a series of voice-mail prompts that ended somewhere in Nebraska, and he'd hung up in frustration. He hoped she'd figured out that the storms had created problems with the phones, because he hated promising to call and not following through.

Lindsay was at work right now, and he considered asking the cabbie to drop him there. But when he saw Lindsay again, he didn't want a teller's cage separating them. He wanted to be able to kiss her senseless, take off every stitch of her clothes and make love until dawn.

What a nightmare of a trip. The storms had messed up the schedule for shooting, and he had virtually nothing to show for all the time spent. On top of that, Pamela had been determined to rekindle the flame. Apparently she'd pulled some strings to get the snorkel layout job because she thought in that tropical setting she'd convince him they were meant for each other.

He was meant for Lindsay, and he'd finally had to tell Pamela that in so many words, to get her to back off. She hadn't been much fun on location after that. The makeup artist had started referring to her as Tropical Storm Pamela.

It was all behind him now, though. He had about thirty minutes before Lindsay came home, time enough to shower and decide how to commemorate this important reunion. He'd bought a single red rose at the airport, and he wanted to think of some clever way to leave it by her door.

The perfect plan didn't come to him until he was standing under the shower in his apartment. After drying off and dressing in shorts and a T-shirt, he emptied the contents of his suitcase into his laundry basket, put the rose on top of it, and placed the basket in front of Lindsay's door. That should send the message he had in mind.

Then he left his door slightly ajar and paced the length of his apartment, too wired to sit down. He hoped she remembered when he was coming back. If she didn't remember, that was a bad sign. If she'd gone out with friends after work, or stopped to run any errands, he didn't know how he'd stand the wait. He'd thought about her constantly for ten days, and at last the long drought was over.

LINDSAY HAD CONSIDERED going to a movie after work in order to delay getting back to the apartment. Hunter was due home this afternoon and, coward that she was, she wanted to put off the inevitable conversation with him. But she needed to show a little backbone to keep her self-respect, so she climbed aboard the bus and headed home, prepared to face the music.

He hadn't called, and although she could blame that on the tropical storms in the Caribbean, she didn't think that was the real reason. It couldn't have knocked out every single opportunity. No, the explanation was clear enough. He'd been too busy with Pamela.

She'd started looking for another apartment, knowing that she wouldn't be able to stay next door to Hunter while he renewed his love affair with Pamela. He might be more careful now that he knew how easily sound penetrated the common wall, but he couldn't possibly be *that* careful. The walls were too thin, and so were her defenses.

For ten days she'd suffered in private, unwilling to hear what Shauna would say if she found out. Shauna had been through enough with her on this score, anyway. So close to her wedding, she didn't need to deal with another stupid sob story, one that was all Lindsay's fault.

With a sense of doom, she climbed the stairs to the fourth floor. Hunter was an honorable and humane man, so he'd want to get this over with fast. He'd be waiting for her. She felt that in her bones.

She spotted the laundry basket the minute she started down the hall, and her stomach lurched. Maybe he was trying to be lighthearted so they could laugh about this. But she didn't feel lighthearted. She felt as if she'd swallowed a helping of hot rocks.

She paused to look down at the laundry basket. *A red rose?* Maybe that was his idea of a sympathy gift. Her stomach churned.

"Hi."

She glanced up to see him leaning in the doorway of his apartment. He looked so damned good, this man who belonged to someone else. He was smiling tenderly at her, probably because he knew that he was about to lower the boom.

Gulping, she forced herself to say something polite. "Nice trip?"

His smile faded. "Oh, hell. You're upset because I didn't call." He pushed away from the doorframe and started toward her. "It was crazy down there, and I—"

"Don't, Hunter." She'd thought she could bear up under the speech, but it turned out she couldn't. "Don't make excuses."

"You're right. I should have found some way. I

should have sent a damned telegram. I'm sorry, Lindsay.''

''Me, too.'' She stared at him, her heart like lead. ''But that's the way it goes, right? Thanks for the rose.'' She turned away and fumbled with her key.

''Wait!'' He grabbed her arm. ''Are you serious? Are you going to let the fact that I couldn't get to a phone ruin everything between us?''

She glanced up at him, determined not to cry. ''You mean ruin our friendship? Because I can't do the friendship thing anymore, Hunter. Not after—''

''Friendship?'' He grasped her other arm, knocking her purse to the floor as he spun her to face him. ''Yeah, that's part of it, but I had some other words in mind. Like *lover.*''

Had she been wrong? Her icy heart began to thaw. Could she possibly have been *wrong?* Her chest tightened as she looked into his eyes, and she had to swallow before she could speak. ''You didn't make up with Pamela?''

His jaw dropped.

''I heard you talking with her on the phone before you left.'' Oh, dear God. Maybe, maybe, she'd been wrong. ''So I thought, when you didn't call, that—''

With a groan he pulled her close, his mouth seeking hers, his kiss hungry and insistent. Hope bloomed in her. This wasn't the kiss of a man who'd been enjoying the charms of another woman for the past few days. It was the kiss of a man who'd missed her as desperately as she'd missed him. She'd been *wrong. Totally wrong!* She'd never been so happy about being wrong in her life.

Eventually he lifted his lips from hers, but not before he'd erased every doubt she'd had. "Does that answer your question?"

Tears of joy welled in her eyes as she held him tight and looked into his warm gaze. "I'm so sorry for doubting you." She cleared the huskiness from her voice. "So very sorry."

"You should be." His grin was slow and sexy. "And you can apologize for the rest of the night, in all sorts of interesting ways. It'll probably take many creative fantasies before I'll forgive you."

"Okay." Desire curled in her tummy. She would love making amends.

He shook his head. "I still can't believe you would think such things after what went on between us before I left."

"I know, but you have no idea how many times I've been dumped by a guy on the rebound, so when I heard you talking to your ex, I just assumed—"

"Rebound?" He blinked. "What rebound?"

She realized that guys didn't always understand the finer points of relationships, so she didn't mind explaining. "Pamela dumped you that night we first made love, so that makes me the one you picked up on the rebound. I can see now that I'm more than that, but in the beginning you were definitely on the rebound.''

"Was I, now?" Hunter started laughing as he maneuvered her toward the open door of his apartment. "This is what you get for eavesdropping, Laundry-Room Girl. Pamela didn't dump me. I dumped her about three weeks prior to that night. What you heard was Pamela having a hissy fit after I said I wasn't interested in getting back together."

Lindsay's head buzzed. "*You* dumped *her?*"

"Yeah." Hunter kicked the door shut. "Want to know who I dumped her for?"

Lindsay stared at him, completely dazzled. "*Me?*"

"You. Now let's get naked. I can't propose when I'm in this highly aroused condition."

"P-propose?" Lindsay didn't think her heart could hold any more happiness, but here came another bucketful.

"Right." He undid the buttons of her dress. "Because the other words I'd like to use in connection with you are…my darling…and—" He hesitated, looking unsure. "And my wife," he murmured.

"Oh, Hunter." She started quivering.

"But let's do this first." He shoved her dress to the floor. "Then later on I'll get down on one knee and everything, I promise. You'll have the whole deal, except for the ring, which I think we should pick out together, assuming you say yes, which you might not. But don't think about your answer now. Think about getting out of your clothes."

The quivering became worse. He was reducing her to jelly, both mentally and physically. She could barely breathe. "Yes."

"Good." He unfastened the catch on her bra. "I'm glad you're going along with the getting naked program, because otherwise I'd—"

"I mean, yes, I'll marry you."

He went completely still as he looked into her eyes. Hope battled uncertainty in his expression. "Really?"

"Really. I love you to pieces, Hunter."

He swallowed. "I'd hoped...but I wasn't...we haven't been involved for very..."

"Oh, I've been involved with you for months." She smiled, tears blurring her vision. "You just didn't know it."

"Same here." He sighed and cupped her face in both hands. "Lindsay Scott, I love you to pieces. I love you more with every day that goes by."

She'd never heard more beautiful words. Her throat closed as gratitude swept through her. Dreams really did come true.

He stroked his thumbs over her cheeks. "Can you imagine how much more we'll love each other in fifty years?"

"It boggles my mind." Fifty years with Hunter. She'd buy her own copy of *Sexcapades,* that was for sure. "Do you think they'll have washing machines in fifty years?"

He laughed. "I don't know, but whatever they invent, as long as it vibrates I'm sure we'll be able to adapt." He tugged her toward his bedroom. "But on this occasion, I plan to give you a screaming orgasm the old-fashioned way. Fortunately, I have it on good authority that my next-door neighbor isn't home to hear us."

Lindsay started unfastening the button at the waistband of his shorts. "Are you sure about that?"

He stopped and gazed at her. "Actually, she is home," he said softly as he pulled her down to the bed. "Home at last."

GOING ALL THE WAY

Carly Phillips

CHAPTER ONE

REGAN DAVIS glanced around Divine Events one last time. The hottest party-planning business in Chicago earned its name, but since she'd been dumped, Regan had no more use for their specialty skills.

She paused at the table in the reception area and took in the large Grecian urn she'd seen many times before. Filled with bird-of-paradise, hyacinth, hydrangea and lush greenery, the flowers created a canopy over the table. Gliding her hand over a set of white photo albums—portfolios of Divine Events' creations—her hand skipped from book to book until she reached a red leather-bound volume. The draping flowers had hidden the album from view until now and she paused, intrigued.

A few feet away, the doorway, fresh air and a new life beckoned to her. Beside her, a crystal bowl full of candy sat available for picking. But not even the gourmet chocolates or the taste of freedom tempted Regan as much as that book.

Why? Why did that single volume entice her so?

Because her life was in the dumps and she was ready for something, anything, to turn it around, spice it up, make it what she wanted it to be. And the scarlet book just oozed scandal and sin. As she remained alone in the room, there seemed to be no reason not to peek, so she sat on the couch, then reached for the heavy book. No title and the leather turned out to be a protective covering for an over-size paperback. She tried to flip through but each page had been sealed, a fact that further heightened her piquing curiosity. She bit down on her lower lip and opened the front of the book in search of the title page.

Sexcapades: Secret Games and Wild Adventures for Uninhibited Lovers. Oh, my.

She slammed the book closed. She was certain a furious blush now covered her cheeks, but her southern breeding took over. She glanced around through lowered lashes. Though voices buzzed from the back fitting rooms and other areas of the shop, no one was in the reception area or entryway. Because she was alone, Regan indulged herself further. Her heart beat out a rapid rhythm and her mouth grew dry as she looked at the first sealed section. "Tie Him Up in Knots: For Women Who Like Being in Control."

An erotic tingling heightened her senses, but she acknowledged that the words on the page hit her on another level. It had been a long time since Regan had been in charge of anything, especially her life. Yes, she'd made a start, but it was long overdue.

Prior to her trip to Divine Events to cancel her wedding plans, Regan had stopped in at Victoria's Secret and purchased the most naughty, racy, sexy nighties she could find. Clothes had to come next. She pulled at the silk blouse buttoned to the top that was making her perspire. No, darn it, the blouse was making her *sweat*. She snorted aloud, disgusted. Her southern manners and refinements were so ingrained, even losing them took premeditated thought.

From being the dutiful daughter to almost becoming the obedient wife, she'd lived her life by the rules indoctrinated in her and her sisters since birth. Her parents already had a banker and two attorneys as sons-in-law, and Regan was to have added a third lawyer to the *perfect* family tree. Regan would have finally become the perfect daughter, not the disappointment. Not the daughter who did things her own way.

Her daddy, the judge, had been thrilled and her mama would have been, if Regan had planned to hold the wedding at the country club in Savannah. That had been a huge disappointment for the Davis family.

Her move to Chicago one month ago was another, but her fiancé had insisted they marry here, in the city where they'd relocated thanks to his being named head partner of the new office. Regan had been too happy to go along. Anything to escape the restrictions she'd grown up with. And now she had to deliver the third blow. She shook her head, unable to stifle a laugh because, before today, Atlanta burning had been the darkest day in the history of the Davis family.

A proper southern belle, born and bred, Regan had been groomed to be a blushing bride. Instead she was a jilted one. Which didn't bother her as much as it should have, considering her life's mission would now be classified as a failure by her loved ones. Her mother would be particularly disappointed. Kate Davis was at her best as a parent when her daughters complied with her southern expectations. Defy them and Kate withdrew, turning into a stranger instead of a mom.

With this broken engagement, Regan's family would be devastated, but Regan was grateful to be liberated from the shackles of propriety and from the fiancé who'd been yet another concession to expectations.

Regan should be desolate. Instead, with her wedding canceled and her fiancé gone from their shared apartment in the Chicago high-rise, she felt relieved—despite Darren's betrayal. They'd used each other—she accepted that now. She'd chosen him to please her family, never mind all the things lacking in their relationship. And he'd picked her because of her daddy's standing in the legal community. Still, Darren had walked out on her first. She was almost tempted to applaud his courage.

And wouldn't her parents be shocked to find out that Darren had grown tired of the proper southern manners schooled into Regan since before her coming out? What a laughable irony. He preferred the loud, tacky, foul-mouthed legal associate he'd hired to work beside him. Regan shook her head. She had no business thinking evil thoughts about a woman who was bold enough to wear miniskirts and dark, sexy-looking lipstick, and to speak in a manner that demanded a man's respect. Not when Regan wanted to be more like her and always had.

She wanted to be free. Free to wear clothing she liked, not clothing society, or her mother, deemed proper. Free to channel her public relations abilities into a career beyond charity work. And free to choose a sexy guy without checking his credentials or pedigree. Heck, at this point she'd settle for being able to think for herself. Living in Savannah had stifled her and she hadn't realized it until she'd moved to Chicago one short month ago—and she hadn't accepted it until now.

But her life could start fresh. New. Now. Darren, the no-good cheating rat, had given her that chance—if she had the nerve to reach out and grab the opportunity.

Sexcapades. She ran her hand over the soft red leather. The scarlet covering. How apropos, Regan thought, and after a quick glance around to make sure she was still alone, she defiantly undid the first few buttons on her silk blouse, giving an unobstructed view of a matching pink lace bra and, she thought proudly, the ample cleavage her sisters envied.

She ran a hand through her carefully set curls, creating what she hoped was the disheveled, comehither look her mother associated with bimbos and tainted women. A quick peek in her compact mirror proved her right. Her cheeks were flushed pink and a quick swipe of lipstick added a sultry appeal. Talk about making do with the bare minimum essentials, Regan thought. But it'd have to do, at least until she could shop for hot, skimpy new clothes to go with her bold new outlook and attitude.

The more she removed the external shackles in her mind and the external ones she put on each morning, the more Regan's courage grew. She glanced down. The directions inside the book were clear, instructing readers to tear out a section that sparked their interest, then live and love!

Her palms grew damp and her hands shook, her

gaze returning again to the "Tie Him Up in Knots" section. Oh, yes, she'd like to tie a man up in knots, to see a spark of desire light in his eyes and know his need was for her and her alone. And, suddenly, she didn't want to wait for the right man to come along sometime in her future. She wanted to grab control now. Before she informed her family about the broken engagement, Regan wanted to take that first step and establish her independence. Starting with a no-strings-attached affair.

At that heady, seductive thought, liquid desire flowed through her veins, pulsing, pounding, assuring her she'd chosen the right course. And she'd start with picking her fantasy. Despite her resolve, southern breeding took over, and her gaze circled the shop to see if anyone would catch her stealing a page. No, she was still alone. She reminded herself that, after today, she'd never see this place or anyone in here again, then she mustered her courage and ripped out the page.

The tearing sound echoed loud and clear in the empty reception area. Regan winced, but when no one came by to chastise her, she folded the paper and slipped it into her purse. Mission accomplished, she thought with pride.

Now she just needed a man.

THE THINGS a guy put up with for his friends, Sam Daniels thought wryly. He stepped out of the fitting room in Divine Events, leaving the monkey suit and the rest of his best-man trappings behind—at least until tomorrow's ceremony. Tonight was the rehearsal dinner and, thank goodness, the bride and groom had opted for casual clothing.

He swiped a hand over his eyes but the bleariness remained. Well, what did he expect after taking a late-night flight out of San Francisco? Before coming home, he'd been on a prolonged trip, as he usually was in his job as a corporate pilot for Connectivity Industries, a large computer company. His most recent stint had been taking the CFO and some underlings to Paris, which had entailed a stay at the Ritz and assorted other perks. Man he loved his job.

After growing up in a hellhole in San Francisco, he'd promised himself he'd get out and stay out. And he had. Sam had a condo in a high-rise in the Embarcadero with a view of the Bay Bridge. Overlooking the city reminded him of how far he'd come. Thanks to his hard work, he'd landed a job that took him all over the world and paid extremely well. The luxuries associated with his career weren't bad either.

The only downside was jet lag and Sam suffered the bone-weary feeling now. He was in no mood for his newest obligation, but, as best man, Sam was duty bound to do right by his good friend, a guy he'd met in flight school. Bill had decided to give up flying and settle down with his soon-to-be wife. Sam snorted, disappointed with his friend's choice, but determined to respect it nonetheless.

Like Sam's mother, Bill's fiancée didn't want a man who wasn't home, one who traveled for a living. Sam just hoped that unlike his old man, Bill didn't wither into a shell of a human being as a result. Sam shrugged. Bill was a grown man and knew what he was getting himself into. But no woman would get Sam tied up in knots, in matrimony or in anything else besides a sizzling-hot affair.

And it had been too damn long since he'd indulged in one of those. Mostly because women claimed they could handle one night—just like they claimed they could cope with his lifestyle—then, before he blinked, they were trying to change him. To convince him what he really wanted was to leave the friendly skies behind in favor of hearth and home.

Like hell.

Despite his personal feelings on the subject, he'd rearranged his schedule in order to hit Chicago a few days before the wedding, but he wanted out of *this* place now. All the flowers and white accessories screamed *wedding* and that made Sam shudder.

He tucked his T-shirt into his jeans and strode through the hall and into the reception area. Only the sun could reflect brighter than all these damn mirrors surrounding him. He squinted his eyes as he set foot in the entryway. Then he froze, mesmerized.

She was a blonde and he'd always been a sucker for blondes. She wore silk, a fabric that reminded him of the feel of a woman's skin. And her fingers glided over a red book in a delicate, erotic way, adding to the intensity that had begun throbbing through his body. And he hadn't even seen her face.

Not that it mattered. If she was in Divine Events, she was either about to be married, a maid of honor or a bridesmaid, which in Sam's book usually meant she was waiting to catch the bouquet and be next in line to tie the knot. At least that's what his sisters and their friends claimed and Sam refused to be trapped. He shook his head and laughed.

At the sound, she looked up, wide-eyed, and met his gaze. Stunned and obviously embarrassed, judging by her pink cheeks, she slid the book off her lap and back onto the table.

He didn't know what intrigued him more, the scarlet book, the pink cheeks…or her. She had large blue eyes with a hint of sadness and secrets, porcelain skin and the most gorgeous bone structure he'd ever seen. And she couldn't tear her eyes from his.

It'd been a long time since he'd experienced such a strong, reciprocal visceral reaction to a woman. Long enough that he decided it was worth exploring further.

He strode to the couch and settled in beside her, laying one arm behind her head. "Hi," he said and leaned close. A floral scent assaulted his senses and inside his jeans he grew hard. Talk about instant attraction. He hadn't been so immediately horny since he was a kid.

She inclined her head so blond strands brushed her shoulder. "Hi, yourself." Her eyelashes fluttered in a move unpracticed yet seductive at the same time. Added to the sultry southern accent, the gesture caused desire to rush through him at Mach speed.

He let his gaze travel over her hands, which remained splayed on her thighs. No rings adorned any finger, just an intriguing tan line on the ring finger of her left hand. From looks alone, she appeared single.

Score one for him, he thought. "So what's a nice girl like you doing in a place like this?" He chose the worst, most obvious pickup line he could think of.

As he'd hoped, she rolled her eyes and laughed, a light flirtatious sound he enjoyed.

When she didn't answer immediately, he questioned her further. "Bridesmaid fitting, maid of honor or planning your wedding?" He ticked off each possibility on one finger.

She exhaled a long sigh. "Try, canceling one."

"A fitting?" he asked.

"My wedding," she replied, her gaze darting from his.

That took him off guard and explained the hint of sadness he'd glimpsed in her eyes. "I sure as hell hope it was your choice or else your fiancé's got rocks in his head." And in his pants. Sam might not be into commitment but what kind of guy walked away from a woman like this?

"I think I'll take that as a compliment," she said.

"I think you should."

Her gaze jerked toward his. For the first time since he'd sat down, her smile reached her eyes. No pain, no sadness, no vulnerability remained. Just pure seductive woman.

Acting on impulse, he reached for her hand, threading his fingers through hers. Her lids opened wide with surprise, her thick lashes fluttering over her huge and—if he wasn't mistaken—hungry eyes. Her shock gone, she obviously liked his touch as much as he enjoyed hers.

And he did enjoy. Her skin was as soft as her voice, as hot as the need gliding through him and telling him not to let this woman walk away just yet. "Was it your idea or his? To call things off, I mean."

"His." She shrugged, managing to give even that everyday gesture a delicate bent. "But he did us both a favor. Even if he is a cheatin' son of a bitch," she muttered under her breath.

But not low enough. "Sounds to me like you're better off without him."

"Tell me something I don't know." She turned towards him. "So what's a nice guy like you doing in a place like this?" A quirky grin pulled at her lips. "Are you the groom, best man or usher?" she asked.

"Best man."

Her gaze boldly traveled over him, from the tips of his old sneakers to the top of his head. "Now *that* I can believe."

"I think I'll take that as a compliment."

She laughed. "I think you should. I also think you need to tell me what you're after," she said, glancing down at their still intertwined hands.

Once again, she'd stumped him. Normally a take-charge guy, he didn't know what to say now.

He was attracted to her. Sexually, he desired her. That had been the start. But now he realized she was hurting and, though it shocked him, he wanted to take away her pain. To hear her laugh again. To know when he flew home on Sunday, he'd leave her happier and with good memories to take away the bad.

But there was no other way to describe what he wanted other than a no-strings-attached affair. His body was primed and ready since laying eyes on her. Problem was, she was vulnerable and he didn't want to cause her any more pain. The choice had to be hers.

Regan looked into the eyes of this gloriously sexy, raven-haired stranger and she melted like chocolate in the hot sun. His face was scruffy from needing a shave and his green eyes glittered with desire. Exactly the type of guy she'd fantasized about when deciding to exert her independence.

Yet, as interested as he'd initially appeared, as bold as he'd been in taking her hand, he seemed hesitant now. "Let me make this easy for you," she said to him, leaning closer. Then she drew a deep, shaky breath. After all, she'd never propositioned a man before and this was all so sudden. As much as she intended to turn off those ingrained expectations, some old-fashioned honesty would come in handy now.

"Obviously I'm coming off a bad situation, so I'm not looking for anything long-term. But I want to take charge of my life and I want to begin now." She paused, meeting his gaze. Her heart pounded from just looking at him, and her breath caught when desire flared in the depths of his intense eyes. "And I want to start with you."

Lifting her hands to his mouth, he pressed his lips against her knuckles. Moist heat licked at her skin and her breath caught in a hitch.

"I'm listening," he said, obviously interested.

If he was this good with his mouth on her hand, she wondered just how good he'd be with his tongue and lips on certain other body parts.

She couldn't believe she was having these thoughts about a man she'd just met, any more than she could believe she was having this conversation with him. But she'd wanted to start *now* and fate had sent him her way. She wasn't about to turn him away. "I have this one weekend before I have to go home to Georgia and break the news to my family about the engagement."

He nodded, light dancing in his eyes. "What a coincidence. I have this one weekend before I return to California. Minus a wedding appointment or two, I can be all yours. What did you have in mind?"

Regan clenched her free hand around the handle

of her purse. Inside sat the folded page from *Sex-capades*. Was this man up for bondage games?

Was she? "I'm tired of being a good girl and doing the proper thing."

"You want to be bad."

She nodded. "Wickedly bad." With trembling hands, she opened her bag and pulled out the sheet of paper that had started her on this insane course, and handed it to... Regan blinked in surprise. "I just realized I don't even know your name."

His gaze darted to the page, then back to her, those green eyes filled with intrigue and hunger. "Well, if you're going to be tying me up, I'd say introductions are in order."

CHAPTER TWO

"REGAN DAVIS." She held out her hand for a shake, which felt ridiculous considering his mouth had already brushed over her skin. Considering her nipples had already puckered into her flimsy bra and even less substantial silk blouse.

"Sam Daniels," he said, his lips twisting in an amused grin. "Seems silly to shake on a deal as intimate as this one, don't you think?"

He'd read her mind. And, yes, she thought it was ridiculous. But proper introductions demanded a proper handshake and Regan Davis had been raised a proper woman. "Damn," she said, forcing the profanity from the back of her throat.

He lifted an eyebrow in question and Regan sighed. "You see, I'm a southern lady, born and raised." She deliberately added to her drawl. "And I want to leave that upbringing in the dust, but if I keep falling back on proper behavior, I'll never have the adventure I want." She'd never make it past Divine Events' threshold with this man, and that would never do because she wanted to end up in his bed!

"Yes, Regan, you will." He pulled her to her feet.

She shivered at the seductive way her name sounded rolling off his lips.

"Just remember we're way past the handshake stage and you'll be fine," he said, twirling the *Sexcapades* page in front of her eyes before folding it and placing it in the back pocket of his jeans. Which, she noted, molded to a perfectly defined behind. She shook her head. Which molded to a perfect male *butt,* she silently amended.

He patted his rear with one hand where he'd tucked in the page. "If you want it, you're going to have to come get it," he said with a suggestive grin.

Now that was an intriguing idea, but before she could respond, they were interrupted.

"Hello, folks." Cecily Divine, owner of Divine Events, strolled into the reception area. "Can I get you two anything?"

"No, thank you, we were just leaving," Regan said, taking charge of the decision for both herself and Sam.

Cecily nodded. "Okay. It's started to rain. Need me to call you a cab?"

If Cecily thought that anything about Regan having met or hooked up with Sam was odd, she didn't show it.

"Regan?" Sam asked, leaving the choice of transportation up to her.

"Actually we can take the el. My apartment is in Lincoln Park, right near the DePaul stop." And one of her resolutions was to become more worldly and stop taking taxis when she could commute by the el.

Cecily shrugged. "Okay, then. I'll leave you two alone and bother some other customers." She walked over to give Regan a quick hug. "You take care, okay?" Stepping back, she then shook Sam's hand. "I'll see you tonight at the rehearsal dinner." Like the efficient whirlwind she was, Cecily disappeared as quickly as she'd come, leaving Sam and Regan alone again.

"Ready?" she asked him.

"Born ready. Since I came straight from the airport, my duffel bag's in the coat closet." He headed to retrieve his things, apparently not the least bit hesitant about leaving with her.

She wasn't unsure either. Still, she swallowed hard.

He returned, duffel in hand and together they started for the exit. He swung the door wide, holding it for her. "Lead the way."

"What a mass of contradictions," she said,

laughing. "Who are you, really? The gentleman holding the door or the one willing to give me control?"

He cocked his head to one side and self-assured sexiness oozed from him in waves. "Damned if I know myself, but one thing's for sure—thanks to that fantasy of yours, by the time the day's over, we're going to know a helluva lot more about each other."

And, Regan had a hunch, she'd learn even more about herself.

SAM WALKED into the entryway of a glass-and-chrome apartment building, took in the obviously expensive decor and let out a long, slow whistle. "These are swanky digs."

Regan waited until they'd reached the elevators and pushed the button before she turned to face him. "According to the real estate agent, Lincoln Park has more restaurants per capita than almost any other neighborhood in the city. I can make reservations every night of the week and never duplicate a meal for a good long time."

"Sounds like a working woman's dream."

She glanced up at him through wide blue eyes. "Not being a working woman, I wouldn't know."

They walked into the waiting elevator and the doors closed behind them. He propped a hand against the mirrored wall and anchored her body between himself and the back corner.

So she didn't work. "What do you do?" he asked.

She lifted one shoulder in a dainty shrug. "I chair committees and benefits, raise money for charity and the right causes. Anything that made my family and fiancé happy, I took on. And, in turn, they made sure I was treated like a princess. Until Darren took on that old double standard. The one my mama accepted from my daddy." She pursed her lips in disgust, making him wonder what she'd reveal next. "You see, cheatin's okay as long as he treats her right." She shook her head. "What do you think of that code of ethics?"

"Cheating's never all right," he said, vehemently. No man should make a vow and deliberately break it. It went against everything Sam believed in. One thing he knew for damn sure—if this woman belonged to him, he'd never stray.

"Are you trying to tell me you're a one-woman man?" She made light of his words, but her expression was one of gratitude.

"I'm telling you if I'm with you, you can be sure there's no one else to worry about." He brushed a strand of hair, damp from the rain, off her forehead.

"Well, good." Her lashes fluttered down in obvious relief. He wasn't surprised his southern beauty was raised in luxury, a far cry from the way he'd grown up. Nor was he shocked she was a kept woman, either by her ex-fiancé or her family. Old southern traditions were hard to break. He didn't hold it against her since she'd as much as told him she'd never known any other way.

But she was fighting her way out now and he admired her for it. He was actually thankful he was able to play a part in her belated attempt at joining the women's revolution. Even if it was just a sexual part. Especially if it was a sexual part. Hell, sex was a great start to a new life and he intended to give her a night she'd never forget.

"An affair's one thing, but I don't want to live a double standard and take someone else's man."

Knowing how solitary his life had been lately, he chuckled. "I can promise you, you're not poaching on anyone else's territory."

She raised her gaze. "What's wrong with the women in...where did you say you were from?" she asked.

"I didn't. But I'm from California, and there's nothing wrong with the women there except for the fact that, like most women I've encountered, they're looking for commitment."

She rested a shoulder against the elevator wall. "And you're gun-shy?"

"I wouldn't say that. I just like my life the way

it is. I'm a pilot and my job takes me around the world.'' He shrugged. ''Being confined isn't my thing. Unless it's like this. With you.'' He stroked a hand down her cheek and watched as her pupils dilated at his not-so-innocent touch.

He let his lips hover over hers, the desire to taste her strong. But not stronger than the need to learn more about her. In the background, the elevator hummed, a metronomic accompaniment to the passion beating through him. Any second now, they'd reach her floor. He turned away long enough to hit the stop button on the elevator.

If she was surprised by his action, she didn't react. ''I'm glad to know you're not the cheating kind.'' She ran her tongue over her lower lip.

Unintentional or deliberately sultry, the result was the same—an electrical current rushing straight to his groin. ''I'd never do such a despicable thing,'' he said, intent on distinguishing himself from not only her ex, but the so-called acceptable traditions of her past.

''Not all men think that way and, damn it, they should,'' she said, punctuating her statement with a stamp of her foot.

She pursed her lips again and it was all he could do not to kiss her senseless. But he wasn't ready. Time would build their need and make anything between them even more spectacular. ''Anyone ever tell you that your southern accent comes out when you're mad?''

She blushed. "Another thing I need to over-come."

"Not in my book. That drawl of yours turns me on." He stepped closer, until he felt her pert nipples through his light cotton shirt.

"*You* turn me on," she said in the most obvious and deliberate *sexy* southern drawl he'd ever heard.

She wrapped her arms around his waist at the same time she let out long a breath, which ended on a thick, sultry moan. His groin, already full to bursting, lodged a protest at being confined in his jeans. He gritted his teeth, because no matter how much he wanted her, an elevator wasn't the place.

"You know what else?" she asked, talking when he wanted to do anything but.

"What?" he managed to ask.

Her fingers tangled in the back of his hair, her nails grazing the sensitive skin on his neck, tugging at his scalp and arousing him in ways he'd never known he could be aroused. Then her hand slipped downward around his ass, teasing him with alter-nately firm, then gentle gropes.

"When I told you I needed to be in control, I meant it." Without warning, she stepped aside, dangling the white *Sexcapades* paper in front of him, just as he'd done to her earlier.

He'd been had.

And damned if it didn't make him want her more.

REGAN LED THE WAY into her apartment. Lordy, she was warm and it wasn't because of the summer heat. The things Sam could do to her body with a look or a simple touch defied logic. But then logic had nothing to do with chemistry. He wasn't into commitment or women who wanted anything from him other than sex. And that was all she needed from Mr. Sam Daniels, pilot from California, who'd be making his trip home and out of her life come Sunday.

A brief glance at the clock in the hall as she tossed her keys onto the counter told her it was quickly approaching dinner time. "Can I get you something to eat or drink?" She turned and was stunned to find him not just behind her, but extremely close.

"You sure can." He bracketed one hand above her head, pinioning her body between his and the wall, much as he'd done in the elevator. Only this time, they were in the privacy of her apartment. No door would be opening, nor would anyone be interrupting them anytime soon.

With his free hand, he tilted her chin upward and

his lips hovered over hers. "I've been dying to taste you since the moment we met."

"I don't see what's stopping you now." And then, because she'd promised herself she'd maintain control, she cupped his face in her hands and brought his mouth down hard on hers.

For two strangers, they fit together perfectly, Regan thought. He kissed her with an intensity that backed up his earlier words. She'd wanted a man whose eyes flared with desire only for her, whose kisses made her tremble and whose body wracked with a need she inspired. She'd found him.

He made kissing into an art form, his lips creating exquisite texture, his tongue finding a home inside her mouth. He tasted like mint and sexy, seductive man, and a ripple of heat seared straight through to her core. Her breasts grew heavy, her nipples tight, and between her legs, a trickle of moisture that was so very welcome settled there.

Her fingers traveled from his stubbled cheeks to the back of his head where they tangled in his hair. She discovered that if she massaged his neck in a certain spot, he groaned and pressed her more fully against the wall, letting her feel his hard body intimately against hers. And she learned that when he nibbled, suctioning her lower lip into his mouth, her back arched and her breasts pushed harder into his strong chest.

She didn't know how long she stood, back against the wall, lost in the pure pleasure of a kiss, but the erotic sensations continued to build inside her, creating a cascading whirlpool of cavernous need. And by the time he broke the kiss, she'd come to the conclusion that with this man, there would be no being in control. She'd just have to jump without a parachute and hope the glorious ride was worth the potential danger.

He leaned his head against hers, his breathing harsh and ragged. "I think I'll take that drink now."

She forced a deep breath into her lungs. "Sure thing. Let me see what I've got." Ducking beneath his arm, she headed for the kitchen and a brief escape to collect herself. If such a thing were possible.

The man could definitely kiss.

Opening the refrigerator, she scanned the meager contents. She was due for a grocery trip. "I can offer you a glass of white wine," she said, looking at the top shelf. "Or..." she knelt on her knees to scan the bottom, "there's a six-pack of beer my ex left behind."

"Beer sounds good. And don't bother with a glass. We're going to rough it," he said, his dual meaning clear.

When they came together, they were combustible

and there'd be nothing genteel or civilized about where they were headed. Regan was glad. Her heart pounded in her chest and she wanted this one experience to prove what kind of woman she could really be.

She pulled out two bottles. "Make yourself at home," she called to him. Knowing he liked her accent allowed her to use it shamelessly.

"I'm one step ahead of you," he said from the other room.

Bottles in hand, she walked around the corner and headed into the living room. He'd already settled himself on the leather couch. He'd kicked his shoes off and left them in the hall and the television remote control was in his hand.

"Looks like the VCR was left on," he said. "Anything worth watching in here?"

She shook her head. "I wouldn't know. I usually watch TV in the bedroom, but Darren used to watch movies with his friends when I'd be out at a charity event." Which was fairly often.

Soon after their arrival in Chicago, her fiancé had handed her a list of organizations his law firm planned to help pro bono, and suggested she start her fund-raising campaigns immediately. Though he couched his reasoning in the fact that it'd help her make friends, she realized now that he'd provided himself with many free evenings to play with his female coworker when Regan wasn't around. She shrugged, pushing the memory back into the past where it belonged in favor of joining her soon-to-be weekend lover on the couch.

She perched herself a respectable distance away. Before she could think about her next move, he grabbed her hand and hauled her beside him. "Next time don't wait for me to ask," he said gruffly, his eyes twinkling as he made his demand.

He wanted her close, she realized and warmth settled in her chest. Because she'd been thinking of Darren, she'd reverted to her formal, let-the-man-be-in-charge attitude. This was Sam and he liked her more forward.

"What kind of charities do you work for?" he asked, hitting the rewind button on the remote.

She curled her legs up on the couch and leaned against his chest. "I wouldn't want to bore you with details."

He shot her an aggravated glance. "If I didn't want to know, I wouldn't have asked."

She nodded, accepting his point. "Darren's law firm provides free legal work for a woman's shelter and many of their residents. I use my people skills to raise money for the cause. That's one type of work I'd done back home that I wanted to continue here. Same with some of the local youth centers."

A warm, approving smile settled on his lips. "I'd

already guessed you had a big heart. I'm glad you proved me right."

"Flattery will get you nowhere." She didn't want lies or even flirtatious, overblown compliments to come between them. What she liked best about Sam so far was his down-to-earth style. She didn't need him praising her as if she was his well-trained dog. As Darren had done.

"I'm already where I want to be—with you. And your choices please me. You have no idea how much people like that need your skills."

She rolled her eyes. "Of course I know or I wouldn't waste my time raising money for them," she said, tired of the same old words Darren had used to push her buttons and steer her towards his choice of charities—the ones that benefitted his firm first and foremost. But Regan hadn't given a fig about whether his law firm benefitted from her effort or whether it helped push Darren up the partnership ladder. She might have been guided by her family and taken the expected path, but she'd stood firm and chosen those most in need of her help.

"I didn't mean that literally," he said his voice taking on a hurt tone. "And when I say those women or kids need you, I'm telling you from first-hand experience. A youth center I used to hang out in when I was a kid was shut down for lack of funds. No one gave a damn that the kids they turned out into the street ended up doing drugs or stealing as an after-school activity.''

His revelation stunned her, because she knew only the self-confident, self-assured man before her. She knew nothing about his childhood or upbringing and was glad he'd offered some insight.

Beside her, his body tensed, putting a barrier between them and guilt settled on her shoulders for misjudging him. ''I'm sorry. I'm just touchy about my lack of real work experience. I thought you were patronizing me like…''

''I'm nothing like Darren,'' he said, reminding her about something she already knew.

She sighed, hoping she hadn't blown her chance with him before she'd even had one. ''Can we rewind and start over?'' She wanted to get back to the easy camaraderie and sexual sparks that had come so naturally before they'd begun inadvertently pushing each other's hot buttons.

He chuckled, breaking the tension, and she let out a relieved breath.

''I'm already there,'' he said. Then, as if to prove his point, he pointed the remote at the large-screen TV and hit Play. ''Let's see what movie Dagwood left for us to watch.''

She chuckled at his chosen nickname. ''I'm a fan of the old *Bewitched* television shows myself.''

He grinned. ''If this Darren's anything like that

Darren, then Endora had herself a point. And based on everything you've told me, *Dagwood* seems to fit the jerk.''

Regan bit the inside of her cheek to keep from laughing aloud. Sam seemed to have her ex-fiancé pegged. As for the movie, she hadn't any idea what kind of movie Darren would have chosen. She didn't even know anything about his taste in television shows, she realized. She knew he preferred dry wine to fruity, and champagne most of all. So much about their relationship had been based on the superficial. She shook her head. She was lucky to be out and on her own now. Luckier still to be with Sam.

She snuggled into him and he wrapped an arm around her, placing the remote on the table and exchanging it for a beer. From the TV, music she didn't recognize began to play, credits she wasn't paying attention to flashed across the screen.

"Want a sip?" he asked.

"Sure." She started to reach for her own bottle but instead he held out his.

She placed her mouth over the opening of the long neck and let him tip the contents so the beer began a slow trickle into her mouth and down her throat. The rim was warm from Sam's mouth and the malty taste was what she could only describe as down-home good, the combination making for a delicious yet erotic taste. Without warning, the brew dripped down her chin and he had to pull the bottle away so she could swallow faster.

She laughed at the mess and lifted her hand to wipe her face, a southern no-no she would definitely enjoy, but he stopped her hand in midair. Taking her off guard, he leaned forward and kissed her, running his tongue deliberately around her mouth, lapping up the beer and arousing her at the same time.

Regan couldn't remember the last time she'd played while fooling around with a guy and the enjoyment hit her from all sides. Easing herself forward, she came down on top of him, her body prone along the length of his. The reminder of how much she wanted to be in control ran through her mind at the same time the *Sexcapades* article taunted her with naughty possibilities.

He threaded his hands through her hair and a low growl of desire rumbled from his chest, reverberating through her, turning her nipples into tight, aching peaks. She needed him to touch her, to feel the weight of his hands surrounding and massaging her breasts. She'd never asked a man for what she wanted, never had the nerve to verbalize her desires. Perhaps it was time.

"Give it to me, baby." A husky female voice mimicked Regan's thoughts.

"Who said that?" Regan lifted her head and met Sam's amused gaze.

"Apparently Dagwood was into porn." He gestured to the television.

Regan blinked, surprised. "I had no idea."

She turned in time to see a couple lying together on a couch. The similarities to Regan and Sam were strong, from the man's jet-black hair to the woman's blond tresses. But unlike Sam and Regan, the couple was completely naked and unlike Regan, this woman wasn't intimidated by her sexuality or need. Nor was the man.

"Ever watch one of these before?" Sam's arms wrapped around her, his hands splayed beneath her shirt against her back.

She shook her head, unsure if she was more embarrassed, startled…or secretly intrigued by this turn of events.

"Want me to turn it off?" he asked, probably in deference to her more delicate sensibilities.

"No," she said softly. Because Regan was coming to realize she didn't have as many sensibilities as she'd once thought.

After all, she'd brought Sam back to her apartment and now she was watching in awe as the woman on the small screen acted out Regan's own fantasies. The woman was taking control by orchestrating their movements and positions, her goal obviously to maximize her own pleasure. Regan's surprise at her ex's movie choice took a back seat to her astonishment over the fact that this enactment actually turned her on.

CHAPTER THREE

HIS SOUTHERN BELLE was turned on. Oh, she'd
been hot for him before the movie but now... Now
she was watching a couple go at it on the television
while lying on top of him and, no doubt about it,
she was squirming. Sam grinned.

His jet lag had all but disappeared, especially
since she'd maneuvered to a sitting position, her
mound nestled firmly over his aching groin. He
might not know her well, but he understood that
this entire experience was new to her. He'd go as
slowly as she needed, but his gut told him that once
she got going, Regan and her *Sexcapades* page
wouldn't need slow.

He lifted her top and slid his hands around her
waist, letting his callused fingers glide against her
soft skin. But she hadn't met his gaze since she'd
realized what was showing on the screen. "There's
nothing wrong with being aroused by a movie."

"I never thought it was proper."

There it was again, that thicker-than-normal
southern accent because she was nervous. He

chuckled. "Neither is picking up a man in a wedding shop, sweetheart, but here we are. Might as well enjoy it, don't you think?"

"Yeah, I do." Her stare drifted to his, the blue irises slumberous, her lashes heavy and her smile widening.

Now this was the woman he'd come home with. "So let's leave proper at the door." To punctuate his point, he gripped her tighter, thrust his pelvis upward and rolled his hips, maximizing not just contact but pure enjoyment.

His body was already hard and aching and the sultry moans and groans emanating from the television only served to inflame his need. And when Regan added to the chorus with a long drawl of delight, he nearly came in his jeans.

"That wasn't proper, darlin'" he said, mimicking her accent and treating her to a wicked wink.

She shook her head and her blond mane tousled around her flushed face. "I do think I like being bad." Desire darkened her eyes and, taking him by surprise, she hooked her fingers into the belt loops of his pants, locking their bodies tightly together. He didn't have to touch her to know that if he drove inside her, she'd be slick, hot and wet—just for him. Just as he was rock-hard for her.

The friction of denim rubbing against his erection wasn't easing his need but heightening it and driving him crazy. Above him, his sexy vixen rode him, capturing his cock between her thighs and driving both herself and him to insane heights.

His breath came in shallow gasps and wave after wave of intense ecstasy pummeled his body relentlessly, taking him closer and closer to the edge. He was beyond thought and nearly beyond reason, but he gritted his teeth and managed to hang on, letting her climax hit. And when it did, he forced his eyes open and watched as she came, her face flushed, eyes closed in sheer rapture and bliss.

Her body shuddered and her thighs squeezed tight, her hips gyrating, her pelvis straining against his erection, milking him and enjoying every last spasm until she was sated. Nearly boneless, she splayed on top of him, collapsing against his chest.

Her breathing came in ragged gasps. "Lordy, Sam, that was awesome."

"There's something to be said for being in control, huh?" He ran his hands through the tangled strands of her hair.

"Oh, yes," she said, her breath hot against his neck. "And there's something to be said for losing it, too."

He agreed wholeheartedly. He clenched his jaw against the unrelieved ache in his jeans. "Think you're ready for more?"

She raised her heavy-lidded gaze and smiled.

"Can't see why not." Then without warning, she rolled off him. "Be right back." She disappeared into another room and returned in seconds, a foil packet in her hand. "Darren believed in bein' prepared," she explained, tossing the condom onto his chest. "Of course, I never thought they'd come in handy once he was gone. Then again…" She pursed her lips in obvious thought.

"What?" he asked, curiosity overriding desire, at least for a moment.

"Then again they didn't come in handy that often when he lived here, seein' as how he was always so tired." She frowned. "Which I suppose is what happens when you're expending energy on another woman." She placed her hands on her hips, which had the effect of pushing out her breasts and making her nipples point through her silk shirt.

"Come here." He crooked a finger and she jumped back onto his lap, assuming her former position.

He'd been planning on dropping his pants and driving into her, anything to slake the need racing through him still. But now that he had her here, he wanted more.

Wanted to taste and devour. He'd propped himself up against the arm of the sofa and she sat astride him. Taking advantage, he levered himself up and pulled her by her blouse, bringing her close.

His gaze never left hers, but his intentions were clear as his lips hovered over one full breast. She had time to object, and when she didn't, he closed his lips around her distended nipple, suckling her through the silk.

She let out a soft moan. "You're killin' me."

"I sure as hell hope not," he murmured, then nipped her with his teeth before grabbing the lapels of her shirt and pulling them apart, ripping the buttons and flimsy fabric, and exposing her lace-covered breasts for his view.

At his dominant behavior, Regan sucked in a startled breath, shocked, yes, but also thrilled at the turn this was taking. She'd wanted a man wild for her and now it seemed she had one.

"Don't be afraid of me," he said, his voice rough and gravelly, the desire she'd so wanted obvious in his gaze.

She shook her head. "I'm not. I'm..."

"Excited?" he asked, a wry but pleased smile on his lips.

Regan nodded. "That's one word. But don't forget this is my fantasy," she said, reminding him of her *Sexcapades* paper. "My show." But even as she spoke, she knew bondage games could wait. She'd let herself experience his idea of control, then she'd take over, in all her dominant glory.

Meanwhile, his hands remained at his sides and

she had to do something about that. Feeling bolder by the minute, she unhooked the front clasp on her bra and pushed the cups aside, baring her breasts to the cool air and his hotter gaze. She grabbed his wrists and placed his palms on her breasts. On the first feel of his strong, heated hands on her softer flesh, her nipples puckered into tight peaks and liquid desire trickled between her thighs, the swirling need building all over again. Lordy, but this man did something to her she'd never experienced before.

He shut his eyes and a low growl rumbled from his throat, but he made no other move to touch her.

"What are you waiting for?" she asked, frustrated.

"Instructions, sweetheart. You said this is your show."

So she had, but she liked his aggressive side. Meanwhile the condom lay on his chest where she'd tossed it earlier.

"I changed my mind. This time," she said, making sure he understood her rules, "I want—" She paused, uncertain how to express her sexual needs as she'd never done so before.

He arched an eyebrow. "Just say it," he urged her. "Whatever you want, tell me." His eyes darkened and, beneath her, his body was rigid and hard, solidly male, just waiting for her okay.

"I want you to take charge."

"And?"

"I want to feel all that power you've been restraining and I want to feel it inside me." Having said that, she expelled a long breath of air, but before she could register whether she was more relieved or more proud of herself, Sam dislodged her from her position on top.

She didn't know how he managed it so quickly, but in the blink of an eye, she lay prone, while above her, he stripped, pulling off his shirt and tossing it on the floor, then getting to work on his jeans.

Regan wasn't about to waste time either. She sat up and let her torn shirt and open bra fall off her shoulders, before swallowing any embarrassment and taking her pants off next. When she finally stopped her frenzied actions, she glanced up to see Sam, condom in hand, staring at her naked body. But she couldn't worry about being modest because her focus was *him*. Long, thick and hard.

"Oh, my." She licked her lips and forced herself to meet his gaze.

That was one way of putting it, Sam thought. He'd never been so damn hard in his life, and the woman who was the cause sat naked in front of him. He'd never seen such a mass of contradictions bundled in one delectable, desirable package.

Southern and shy one minute, aggressive and dominant the next, willing not just to indulge in what she wanted, but to let him take control as well. Which was the real Regan?

And why did he want so badly to find out?

He moved over her, straddling her until his erection touched her downy thatch of hair and her damp desire moistened his skin. He shut his eyes, absorbing the incredible feeling of this moment—the moment just prior to when he'd slide inside and feel all that slick heat meant just for him. Without warning, she plucked the foil packet from his hands and he opened his eyes as she ripped it open and tossed the wrapper somewhere on the floor.

"May I?" she asked, holding the condom in her delicate hands.

He chuckled at that. "You most certainly may." Hell, she could do anything she wanted to him and more, with his permission, without his permission, it didn't matter, he was so wild with wanting her.

Determination etched her features as she placed the condom on the head of his penis and rolled the latex over his straining shaft. Only determination, and the knowledge that he'd rather be inside her body, kept him from pumping into her hand and coming right then.

"I do believe I got it right," she said, a satisfied yet wicked grin on her face.

His vixen was enjoying this and he couldn't be more pleased. But now it was his turn to control the show. "Raise your hands."

Her eyes opened wide with curiosity. "Why?"

"Because you wanted me to take over and I'm doing it," he said, his voice gruff with the force of his restraint.

Without another question, she raised her hands over her head. Leaning forward, he rained hot, devouring kisses on her uplifted breasts, then switched to hot strokes of his tongue, working his way upward to her lips. He could kiss this woman forever, but more urgent needs beckoned, and, breaking contact, he lifted his body, splayed his hands on her thighs and waited until her gaze met his.

Never breaking eye contact, he slipped his finger inside her, parting her feminine folds. He told himself he wanted to make sure she was ready for him this first time, but he knew better. He wanted to feel her. Now he lubricated the condom with his finger, rubbing her slick essence over the head of his shaft, her eyes eagerly following his movements, her arms still over her head. Apparently not only did she like being in control, she followed orders equally well.

She was delicate and rare and he promised himself he'd take things slowly as he nudged the head of his penis inside her. She let out a long, satisfied moan and slow was no longer an option. Nor, he sensed, as she bent her knees, deliberately pulling him deeper, did she want it to be, and he thrust inside her with a hard, fast, penetrating thrust.

"Wow," Regan said, her voice causing him to focus.

"Hell yeah," Sam muttered, agreeing. He'd found heaven on earth, he thought and clenched his jaw tight, savoring the sensations rippling through him.

But he wanted her to savor them too, and there was only one way to guarantee such tight, intimate contact throughout. He needed to be able to thrust as hard and deep as she wanted, as he needed. "Hold your knees," he told her with a wink. "It's going to be a bumpy ride."

She grinned. "Whatever you say, Sam. After all, you're the pilot." Lowering her arms, she grasped her knees with her hands, holding her legs open wide, giving him leverage, providing him complete access and affording him ultimate trust.

As for Sam, he was lost in her slick, wet heat and the friction of their bodies as they found a perfect rhythm. While he braced his arms on either side of her head, he pumped into her, harder and faster with each successive thrust. Regan met him with her body, accepting him deeper, her pelvis grinding in a circular motion. From her soft moans and frantic movements, her release was obviously close.

So was his and when it came at the same moment she did, Sam let go as he hadn't done with any woman. Ever.

CHAPTER FOUR

REGAN PULLED the sash of her silk robe around her waist and tied it into a bow, then, drawing a deep breath, she joined the man she'd left in the next room. When she stepped into the den, Sam sat on the couch, wearing jeans and nothing else. He'd shut off the television and the shocking movie they'd found in the VCR. She was still surprised, not just at the porno movie, but at her reaction to it and the resulting shedding of inhibitions that had followed.

Feeling her body begin to heat all over again, she pulled her lapels closer.

"It's a little late for modesty, babe." Sam crooked a finger her way.

"You've got a point," she said, joining him on the sofa. "I was thinking you must be hungry."

He leaned his arm over the back cushion and shot her his most wicked grin. "You could say I worked up an appetite."

She laughed. "Are you always so incorrigible?"

"Only when I have the perfect audience."

She rolled her eyes. "Well, Chicago has the best deep-dish pizza ever created. We can go out if you like." Regan didn't know what else to offer this man who she'd been intimate with yet still didn't know well enough. And she wanted to know more.

"I'd rather bring in. We have such a short time together."

He was right. It was late Friday afternoon leading into evening and he was gone on Sunday. Before she could reply, he continued.

"And I'd rather not share you with anyone, including a waiter." His fingers dipped into her robe, reached under the silk and tickled her shoulder.

His words pleased her as much as his caress. "That sounds perfect to me, as long as it's not really an excuse to avoid being seen with me in public," she said, jokingly. She'd love more intimate time with him here.

"As if. Any guy who lays eyes on you, I'd have to consider competition and I'm really not in a dueling mood." His eyes danced with laughter, but there was a hint of possessiveness in his tone she enjoyed, too.

"I'll get a menu." Rising, she headed for the kitchen drawer, where she kept her stash of take-out menus, when the doorbell rang. "I don't know who that could be."

GET 2

HOW TO GET YOUR
2 FREE BOOKS AND FREE GIFT!

1. Peel off the MIRA® sticker on the front cover. Place it in the space provided at right. This automatically entitles you to receive two free books and an exciting surprise gift.

2. Send back this card and you'll get 2 "The Best of the Best™" books. These books have a combined cover price of $11.98 or more in the U.S. and $13.98 or more in Canada, but they are yours to keep absolutely FREE!

3. There's no catch. You're under no obligation to buy anything. We charge nothing — ZERO — for your first shipment. And you don't have to make any minimum number of purchases — not even one!

4. We call this line "The Best of the Best" because each month you'll receive the best books by some of today's most popular authors. These authors show up time and time again on all the major bestseller lists and their books sell out as soon as they hit the stores. You'll like the convenience of getting them delivered to your home at our special discount prices . . . and you'll love your *Heart to Heart* subscriber newsletter featuring author news, horoscopes, recipes, book reviews and much more!

5. We hope that after receiving your free books you'll want to remain a subscriber. But the choice is yours — to continue or cancel, anytime at all! So why not take us up on our invitation, with no risk of any kind. You'll be glad you did!

6. And remember...we'll send you a surprise gift ABSOLUTELY FREE just for giving THE BEST OF THE BEST a try.

SPECIAL FREE GIFT
We'll send you a fabulous surprise gift, absolutely FREE, simply for accepting our no-risk offer!

Visit us online at
www.mirabooks.com

® and TM are registered trademar
of Harlequin Enterprises Limited.

BOOKS FREE!

THE BEST OF THE BEST™ — Here's How it Works:

Accepting your 2 free books and gift places you under no obligation to buy anything. You may keep the books and gift and return the shipping statement marked "cancel." If you do not cancel, about a month later we will send you 4 additional books and bill you just $4.74 each in the U.S., or $5.24 each in Canada, plus 25¢ shipping & handling per book and applicable taxes if any.* That's the complete price and — compared to cover prices starting from $5.99 each in the U.S. and $6.99 each in Canada — it's quite a bargain! You may cancel at any time, but if you choose to continue, every month we'll send you 4 more books, which you may either purchase at the discount price or return to us and cancel your subscription.
*Terms and prices subject to change without notice. Sales tax applicable in N.Y. Canadian residents will be charged applicable provincial taxes and GST. Credit or Debit balances in a customer's account(s) may be offset by any other outstanding balance owed by or to the customer.

If offer card is missing write to: The Best of the Best, 3010 Walden Ave., P.O. Box 1867, Buffalo, NY 14240-1867

BUSINESS REPLY MAIL
FIRST-CLASS MAIL   PERMIT NO. 717-003   BUFFALO, NY

POSTAGE WILL BE PAID BY ADDRESSEE

THE BEST OF THE BEST
3010 WALDEN AVE
PO BOX 1867
BUFFALO NY 14240-9952

NO POSTAGE
NECESSARY
IF MAILED
IN THE
UNITED STATES

She glanced through the peephole, saw her ex-fiancé and groaned. "This is trouble."

Sam came up behind her. "What kind of trouble?" he asked.

"Trouble named Darren."

"Want me to wait in the other room?" His voice left no doubt he'd rather not disappear.

But he'd obviously respect her choice and she appreciated the offer. "Don't worry about it. He's probably here to pick up some things he left behind."

"Like his tape?" Sam asked wryly.

"Oh, Lordy, no. I doubt he'd have the nerve to ask for that."

"Then why don't we just offer it to him?"

She turned around to smack him lightly for his joke, but he grabbed her instead and pulled her into a ravishing kiss. A mind-blowing, tongue-tangling, arousing kiss. One that seemed to go on and on, until the doorbell and persistent knocking interrupted them.

"Open up, Regan. The doorman said you were home," Darren called impatiently.

And he should have called up for permission instead of giving Darren entry privileges, Regan thought.

"Go on and let him in," Sam suggested. "Now that you look well and thoroughly kissed."

A heated flush rose to her cheeks, but she had to admit an ornery part of herself, a part previously ignored in favor of proper behavior, relished the thought of being caught in her apartment with a sexy man—after they'd made love.

Regan opened the door to an irate ex-fiancé. Darren's face had turned red and his hand was in the air to knock again. "It took you long enough."

"I didn't know I had to operate on your timetable anymore," she told him. "What are you doing here?"

"I left some things." He stepped inside without being invited.

"And I told you to call first." But apparently he was only worried about manners when it came to his fellow partners and friends, not her.

"I was in the neighborhood." He started for the den, and when Regan turned around, she realized Sam had disappeared into another room.

She sighed. Well kissed or not, it didn't matter, since Darren hadn't spared her a second glance. His only concern was his box of things, which he apparently thought she'd left in the hall closet since he'd stopped in front of it, ready to rummage through.

She perched her hands on her hips, piqued he'd treat her as if she were invisible in her own home. "Darren, you don't live here anymore, so it's rude of you to come stomping in as if you own the place, don't you think?''

"Last I heard, my firm's still footing the bill. Now where are my things?''

She clenched her teeth. "I hardly think that excuse would hold up in a court of law.''

Ignoring her, he opened the closet door, only to have a large hand slam it shut.

"You heard the lady," Sam said, obviously having decided to take control.

At the sound of a male voice, Darren turned fast. "Who are you?''

Sam, still dressed in jeans and nothing else, stood with his arms folded over his broad chest and stared at Darren. "I'm the man who's been invited here." He looked Darren over. "Unlike you."

Regan bit the inside of her cheek, enjoying this display of testosterone.

Darren turned toward her. "Regan, I realize I hurt you but picking up a stranger…that's beneath you. And your parents would die of humiliation."

At his words, Regan cringed, and knowing he'd intentionally gone for her weak spot didn't help soften the blow. After all, her folks had barely accepted her living with Darren. They'd only allowed it because they favored him as their soon-to-be son-in-law and he'd done an admirable job of sweet-talking them into accepting the arrangement. If they knew she was having a weekend affair, her mother would probably take to her room with a migraine and her father would... Well, it didn't bear thinking about, she thought with a shudder.

But before she could reply to Darren, Sam grabbed her hand, caressing the inside of her palm with his thumb, reminding her of all the positives in their relationship. Brief or not.

"Look, Dagwood, you have no idea how long I've known Regan or what's between us." Sam leaned closer to her ex-fiancé. "And between us guys? You don't want to know." He squeezed Regan's hand in a gesture of support she appreciated.

Darren scowled. "I want my things."

Regan shrugged. "Well, I could have saved you a trip if you'd called like I asked. I put them in storage. I didn't want them cluttering the apartment."

"But you knew I was coming by for them," he said, a man used to her doing his bidding.

"And you knew you were engaged, but that didn't stop you from relegating me to the basement, so to speak. I'd say we're even." She rubbed her hands together. She was embarrassed to admit revenge felt good.

Especially with Sam by her side.

"You've changed, Regan." Darren shook his head slowly back and forth, in a gesture she found more irritating than she remembered. "And your parents won't be pleased," he added.

"Then don't tell them," Sam suggested.

"They'll find out we're finished regardless of who tells them," Regan said. "And you're right. I've changed—enough not to care if they're disappointed about any choices I make," she told Darren, proud of every word she spoke. And meaning it despite the obvious repercussions.

Sam grinned at her, obviously pleased as well. Then he prodded Darren towards the front door.

She watched, mesmerized. Sam was a gentleman in more ways than a man like Darren could understand, or even her parents could for all their so-called social graces. Sam was a gentleman in his heart, where it counted. Breeding couldn't create a decent human being. Sam won on the inside.

And on the outside, there was no comparison between Sam and Darren, at least none that Darren could win. He was slighter and paler than Sam, and Savannah's Golden Boy looked lost beside Regan's pilot.

Her pilot had, in one short afternoon, brought out her naughty side and taught her she had more courage and self-confidence than she'd imagined. Enough to stand up to the disappointment sure to come from her family once they learned of her broken engagement and subsequent affair. But was she now brave enough to stand on her own?

"Darren, wait!" Regan called out, before Sam could shut the door behind him.

"I'm sorry, but you can't talk me out of it, Regan. I have to talk to Kate and Ethan," Darren said, speaking of her parents. "They'll want to know you've fallen into a downward spiral. They'll bring you home. Or send you on vacation and hide the embarrassment until this blows over," he said.

"No, you twit," Regan heard herself say. "You forgot your tape," she said, ejecting the porno video and running to hand it to Darren with a bow and much fanfare.

Red-faced, he snatched the tape and stormed out.

Sam slammed the door closed behind him. "Jackass," he muttered.

"Well said." Regan grinned. "I didn't think I'd feel like celebrating after Darren left, but that was amazing." She laughed and spread her arms in the air and spun around.

Freedom had never felt so good.

"Enjoyed that?" Sam asked, flipping the dead bolt closed.

"Heck, yeah! I got to him." She shook her head, amazed. "It's not that Darren cared that I was with anyone else—I mean, he dumped me first—but the look on his face when he saw you, and then when I handed him the tape, it was priceless."

Sam's eyes sparkled with laughter and innate understanding. "You humiliated him in front of another guy. That's as good as trumping his cheating ass, that much is for sure." He pulled her into his arms. "Stand proud, Regan. You showed him he didn't defeat you."

"I did, didn't I?" She laughed. "I also worked up an appetite." Pulling him toward the room where she'd left the menus, they agreed on a vegetarian deep-dish pizza and Regan called to place the order.

Forty-five minutes later, they were eating a late meal at her small kitchen table. Sam had to leave in a few hours—for a while, at least—but she refused to think about that now. Not when she was more relaxed than she'd ever remembered being, including at meals with her family and during those alone with Darren. Sam didn't watch which fork she picked up first, or if she even used a fork or placed the napkin in her lap. Little by little, she was shedding the burden of the rules by which she'd lived her life and they were taking on less importance.

Sam had come along at the most opportune time and she'd never forget him or this life-altering weekend he'd given her.

SAM WATCHED as Regan devoured her pizza with gusto, delicately licking sauce off her fingers before moving on to the next bite. The episode with her ex had revved her up and the resulting adrenaline rush was inspiring to watch.

Pushing the pizza box out of the way, he leaned forward on his elbows. "Tell me about your family. Why Dagwood used them as leverage to hurt you," he asked, violating his cardinal rule by asking about her personal life.

An affair ought to be just that, simple and easy to walk away from, but he was too drawn to this woman to leave things between them purely physical. Not that the physical wasn't spectacular—it certainly was. Unfortunately it wasn't enough for him.

"Honestly, you don't want to know." She met his gaze through lowered lashes, obviously embarrassed by his question.

"Honestly, I do." He held out his hand and waited until she joined her palm against his. "I want to know what brought you to this point. What brought us together."

She bit her lower lip before speaking. "Well, as you might imagine, I have a controlling family. Certain...expectations. And I was supposed to fulfill them. My sisters already had. My folks had no trouble with them." Regan's eyes glazed over as she remembered. "But in here I didn't want to be like my mother or sisters." She tapped her heart. "So instead of marrying young and the person handpicked by my father, I found something wrong with every man he chose. Disappointing them at every turn."

Sam shook his head. "This all sounds so antiquated."

She laughed. "You just described my family. And all my parents' friends' families. It's real debutante society where we're from. And as much as I told myself I accepted it, I really rebelled. I rejected everyone they pranced in front of me. They called me picky. I called it being selective." She rose and began cleaning up the remnants of dinner.

Without thought, he stood and helped. "Personally I don't think you should have to marry someone to make your family happy. And your family shouldn't expect you to conform if it makes you unhappy." He folded the empty pizza box in half and stuffed it into the garbage bag she held out. "Let me throw this in the incinerator and we'll finish talking."

As he took the garbage down the hall, for the first time, he allowed himself to think about the man Regan had been engaged to. An obviously born-to-money guy with an attitude to match. A guy who'd grown up with everything Sam had lacked, but one who had no character, who didn't take responsibility for his own actions, who would humiliate a woman if it made himself look better in the eyes of her family and the people back home.

He was unworthy of a woman like Regan and Sam was glad she'd gotten out, even if she had been hurt in the process.

She was obviously pleased too, which made their joining even better. She might have turned to him on the rebound, and he might have accepted a stranger's invitation to have sex, but in a few short hours, they'd progressed way beyond that.

He stepped back into the apartment and closed the door, locking it behind him. Regan had finished cleaning and shut off the lights. Only the soft glow from a lamp lit his way. As he entered the family room, he found the silk robe that Regan had been wearing. He took it as an invitation and when he bent to retrieve the garment he paused, bringing the soft silk to his face. He inhaled Regan's fragrant scent, letting his body become fully aroused, before heading for the bedroom he hadn't yet seen. He hung the robe on the doorknob and, strung tight, he stepped over the threshold.

"Regan?" he called out.

"I'm here." One hand on the wall, she stepped out from a doorway, a vision in a black silk teddy.

The outfit was an incredible contrast to her light

blond hair and fair skin, a complex contraption that teased him with possibilities. Straps crisscrossed her shoulders. Sheer lace covered her breasts and revealed her pert nipples and luscious flesh. His gaze traveled lower. Her stomach was uncovered, her belly button tempting him and making his mouth water with the urge to lick, suckle and taste. And lower, lace covered her feminine secrets, but the triangle of blond hair was visible beneath the sheer material, making him harder. And he hadn't thought that was possible.

His mouth watered at the sight, but, at the same time, he knew they hadn't finished their discussion and there was so much about this woman and her facets he wanted to know about.

He stepped forward. "You don't look like any spinster I ever met."

"Why thank you, Sam."

"You're welcome."

She crooked her finger his way, mimicking his gesture earlier. Desire glittered in her eyes and an invitation was clear in her body language.

"How'd you end up in Chicago?" Talk about fitting everything into a short amount of time, he thought wryly, asking the question as he started toward her, intending to accept her invitation with a resounding yes.

Regan sat on the bed, her movements orchestrated and seductive as she crawled over the cream-colored comforter and stretched out on top. Waiting for him.

"Darren's a lawyer," she explained, crossing one leg over the other, teasing him for a second with the hint of exposed flesh. "He was put in charge of a new Chicago office, so we settled here. The wedding was to have been here, too."

"And your family accepted that?" He unzipped his fly and pulled down his jeans.

Regan nodded. "Mama was so happy I'd finally landed myself a man, she was even willing to accept a northern wedding." She patted the mattress beside her.

Kicking his jeans to the floor, he eased himself onto the bed, the comforter as cool as his body was hot. "How old are you, that they had you pegged a spinster?" An outdated word if he'd ever heard one, but then most of her family's values seemed antiquated to him.

"How old do I look?" A grin lifted the corners of her mouth.

He chuckled. "That's a loaded question, sweetheart. And one I refuse to answer on the grounds I might get myself in trouble."

She pulled open the nightstand drawer and, leaning over, she reached inside. He figured she was getting a condom and with the view of flimsy lace barely covering her backside, man was he ever ready.

"I'm twenty-five," she said at the same time she turned back towards him, a sash from her robe in her hand.

He raised an eyebrow, fairly certain of what she had planned, which made keeping his mind on conversation extremely difficult. "And at the ripe old age of twenty-five, if your parents thought you were having an affair, would they really worry about scandal?"

"Oh, yes." She nodded seriously. "If my mama even found out I wasn't a virgin, she'd have sent my daddy after poor Robby Jones with a shotgun."

"But wouldn't that have caused a scandal?" he asked.

"An acceptable scandal as long as it ended in marriage." She crinkled her nose in disgust. "It's hard to explain the way my parents think if you haven't lived it." She sighed dramatically.

She was right about that. Since he came from a neighborhood that *was* a scandal, Sam couldn't understand it.

"What if they disapproved of the man in question? Would your father actually use the shotgun?" Sam laughed but behind the joke, he was serious. After meeting Dagwood, he could envision Regan's parents going ballistic if they thought a man was beneath their daughter.

A scenario he'd never have to deal with since he was heading back to California on Sunday. Less than two days. So why did the thought of that disapproval eat at his gut?

She pulled the ends of the sash, the snapping sound drawing his attention away from his thoughts. "Don't worry, Sam. My daddy's not coming after you to force you into marriage."

"Because I wouldn't meet their expectations?"

She glanced at him, obviously as surprised as he was by his question. It had been years since his background had bothered him and it shocked the hell out of him that it did so now. And because of a woman.

This woman.

"Sam?" Regan asked, suddenly realizing she had to tread cautiously because she was dealing with his feelings. She didn't know enough about him, but was grateful to learn his vulnerabilities. Grateful for the chance to prove he could trust her with them.

"What is it?" he asked gruffly.

"You meet every expectation I ever had," she said, her smile widening as she spoke the truth.

When she'd turned down various men, each man that her parents had pushed her way, she'd always kept in mind that, as a husband, she'd have to look at this man across from her in bed every day. And southern propriety be damned, she'd at least wanted him to make her hot. Darren had been good-looking, but he'd fallen short. The sex hadn't been spectacular nor had he made her feel desirable. Still, she'd given in to her family's haranguing and accepted Darren's proposal. She'd been a fool, she realized now.

"And just what are those expectations?" he asked. "Just what am I?"

"You're kind and chivalrous." He'd exhibited those qualities tonight, both before Darren's arrival and during. Regan rose to her knees in front of Sam, wanting him to hear how special he was. "Not to mention you're handsome as sin, sexy and you turn me on. And if that's not enough, you know how to follow orders. Raise your hands," she instructed.

His sensual gaze never leaving hers, he did as she asked, never once questioning her command.

Once she had his hands positioned by the iron headboard, she tied the sash around his wrists and shackled him. Regan knew, as did Sam, he could break his bindings easily.

But what fun would that be?

CHAPTER FIVE

REGAN HAD HIM just where she wanted him and damned if Sam didn't like it there. He enjoyed the look of determination in her eyes and the way she took control of their situation. Of course, he stopped being amused when she turned hot and predatory and all he could think of was what she intended to do to him.

"You've been really good to me, Sam. From just being kind, to helping when I stood up to Darren, to just being you." Her smile reached her eyes and, in doing so, touched his heart.

Just as quickly, she moved to straddle his legs, settling herself on his thighs, the only thing between them his aching member.

He swallowed hard. "Being good to you is easy, sweetheart."

"So is returning the favor." At that moment, she wrapped her hands around him and he clenched his jaw, trying to concentrate instead of giving up to sensation. Not yet.

He'd learned much about her today, and he'd

shared more with Regan than any woman before. But because Dagwood had hurt her so badly and because he'd driven her to this ultimate act of rebellion against her past, Regan wasn't thinking about Sam as anything more than a weekend fling. Perhaps it was that very fact that made him think this was the first woman who could make him want more.

And, to start, he'd prefer any favors she returned to be based on more than physical need. But when she began to pick up a persistent rhythm, running her palm up and down his straining shaft, he knew any more thinking would have to wait. She let her hand glide up, then down, the friction intense and hot, increasing with each successive slide of skin against skin.

He swallowed a groan, lifting his hips and thrusting himself harder and faster, wanting to complement her rhythm but with his wrists bound his movements weren't anchored and he was unable to accomplish much.

"Relax," she said softly. "And I promise to make you feel so good."

She was an angel, but one dressed for sin as she tossed her blond hair in a seductive movement and lowered her head, closer and closer to his erection until he had no doubt what she intended.

He gritted his teeth, knowing that if she touched

him, he wouldn't be able to stand it for long. When her lips caressed the head of his shaft, he knew he was right. He expelled a long hiss of breath, but she showed him no mercy as her lips opened over him and, using her tongue, she drew him into her mouth.

"God," he muttered as her tongue swept over his tip and down his straining shaft.

From there, physical sensation took over and he gripped the headboard as she worked him with her mouth, then, without warning, added her hands. Using the moisture she'd created with her lips, she glided her palms up and down, bringing him closer and closer to release. His hips bucked, his body strained and finally he came, a tidal wave of utter completion overtaking him.

When he came back to reality, his breathing still labored, Regan was untying his hands. "You could have released yourself anytime, but you didn't," she said, surprised.

"I knew you wanted to be in control."

She tossed the sash to the end of the bed. "I knew you'd follow orders well."

"And, man, was I rewarded." He leaned his head against the headboard and looked at her.

When she met his gaze, her eyes were wide, her expression honest. "I've never done that before," she admitted.

She'd taken him off guard. Twice. Because when she'd initiated bondage games, he'd assumed she wanted to be in control of her pleasure. Instead she'd commandeered his.

And now this. "Never?" he asked.

She shook her head.

"Not even with—"

"Nope." She looked at him, her tousled hair falling over her cheeks. "Could you tell?" she asked, and lowered her lashes.

Like a bombshell hitting him in the gut, he knew he'd fallen hard for this woman in a way that exceeded anything he'd felt before or had even considered possible. "No, babe, I couldn't tell. You were incredible."

"Well, that's good to know." She flipped her hair off her face and began massaging his wrists, obviously keeping herself busy so she wouldn't have to face him or her embarrassment.

Her sudden shyness was completely at odds with the sexy vixen in the silk teddy. Her contradictions intrigued him and he knew he could never be bored with this woman.

Sam sure as hell had never thought he'd buy into love at first sight, but he believed in it now. She'd blown him away the minute he'd seen her at Divine Events and everything he'd seen and learned since then had only cemented his first impression and growing feelings.

He grabbed her hands, stopping her from continuing her soft massage of his wrists. "Do you know what I want?" he asked her.

"No." She bit down on her lower lip.

"I want to pleasure you. I want to strip you out of that skimpy outfit and devour you until you scream, and then I want to make love to you until you scream some more. Oh, and did I mention, I want you tied up when I do?" He raised an eyebrow, waiting for a response, even as he knew what it would be. After all, she'd proven herself up for a challenge.

"I like the sound of that," she said, in her husky southern voice.

She was eager and willing. As proof, she picked up the silk sash and draped it across his chest, making contact with his nipples—on purpose, he was sure, and then she held her hands out toward him, palms up. "So what are you waiting for?" she asked. "Go for it."

He grinned and began tying up his angel. Sam had never thought much about love, only about maintaining the life of travel that meant so much to him, the life he'd seen his father give up. He'd never wanted to be stifled in that same way. Women had always signaled trouble to him. To him, women meant staying at home and giving up your dreams.

At first glance, Regan seemed the kind of female who'd demand just such a thing, but she was deep, thoughtful and understanding. He wondered if he'd finally found someone who could accept and understand his needs, his dreams. He wondered too if she'd even want to.

A glance at the clock told him he didn't have much time left in which to find out. But his gut told him all things were possible and he trusted his instincts. After all, he was beginning to know her well.

Now it was time she learned more about him. Just as soon as he returned the favor and took Regan where she'd just taken him. To heaven and back.

REGAN SAT cross-legged on the bed, her light robe all she had wrapped around her to keep her warm. With Sam showering and getting ready to leave, she was more chilled than she had a right to be. And that scared her considering she'd only known him a couple of hours.

He stepped out of the steam-filled bathroom, a pair of boxers on his hips as he ran a towel over his damp hair. Her gaze traveled the length of him, appreciating his masculine physique all over again.

"If you keep looking at me like that, you'll be flat on your back and I'll miss the rehearsal dinner," he said, shooting her a wink.

"Now that's something I wouldn't mind." She let out an exaggerated sigh. "But they'd miss you at the dinner." Just as she'd miss him when he left. "So tell me about this friend of yours who's getting married." She tried to keep conversation casual and not let on about the inner turmoil roiling inside her.

"Bill?" Sam asked, leaning down to pull clothes from his duffel bag. "We were buddies in flight school. Two cocky kids who couldn't wait to fly." He stood, clothes in hand. "Of course for me, flying meant freedom. I worked my ass off to pay for college, juggling as many jobs as I could handle and still get through school. I was determined to have an education in case being a pilot didn't pan out. Then I worked on getting my certification." He shrugged. "That's when I met Bill. We bonded instantly. First off, we both came from working-class backgrounds and things hadn't been handed to us." He winced, instantly catching his mistake. "That didn't come out right."

She laughed though, not at all insulted. "Just go on, sugar. I know who and what I am." And she was fascinated by this insight into him.

He grinned sheepishly. "Well, anyway, my dad was a trucker who loved being on the road, but my mother hated not seeing him, so he gave up his freedom in exchange for a desk job with the same corporation who'd employed him as a driver.'' Sam lowered himself to the edge of the bed as he continued to tell his story. ''It nearly killed my father to stay in one place, and as much as he loved his family, he resented us for tying him down.''

''That must've been hard for you.''

He inclined his head. ''It was. And I guess I decided young that I wouldn't be tied down, too.'' He paused and met her gaze, heat flaring between them. ''Unless it's by a beautiful woman with only seduction in mind,'' he said, his voice taking on a husky undertone.

She laughed at his double entendre, but his words stayed with her and she glanced out the window, wondering what Sam saw from his perspective as he flew a plane. The lure of that kind of freedom must be potent. After years of feeling constricted by others, she understood his needs and what drove him. ''So you equated flying with freedom.''

He nodded. ''I thought Bill did, too. Apparently I was wrong, since he quit his job as a corporate pilot and is settling in Chicago with his soon-to-be wife.''

''To each his own, I guess.'' She looked at the clock and realized she was keeping him talking when he needed to finish up and move on. "You should get dressed."

"I will, but I wanted to talk to you about something first. This rehearsal tonight, it's casual and informal." He pointed to the pair of khaki-colored chinos and the burgundy polo shirt in his hand.

She leaned back into the pillows. "Sounds nice," she murmured inanely, not sure what else to say.

"It should be, but I won't know many people there and..." His voice trailed off. "Come with me," he said at last, taking her completely by surprise.

She ran a hand through her mussed hair. "I...wasn't invited," she said, falling back on her southern proprieties as an excuse.

"*I'm* inviting you. Bill said to bring a guest if I was seeing anyone. At the time I wasn't, but now I am." He raised his shoulders as if things between them were that simple. His eyes twinkled with possibilities and, damn him, hope.

She didn't want to dash his expectations, but this was all too much, too fast. She was scared to death of what she was feeling for this man so quickly. Coming off a broken engagement she hadn't even told her family about yet, she was falling for a sexy stranger she'd picked up in the wedding planner's, of all places.

Talk about reasons for mortification! Yet she wasn't ashamed of Sam. Only afraid of her own feelings. She met his gaze. "I wish I could but—"

He leaned closer, placing his hand on her leg. Fiery darts of heat immediately set off in her body, her breasts peaking and dewy dampness settling between her thighs. That easily, he turned her on. That quickly, he'd touched her heart.

"Come on, Regan. It's not like we'll have that much time together this weekend, so why not make the most of what we do have?" he asked, giving it one last shot.

"I wish I could." She curled her legs, wrapping her arms around her knees. The effect was to pull away from his touch and, as much as it hurt her, shut him out. "But...I can't." She forced the words from the back of her throat.

"You mean you won't." He straightened, then rose from the bed. "What the hell. It was only supposed to be a quick fling, right? It was stupid of me to push for anything more." He closed himself in the bathroom to get dressed.

Regan swallowed hard, pain rippling through her chest and throat. It wasn't supposed to be like this. Yet here she was filled with more conflicting emotion than she had been when Darren had broken their engagement and admitted he'd been fooling around. She wrapped her fingers around the comforter and shut her eyes tight.

She kept them closed until the bathroom door opened and Sam walked out, dressed to kill in his casual outfit, smelling of his sexy cologne, a cool, disappointed look in his eyes. A look she had never seen before, since, from the moment they met, his gaze had been heated, warm and welcoming. She hated the change, yet acknowledged she was the cause.

"Time for me to go." Duffel in hand, he strode toward the bed and leaned close. "It's been fun, darling." Without asking, he closed the distance and sealed his lips over hers, kissing her long and hard.

She had no right, but she parted her lips anyway, deepening the kiss and the connection, so that when he finally pulled away, his breathing was labored. "You're a mass of contradictions, but I do understand," he said.

She raised her eyebrows. "You do?"

He nodded. "I'm the one who's always been looking for freedom, remember?"

She forced a smile. "Yes, I believe I do." She also realized he was letting her off the hook for her decision, for which she was grateful. "Have fun tonight."

"I will." He rose to his full height.

"Where are you staying? Because if you don't have a hotel reservation, this side of the bed is yours," she said, patting the free end and setting herself up for the same rejection she'd just given him.

He chuckled. "Now who doesn't want to be seen in public with whom?" he asked, teasing her with her own words from earlier in the day.

She shook her head in denial. "I promise you, that's not it." She just wasn't ready to admit a more intimate connection between them. Sex was one thing, she told herself; attending a wedding as a couple was something else entirely. But she was lying to herself. Because the truth was she felt too overwhelmed to deal with her emotions. She hoped a little breathing room would help her figure out her feelings.

"I know." He took two steps, then turned back, meeting her gaze with his deep, compelling one. "Mind if I leave my bag?"

She exhaled a long sigh of relief that their time together wasn't over yet. But when he walked out the door, her keys in hand, leaving her alone with her thoughts, he left her completely alone in a way even Darren hadn't.

Lordy, she was a mess, but she'd better get her act together fast. She needed to find out who she was before she could allow herself to get involved with another man. But as the long, solitary night ticked away, she was forced to admit she was already involved. Deeper than she'd have believed possible.

CHAPTER SIX

SAM LET HIMSELF into Regan's apartment way after midnight. The rehearsal dinner had run long, the guests only too happy to party, drink and have fun. Then, after Bill had walked his fiancée, Cynthia, to her car, he'd insisted they go out for a drink. Sam couldn't deny his friend on his last night of bachelorhood, so they'd hit a local bar, where Bill had indulged and Sam had nursed a beer and thought about the woman he'd left behind.

He stripped off his clothes, including his boxers, and slipped into bed beside her, immediately pulling her close.

"Sam?" she murmured drowsily.

"Mm-hmm." He took it as a good sign that even in sleep she recognized him and didn't mistake him for Dagwood. Obviously her ex played no part in whatever fears or reservations she held about her and Sam. "It's me," he told her. "Go back to sleep."

"'Kay." She wiggled closer, her behind snuggled into his groin, her body fitting perfectly with his.

He buried his face in her hair, letting her fragrant scent surround and soothe him. Arouse him, too, but amazingly that wasn't what he needed from her now.

Sam might not choose to give up his career as Bill had done, but damned if watching the soon-to-be bride and groom together hadn't made him long for the closeness they shared, and the knowledge that they'd face the future together. Sam wanted those things with one woman only, and she lay sleeping in his arms now.

True, he hadn't known Regan long enough to ask that of her, but he wanted the opportunity to see where things could lead, and he doubted they'd stand a chance if she remained in Chicago. He was based in San Francisco as was Connectivity Industries. He had to be available at a moment's notice and be willing to travel when the need arose. Sam still needed the sense of freedom flying gave him. He just wanted to know Regan would be there when he came home.

And from the reactions of most women, he knew how big a sacrifice he'd be asking of her. Not only would she be moving to a new state with no family or friends, but he wouldn't always be there to ease the transition.

If he thought asking her to go to a rehearsal dinner had been a shaky proposition, he couldn't imagine her reaction to this particular question. But by the time Saturday night or Sunday morning arrived, he'd have no choice but to broach the subject—or head home alone.

REGAN AWOKE to a warm body covering hers. She couldn't say she minded the delicious feeling; in fact, she savored it. She'd heard Sam come back last night and, if she were completely honest, she hadn't fallen into a deep sleep until she'd known he'd returned.

Now she lay on her stomach with Sam above her, cradling her in masculine heat. "What are you doing?" she asked.

"Waking you up." He brushed her hair off her cheek and began kissing her neck, grazing softly with his teeth and then stroking her with warm laps of his tongue.

She shivered at the sensual assault and her body arched, her pelvis accidentally rubbing against the mattress, the contact having the erotic effect of arousing her even more. "Mmm. You're going to make me immune to alarm clocks," she murmured.

"If that means you need me to wake up in the morning, that's fine with me."

Before she could tense at his words, he began a

slow nibbling on her earlobe, certainly meant to distract her. It worked. She let her lashes flutter closed and allowed him to arouse her with his mouth, his tongue, teeth and oh-so-able hands, knowing all along this might be their last time together.

He worked his way down from her earlobe to her neck, pausing to kiss, caress and touch every part of her back. All the while, her body writhed and her feminine mound ground into the mattress, her climax closer and closer with each rotation of her hips. Her breathing came faster and a soft moan rose from her throat.

Without warning, she felt his hands clamp down on her thighs and she stiffened, startled.

"I want you to trust me, sweetheart." His breath rushed over her neck; her skin tingled with heated awareness.

"I do." She swallowed hard. She trusted him with much more than just the use of her body, she thought, her heart thumping hard in her chest.

His touch gentled as he spread her legs wide. Her adrenaline picked up speed as his fingers dipped between her legs, moistening her with her own juices, and then she felt him beginning to ease himself inside her.

She shut her eyes and let out a slow moan, he felt so amazing.

"Are you okay?" he asked.

"I'm go-oo-d," she said, drawing out the word. Very good, she thought. How could she not be when his big body surrounded her in warmth and he was so excruciatingly gentle inside her?

He brushed her hair off one side of her face and nuzzled her cheek. "I want you better than good, babe," he said, taking himself deeper still.

She clenched her thighs tighter around him, letting the swirling vortex of desire inside her build. With every slow, careful push he made, he brought her closer to the breaking point. She needed him to move, to thrust inside her hard and fast. Her body shook, trembling with unslaked need and she dipped her head into the mattress to keep from crying out.

"Tell me what you want." Sam's husky voice reverberated in her ear. "You told me you need to be in control of your life. You can have that with me. So tell me what it is you need."

No man had ever given her that right, that freedom, and suddenly she understood how he felt when he was flying. She fully comprehended *why* he needed that freedom. And the fact that he was offering it to her now made her want to cry, even though she didn't know if she could make herself utter the words out loud.

Between her thighs, she felt him pulsing inside

her, his own body shaking with the force of his own restraint. He understood her in ways no man had before and she needed him in ways she'd never needed another man. And silently, only to herself, she could admit it wasn't just sex between them, even if, at the moment, that's all her body cared about.

He seemed to understand that fact as he slipped his hand around her, cupping her breast in his hand and taking hold of her nipple, rolling it between his fingers gently but persistently until desire mixed with the pain of need.

"Trust me enough to tell me what you want, Regan, or what do we really have between us?" he asked.

She swallowed hard, knowing he was right. Hadn't she just admitted it to herself? "I need you. Hard and fast," she said, a tear dripping down her face and her voice breaking, so great was her need.

"Finally." The word came out on a groan as he thrust into her all the way.

He was big and solid and this position allowed him to fill her in a completely different way. She *felt* him, she thought. Because she wasn't focused on his face. Because after thrusting deeply once, he'd paused, and she'd really felt the connection of their bodies. And the longer he waited, the more she contracted around him and the more intense the swirling sensations of desire became.

He did as she asked and started to move, showing her no mercy as he began thrusting hard and fast, his body joined with hers. Between the slick movement of his penis inside her, and the rhythmic contact of her mound against the mattress, climax soon beckoned. Shocking herself, she cried out, feeling the unreal sensations build higher and higher until they peaked, taking her over the edge and into blessed oblivion. All the while, he continued his relentless movements until she was sated, her climax ended, all but the contractions still pulsing around him.

She'd come, but Sam wasn't done. Not by a longshot. He had so little time to bind this woman to him and though he knew he'd made a huge leap just now, he wasn't finished. And he wasn't just talking about his own release, which somehow he'd managed to contain.

He pulled out of her just long enough to roll her boneless body onto her back.

She opened her still-glazed eyes and met his gaze. "You didn't come yet, Sam."

He grinned. "You noticed."

"Everything about you," she admitted.

He withheld a grateful sound. "How are you feeling?" he asked instead.

"Amazing." She'd obviously learned her lesson about the too-bland word *good.*

He leaned down and kissed her on the lips as he'd been dying to do the entire time they were making love. For the first time, Sam refused to think of it as just sex.

Taking him by surprise, she grabbed his hips. "Let's go, lover boy," she said in a teasing, sultry southern voice. "It's your turn."

He chuckled. "If you think you can handle me again."

"Anywhere, anytime." Her voice turned intensely serious.

Good, he thought. He'd gotten to her. Now to make it last. "Want to know why I didn't come earlier?" he asked her.

She nodded.

"Because I wanted to see your face when I come. Because I wanted you to see mine." He rose over her. "And because I never want you to forget," he said, joining their bodies again, feeling every slick, moist inch of her.

And from her wide-eyed stare, she felt him as well. Satisfied he'd accomplished his goal, he began to take them both over the edge, doing as he'd promised. He watched her as she came, and he noted with satisfaction she also watched him.

But that didn't mean he'd made the progress with

her that he wanted. In fact, he had no idea what Regan wanted from him, and after turning down his invitation to a simple party and after he'd pretty much bared his soul while making love, Sam decided the ball was now in her court.

If she wanted more, she'd have to come to him.

REGAN WAS ALONE again and she hated it. She paced the bedroom, trying in vain to ignore the rumpled sheets on her bed, the duffel bag in the corner, and the potent scent of Sam's cologne that remained. It wasn't as if she didn't know how to be alone, or as if she couldn't function as a single person. After all, she'd been on her own for years, even if she had been bowing to convention. But the simple fact remained, she missed Sam.

A not-so-smart realization, considering the man was leaving in the morning. And though he'd hinted that more existed between them than just sex, she would be dreaming if she allowed herself to believe him or believe that his words would last beyond their affair. First off, they'd just met. What could they really know about one another or have in common? Second, they lived miles apart. And third, he didn't want to be tied down as his father had been. As his best friend would soon be.

Her heart rebelled against her objections, but, before she could think things through more clearly, her thoughts were cut off by the jarring ring of the phone. With a groan, she picked up the receiver. "Hello?"

"Regan, darling, I'm worried sick. Please tell me Darren's hallucinating and you aren't consortin' with a man who isn't your fiancé." Her mother's pleading voice sounded on the other end of the phone. "Please tell me the wedding's going on as planned." Kate sounded near hysteria and from the slanted viewpoint she'd obviously gotten from Darren, in her mind she had good reason.

Her mother would believe Darren, if only because Regan had consistently disappointed her—unlike her other daughters who'd always done the right thing, in the right time frame. Regan had come close to pleasing her family, but she was about to destroy any last illusion they might have held about her finally falling in line as the perfect daughter.

Unless Kate could see past social standards and understand what was in Regan's heart, she and her daughter were destined for a rift that would be difficult to breach. As much as Regan longed for a mother who would console, she didn't hold out much hope. Just enough to make her hold her breath.

But Darren had set the stage for disaster, and if he were standing in front of her, Regan would throttle him without second thought. "Mama, listen, things aren't what they seem," she said, hoping to explain Darren's mass of lies.

Kate exhaled a loud breath of air. "Thank goodness. You mean you aren't sleepin' with a strange man?"

Regan shook her head and leaned against the kitchen counter for support, having the distinct feeling she was going to need it. "Mama, I'm twenty-five years old. I—"

"I'll take that as a yes," Kate said, her wail of despair cutting off Regan's next words. "Oh, I knew I never should have agreed to let you go to Chicago before the wedding. If you'd just been home, where we could keep an eye on you, none of this would have happened."

Since Regan had already pointed out her age, she figured reminding her mother was a futile point.

"Don't you realize poor Darren's beside himself with worry?" Kate asked. "And your father, well, I haven't figured out how to break the news to him. You finally found yourself a good man but you couldn't hold onto him, could you?" Kate asked, full of reproach. Full of disappointment that, thanks to Regan, she'd have to be embarrassed in front of her friends. Yet again.

Regan opened her mouth to argue, but realized she'd be fighting an old battle, one she couldn't win. It reminded her of the time she'd refused to attend a country club gala with her father's best friend's son because the last time she'd been alone with him, he'd tried to force himself on her. Her parents hadn't believed her then, instead opting to think she was being typically picky, obstinate and stubborn, defying them on purpose. There was no way her mother would believe her now. No way she'd even try.

Kate had always loved the idea of having daughters she could parade in front of her country club friends, during their coming outs, their engagements, their weddings, all on schedule, *just like her friends' daughters*. But when Regan had turned out to be an individual with her own likes and needs, Kate hadn't known what to do with her. She hadn't ever tried to figure Regan out. And since her father had relegated raising the girls to Kate, neither had he.

Still, they were at a crossroads now and Regan couldn't allow Darren's view to stand. Regan intended to start with the truth. "Mama, listen to me," she said, patiently, wanting her mother to see her point of view. "Darren broke up with me over the weekend. He was cheating on me with—"

"One of his associates," Kate said, taking Regan by surprise. "I already know. Darren warned us you'd be defensive and come up with a story like that to blame him. He said you've been that way since the move to Chicago. He's had to work long hours to establish the new office, but you didn't understand. You've been cold and distant and turned to another man for attention.''

Regan leaned back, deliberately knocking her head against the cabinet, but it didn't cause her to mercifully black out or make her mother's ridiculous faith in Darren disappear.

"I have a plan," Kate said.

Regan rolled her eyes. "I really don't want to know."

"Of course you do. Your daddy can talk to Darren and I'm sure he'll take you back."

She shook her head. "I don't want Darren back even if he would take me, which he wouldn't. Didn't you hear what I said? Darren was cheating on *me*. He doesn't love me and—"

Her mother let out an exasperated sigh. "Love's got nothing to do with a good marriage, Regan Ann Davis. The point is to marry someone of equal stature and live the life you were meant to have. End of story."

End of story for Kate, maybe, but not for Regan. "Don't you care that Darren's been unfaithful?" she asked, hating the little-girl voice that begged for her mother's approval.

But whatever Regan needed from Kate, she'd

never get it. Not when Kate accepted so much less for herself than she deserved. But not Regan. Not anymore. And no more pretense, either. She was through trying to be someone she wasn't or couching the truth to avoid hurting her parents' feelings.

"I suppose I should have spoken to you about men and their needs long before this," Kate said, resigned. "Men cheat. It's their way. But if you accept it, you'll have everything you ever want in life. Everything you deserve."

Regan twisted the phone cord around her finger as her mother spoke. "What things are those? Money? A big, cold, lonely house? Is that what I deserve?" Is that what Kate thought *she* deserved?

Tears welled in Regan's eyes as her childhood came back to haunt her. Memories of her mother crying in her bedroom when her father failed to come home; memories of Regan and her sisters singing lullabies to each other, each one louder than the last in order to drown out the sound.

Well, Regan wanted more for *her* children. She wanted more for herself.

"Those are important considerations, honey-child," Kate said, calling Regan by her childhood nickname. "Just what are you without them? Who are you without money? Stature? Standing in the community, and your good name?"

Regan swallowed hard, the answer coming to her

without thought. "I'm me," she said in a soft but determined voice. "I'm Regan Davis." And that was good enough for her.

It was also good enough for her pilot. In one short weekend she'd gone down a road of discovery, learning her inner strength and her true desires.

She'd been on her way since her trip to Victoria's Secret and her subsequent discovery of the *Sexcapades* book in Divine Events' lobby.

But it had taken Sam and his quiet acceptance for her to complete her quest for self-discovery— Regan liked the person she was. She liked the woman with fewer inhibitions who didn't worry about what people thought and who acted on her baser instincts.

Regan had thought she had to find herself and figure out who she was and what she wanted in life, but she had already known. All she had to do was be willing to step outside the protective cocoon created by her family then maintained by Darren, and venture into the big, bad world by herself.

And once she did, once she established her own identity, maybe her parents would see her differently. Maybe not. But at least Regan would be happy within herself. No matter how sad she was now.

"Regan are you listening to me?" Her mother's shrill voice traveled through the phone line and forced her to focus. "I said you need us and you need Darren. Call him and apologize. I'm certain with some smooth talking by your father, Darren will take you back."

"No." Regan verbalized her defiance for the first time, despite knowing that being proudly independent would never be something that would draw out her mother's love and approval. Nothing would, short of caving in. And that Regan wouldn't do.

"Excuse me?" Kate asked.

Regan imagined her mother straightening her spine and taking on her haughty air. "I said no. I won't apologize. I don't want Darren back, even if he did want me. Which by the way, he doesn't."

"Nonsense."

"Try asking him next time he calls to snitch on me, okay? He broke up with me." And, boy, was Regan glad. "But at least it made me realize that I have more self-respect than to settle for a man who doesn't want me. Doesn't love me. And certainly doesn't respect me."

She swallowed a laugh since Darren certainly wasn't banging down her door begging for a second chance. But her parents didn't realize that. They were too intent on finding fault with their daughter, while Darren played into their fears. He knew them well enough to play the game his way—and win.

"If you refuse to cooperate now, I'm not going

to be able to bail you out of this,'' her mother warned.

Regan straightened her own shoulders. "I'm not asking you to." She swallowed hard, accepting her mother for who she was and hoping that one day her mother would do the same for her.

Silence descended for a few moments before Kate resorted to sniffles and probably tears. "You're going to disappoint your daddy, Regan, and I won't be able to hold my head up at the country club." Kate wasn't threatening, she was stating bald fact, and Regan understood how disappointing and devastating her act of rebellion was for Kate.

Once Regan hung up, there'd be no turning back unless she crawled. And *that* day would never come. She blotted tears from her eyes. "I'm sorry, Mama."

Not for becoming her own person, but for the pain she was inflicting on her parents who knew and understood no other way to live.

The click and resulting dial tone on the other end confirmed Regan's hunch of how the conversation would end. She hung up the phone, her hands shaking, then hopped up and sat on the kitchen counter.

Though she was well and truly alone now, as a result of taking a stand she no longer felt bereft or empty. She had herself. And she would survive without her family's support or her fiancé's money. She had enough PR background to finagle a job somewhere and she could talk circles around anyone to raise money. Regan had faith in herself, she realized for the first time.

And she had Sam to thank for helping her to come to that realization. Sam Daniels, a man who allowed her to be herself—and loved her anyway. She'd bet her life on it because she loved him. Her mouth grew dry and her heart pounded in her chest as she allowed herself to think the words for the first time.

She loved Sam. And she did believe he loved her, in his own way. Not that she deluded herself into thinking that love changed who or what he was—her pilot who needed his freedom in order to survive. As much as he accepted her, she also accepted him.

She wondered if his solitary view of the world left any room for her. For them. And she realized there was only one way to find out.

CHAPTER SEVEN

As Sam finished his toast to the bride and groom, he raised his glass. "And here's to a lifetime of health, happiness and kids who look like Cynthia," he said, ribbing Bill. "Cheers."

The crowd broke out in applause and Bill stepped away from his bride long enough to give Sam a warm hug and pat on the back.

"Be happy," Sam told his friend. Not only did he mean it from the heart, he finally understood how such a thing as "happily ever after" was possible.

For years Sam had believed commitment, marriage and even a woman's desires would never mesh with his own. He thought his parents' situation was a living, breathing example and the women he'd come into contact with had never proved him wrong. Until now.

In his male arrogance, Sam had figured he'd never be the one with anticipation and nerves churning his gut. Had never thought he'd want a woman so badly, he'd be willing to do almost anything to keep her in his life.

He'd just never met the right woman.

Now he had, and he wasn't worth shit without her. Hell, he'd been propositioned by one bridesmaid and felt up by another and, though both were attractive, neither had interested him. Not even for prolonged conversation. Sam knew he'd spend a damn long time trying to get over Regan, his "one-night stand."

He made his way to the bar, ordered a Scotch, then headed for the front entryway to get away from the noise of the band and the throngs of people. He stood, shoulder propped against the wall, and watched from the doorway of the Grand Ballroom as the bride and groom danced to a slow song.

"Funny, but I would have pegged you as the type of guy who'd be in the middle of a party, not hanging out on the sidelines."

Regan's voice took him by surprise, and he figured he must have wanted her so bad, he was hallucinating now. He turned to see her standing behind him wearing a knee-skimming black dress with a shawl collar, a full face of makeup she didn't need, and her hair pulled back into a twist, looking like a million bucks.

"What are you doing here?" he asked, still shocked and not daring to hope for anything.

She shrugged, her fingers curled tight around a small black purse. "I'm looking for you."

The ballroom doors swung open, interrupting them. He grabbed her hand and pulled her toward the back hall where the restrooms and pay phones were, so they could be alone.

"So, how'd you find me?" he asked, because they'd never discussed where the wedding was being held.

She let out a long, feigned sigh. "Sadly, I resorted to snooping through your bag. How else would I find the invitation and information?" She shook her head in a dramatic fashion. "Oh, the shame."

He chuckled. "And what made you decide to come looking in the first place?" After she'd turned down his request to accompany him to the rehearsal dinner, he deliberately hadn't invited her to the wedding.

Bill had laced into him for that omission the entire time they were changing into their tuxedos earlier. Because Sam been dumb enough and drunk enough to spill his guts to his friend over drinks the night before, he'd set himself up for a lecture today. Never mind that he probably deserved one for taking the risk of losing her, Sam believed the next move had to be Regan's.

And he hoped like hell she was making it now.

He placed a hand beneath her chin and raised her head until their gazes met and locked. "I forgive you for snooping."

"Whew." She lay a hand across her forehead in Scarlett O'Hara fashion. "I thought I might have to work a little harder for that one." She smiled at him, but the gesture didn't match what he saw inside.

He raised an eyebrow, not trusting her light tone and flippant demeanor. Not when up close her eyes were red and puffy beneath the makeup and her voice shook beneath the brave exterior. "What's going on, babe?"

Her shoulders lowered and she let out a long breath. "I'm not pulling this off, am I?"

"Depends. You found me and I'm glad. But something's wrong and I want to know what it is." With his plane leaving in the morning, Sam knew they had no time for games.

A group of women shuffled out of the ladies' room, giggling and making too much noise. "So much for privacy," he muttered. "Follow me." Taking her hand again, he led her into the bride's room and locked the door behind him.

They might be surrounded by stray panty hose,

hair spray and things, but they were finally, bless-edly alone. He sat on a bench, then pushed a pile of clothing onto the floor and patted the space be-side him.

Regan joined him. "My mother called," she said as soon as she was seated.

"Darren let her in on his version of events, huh?" It wasn't hard to hazard the guess.

She nodded. "He made it sound like he was the wounded party, and I'd caused the breakup because he found me with another man. The nerve of the louse!"

Sam had to agree and waited for her to go on.

"Mama suggested I go crawling back and apol-ogize." She snorted, rolling her eyes. "As if I ever would."

No, Sam didn't see Regan crawling back to any man, but she *had* come looking for him and, despite his best efforts, hope expanded in his chest. "What happened next?"

"Well, Mama wasn't much interested in my ver-sion of events. She said even if they were true—as if I'd lie—that men cheat. That it's their way." Regan narrowed her gaze, then leaned closer until they were mere millimeters apart. "Which brings me to my question." She pursed her lips.

Luscious lips coated with shimmery gloss. She also smelled delicious and he got a damn hard-on just being near her. He figured he'd be eighty and still get horny anytime she came near.

"What are you laughin' at?" she asked him, kicking his shin with her foot.

Damn it, was it his fault the woman made him happy?

"There's nothin' funny about this," she said, furious with him and so very southern in her anger.

He stroked a finger down her cheek, trying to calm her and ignore the throbbing in his shin and the growing need filling certain other body parts. "You make me smile, Regan. There's nothing I can do about that, but if you're going to injure me every time I do, we're going to have a problem."

She dipped her head. "Sorry."

He chuckled. "Apology accepted. Now, what did you want to ask me?"

She clasped her hands behind her. "I wanted to know…" Her voice trailed off, her face flushed pink. "You're either going to laugh or think I've gone plum crazy."

"I promise I'll do neither." They'd obviously reached a crossroads and he wasn't about to blow it. "Go on," he said in a gruff voice.

"If you were mine…I mean, if I was yours… If we belonged to each other, would you find cheatin' acceptable? Necessary? A man's way?"

Through her rambling and obvious embarrassment, he understood how serious she was with her question. She wasn't just asking his opinion on cheating, because they'd covered that topic already, but she was trying to find out, in her adorable, roundabout way, whether he wanted more with her than the weekend they'd shared.

He already knew his answer. Sam's perspective had changed enormously since flying into Chicago yesterday morning and this bundle of nerves questioning him now was the reason.

For both of their sakes, he decided to tackle things head-on. "From the day I laid eyes on you, you spoiled me for anyone else. That's the way it's supposed to be between a man and a woman." He cupped her cheeks between his hand. "Between a couple. I never knew it before, but once I met you, it all became clear."

Her eyes grew wider. "So me and only me would be enough for you?"

"That goes both ways. I wouldn't expect anything less from you."

"I can live with that." She nodded, her big eyes solemn and serious, a happy smile pulling at her lips. "You spoiled me for any other man, too."

"Good. Now I have a question of my own." A huge question, one that had been niggling at him for a while now. "What happens if your parents' disapproval becomes too much? Have you thought through what you want out of life?'' He was who he was, after all—a pilot from the wrong side of the tracks. He wanted her to know the obstacles up front.

She glanced down at her hands. "My parents have never cared about what I want, only what they think is right. It took me leavin' Atlanta to realize it, so I can thank Darren for that, at least." She ran her tongue over her glossed lips. "But I'm finished livin' life for anyone but me."

"And what about what *you* want?" He grasped her hands in his, knowing they'd come to the crux of things. "I can't give up flying—"

"Who asked you to?" she said, sounding offended at the prospect.

He swallowed hard, daring to believe at last that this woman really did understand and accept him. "I can't leave California, either. The corporation I work for is based there. And I know it's a lot to ask after just one weekend, but if you're willing to move to San Francisco, I believe we have a chance."

She rolled her eyes again. "So do I or I wouldn't be here."

He wanted to grin, to laugh, to kiss her senseless, but he couldn't. There was more. "I can take you with me on certain trips. It's allowed and this way we wouldn't be apart for long. Still, you'll be alone

a lot when I'm gone, no friends—at least at first,"
he warned her. "But my family's there and they'll
really like you. My sister will make you feel at
home, and—"

"I'm a big girl, Sam." She wrapped her hands
around his neck, her fingers tangling in his hair. "I
know how to make friends and I can occupy myself
easily. I know what I'd be getting myself into."

"It can get lonely," he said, repeating the words
he'd heard his mother utter often enough.

"I like my own company." She straightened her
shoulders and met his gaze. "Sam, are you trying
to scare me off?"

He shook his head. "But if you're going to walk
away or make demands, better now than later."

"Silly man." She caressed his cheek, holding his
face in her hand. "There'll be no later. I love you.
I told you I believe we can make this work and I
meant it."

"Well, hell." What else could he say?

She smiled wide. "I want you to know, I don't
expect you to support me. I'll get a job. I've got
great PR skills. I know how to raise money and—"

"Do you want to work?" he asked. "Or do you
want to keep doing your fund-raising? Because I
can afford to support you. Hell, I want to support
you. So if that's what you want, I can hook you up
with the right charities. And that way when this

thing between us works out like we know it will, you can have my kids and not have to worry about giving up a job—''

''Who'd have believed Sam Daniels is rambling? We have so many decisions to make, but the important ones are ironed out. Right?'' she asked.

''Right.''

''So do you have anything else to add?'' she asked, laughing and happy. ''Because it seems to me the most important thing's gone unsaid.'' Her eyes glittered with ultimate happiness and certainty, and though he hadn't told her yet, she obviously already knew.

''I love you,'' he said, his words the most serious he'd ever spoken.

He didn't think it was possible, but her smile grew wider. ''I love you too, Sam.''

He pulled her towards him until he captured her mouth, parting his lips and making her his with the deepest, most intimate, primal kiss he could manage. After all, he was sealing the most important bargain of his life.

Later, when he finally broke for air, Regan said, breathlessly, ''Now do you want to know why else I came looking for you?''

Sam stroked her hair, dying to undo the knot, but knowing if she was going to meet his friends, she'd want to look her most southern perfect. "I want to know anything that's important to you."

She glanced at him with those huge eyes. "I want you to make me a member of the mile-high club," she explained.

He groaned. One thing he knew for sure. With Regan in his life, she'd keep him on his toes and he'd never be bored.

He held her hands in his and promised. "Babe, you have got yourself a deal."

HIS EVERY FANTASY

Janelle Denison

CHAPTER ONE

LEAH BURTON stood just outside of Jace Rutledge's auto shop, her heart beating triple time in her chest as she gathered the courage to approach Jace with her shameless proposition.

In all of her twenty-five years, she'd never been so brazen. But in the span of a few hours she'd gone for broke. First, she'd daringly stolen a page out of the *Sexcapades* book she'd found on the coffee table at the wedding planner's office. Then she'd made a spontaneous decision to seek out what really should go on between a man and woman in the bedroom. Because she certainly wasn't getting anything in that department from her soon-to-be fiancé, Brent. In fact, he seemed immune to her efforts to tempt him beyond lukewarm kisses, affectionate hugs and his gentle insistence that he respected her. He had no doubts that it was best to wait for their wedding night to make love.

If she accepted his offer of marriage, she thought, and leaned wearily against the cool metal siding of the building. She'd been stunned by his unexpected

proposal a week ago during a candlelit dinner at
one of Chicago's finest restaurants since after all,
they'd only been dating for six months. Though she
had to admit, from the moment they'd met, Brent
had literally swept her up into a whirlwind court-
ship that included expensive dinners, lavish dates
and social events, and extravagant gifts. Including
the gorgeous, two-karat diamond engagement ring
he'd presented her with when he'd asked her to
marry him.

Even though at times she felt more like a convenient social hostess than a true girlfriend, and she
knew their relationship was based more on a subdued compatibility than on passion, she couldn't
help but consider his proposal. Despite being a bit
on the staid side, Brent was offering her that elusive
something she'd spent the past few years searching
for—a man who wanted to settle down and get
married.

As an investment banker, Brent's career was sta-
ble and secure, which she considered a bonus. She
loved kids and couldn't wait to have a family of
her own, and she wasn't getting any younger. Brent
had assured her that he wanted the same. He'd said
all the right words during his proposal, and while
she told herself her emotions for him would flourish
as time passed, she hadn't been able to bring herself

to answer with an unconditional yes. Instead she had given him a quiet, solemn, "I'm not sure."

Leah winced as she recalled the disappointment she'd seen in Brent's gaze, but he'd been incredibly gracious and understanding about her uncertainty. He'd reached across the table, squeezed her hand and told her to think about his offer while he was out of town for a week-long business trip. She could give him her answer when he returned on Sunday afternoon.

Which left her with only this weekend to figure out what she wanted in her life and in her future.

But one thing was clear—that missing intimacy between herself and Brent was causing a whole lot of doubts about herself and their relationship. And his lack of sexual interest made her painfully aware that she wasn't inspiring wild passion in Brent, nor was he doing it for her, either. Not in the way a certain someone else could light a fire within her with just a glance.

She exhaled a deep breath and at the same time damned that book of erotic invitations she'd come across. The contents of the book had played on all her feminine insecurities and had compounded the doubts in her mind about herself and Brent. She'd gone into Divine Events that afternoon hoping that being surrounded by every aspect of planning a wedding would give her the boost of excitement

and feeling of absolute certainty she needed to accept Brent's engagement ring.

Unfortunately, her impromptu trip to the wedding planners had only increased her anxiety.

While she'd been waiting in the reception area
to meet with Cecily Divine, a red leather-bound
book on one of the tables in the entryway had
caught her attention. There was no title on the outside of the volume, and curiosity had gotten the
best of her. She'd opened the cover and discovered
the titillating world of *Sexcapades,* a sizzling-hot
book for lovers all about shedding inhibitions,
pushing boundaries and taking risks.

Inside, there were sealed pages of provocative,
daring invitations. Some were even missing, as if
other customers had helped themselves to a page
to spice up their sex life. Right then and there, Leah
took a risk of her own, and when no one was looking, she'd ripped out an invitation and had come
away with "The Dance of the Seven Veils."

Once she'd reached the safety and privacy of her
car, she'd opened the sealed page and read the provocative instructions, which included baring herself
to her lover, body and soul. She'd shivered, certain
she didn't have the nerve to pull off such a bold
stunt, but the fantasies dancing in her head had
taken on a life of their own. Except, in her mind it
hadn't been Brent whom she'd performed the se-

ductive striptease for. It had been Jace Rutledge,
her brother's best friend since junior high, and a
man she'd been half in love with for years.

That's when she realized her feelings for Jace
were partly contributing to her inability to make a
firm decision about Brent. And she knew that before she could commit herself to Brent—or any
other man—for the rest of her life, she had to get
Jace out of her system once and for all, so she could
move on without any "what ifs" or regrets haunt-
ing her.

Jace was the guy she'd always desired from afar,
but could never have. Not in the emotional, forever
way that mattered, regardless of her strong attraction to him. Over the years they'd become good
friends and spent time together on a casual basis.
But ultimately, he was a bad boy who'd always
played the field, who was content to remain a confirmed bachelor. And she'd heard enough talk between Jace and her brother to learn his MO when
it came to dating. No strings attached. No commit-
ments involved. And he'd made it clear that he had
absolutely no interest in marriage.

Which actually made him the perfect candidate
for what she had in mind. After having her sexual
advances toward Brent subtly turned down with
placating excuses, she was determined to validate
her sexuality. She also needed to know that she had

the nerve and fortitude necessary not only to seduce a man, but to strip for him as well.

With an erotic invitation tucked into her purse, she intended to learn what men really wanted from women, what turned them on, and to uncover what *she* found sexy and arousing. In the process, she hoped to find out what kind of man she wanted in her life. And there was no one better to experiment and indulge in those seductive desires with than Jace. Not only because she had the hots for him, in a way she didn't for Brent, but also despite his playboy reputation, he was one of her best friends, and someone she trusted with sexual tutoring and advice. She also trusted him to keep everything private between the two of them.

One weekend of Jace's time was all she'd ask. One weekend was all she'd give herself to be free and to satisfy the fantasies about him that slipped through her mind on a too-frequent basis. Then, armed with new knowledge, skills and confidence, she'd reevaluate her relationship with Brent. Her obsession with Jace would be behind her, so thoughts of him would no longer cloud her decision.

But, first, he had to agree to her request.

Biting her lower lip, she considered every last detail of her plan. So far, she hadn't told a soul about Brent's proposal—not even her best friend, her brother or her family, and she didn't intend to enlighten Jace either, or mention all her thwarted attempts to entice Brent. No, she'd tell Jace she just wanted the male point of view on how to spice things up sexually.

Squaring her shoulders, she turned the corner of the building and stepped into the auto repair garage Jace had bought six years ago and had since cultivated into a very successful business. There were eight bays, all filled with various vehicles in different stages of repair, and she glanced down the line of cars and the mechanics working in the garage in her search for Jace.

She waved to Gavin, one of Jace's workers and the garage manager, who smiled at her and pointed toward the front end of a BMW. She followed his directions and found Jace with the top half of his body bent over the engine, a wrench in hand as he worked on tightening a bolt.

Stopping a few feet behind him, Leah gave in to the pure pleasure of admiring his fine backside and decided that no one filled out a pair of faded jeans like Jace Rutledge. The soft, well-worn denim, complete with streaks of grease where he'd absently wiped his hands, molded to his toned butt and hard thighs, and the waistband rode low on his lean hips in a very enticing way. The blue work shirt he wore stretched over the muscles bisecting his back and bunching across his broad shoulders as he gave the wrench another firm tug.

He was an earthy, physical kind of man, in every way that mattered. He didn't mind getting down and dirty to get the job done, and he seemed to enjoy the exertion and labor involved in his line of work. Unlike Brent, who was polished and meticulous and wouldn't be caught dead with grease on his hands.

Jace straightened, six-feet-two of impressive, overwhelming male, and turned around to reach for a different-size wrench. He came to an abrupt stop when he caught sight of her, and a slow grin lifted the corners of his mouth, accentuated by a disarming dimple that had been charming those of the female gender since middle school.

Her pulse fluttered and a slow heat thrummed through her veins, a normal reaction whenever she was around Jace. He was so breathtakingly gorgeous, so inherently sexual, that any woman would have to be blind not to be affected by his virile good looks and confidence.

His facial features were Brad Pitt handsome, and his deep-green eyes lit up with genuine delight upon seeing her. "Hey, Leah," he drawled, his voice low and smooth and incredibly sexy. "How long have you been standing there?"

Long enough to look my fill of you. "Not long,"

she replied, and returned his smile with a casual one of her own, though she was feeling anything but nonchalant, considering the reason for her visit.

Grabbing a rag instead of one of the tools lined up on the workbench, he wiped his big, callused, working-man's hands on the towel, leaving dark smudges behind. "What's up?" He tipped his head, causing his roguishly long, sandy-blond hair to fall across his brow as he studied her for a quick moment. "Is everything okay, Leah?"

Depends on whether you'll agree to my proposition, she thought, and shifted nervously on her feet. "Would you happen to have a few spare minutes to talk?"

"For you, I have all the time in the world." He winked at her. "Just let me get cleaned up a bit, and I'll meet you back in my office."

"Thanks." She watched him disappear down a hallway that led to the men's room before she headed into the adjoining reception area of Jace's Auto Repair.

Leah said hello to his longtime secretary, Lynn, and continued on to the back room where Jace had set up a small but efficient office for himself. Other than the chair behind his desk, there was no place to sit, but she had too much restless energy swirling inside her to be idle. So, instead, she paced along the small strip of gray industrial carpet in front of his desk and in her mind rehearsed her request.

He entered the office minutes later, all cleaned up in a different T-shirt and jeans, and all traces of grease gone from his forearms and hands. The familiar, arousing scent of orange citrus clung to him, which was from the special solvent he used to cut through the grime that came from working on engines and automotive parts.

He handed her a bottle of chilled water, which he knew she preferred over soda, and popped open his own can of cola. "So, what brings you by?" he asked, his warm gaze connecting with hers. "Not that I'm not glad to see you, but you seem…distracted. Like something's on your mind."

As a longtime friend, he'd always had the uncanny ability to read her moods. "There is something on my mind," she admitted. He waited patiently for her to continue, and she rolled the cold bottle of water between her warm palms. "Actually, I need your help. That is, if you're willing to…assist me."

Setting his drink on his desk, he turned back toward her and gently grasped her shoulders, his attention undivided and direct. His touch was firm, and the way his thumbs idly stroked the bare skin of her arms caused an insidious, forbidden heat to steal through her and settle in her belly.

She'd always known that Jace's touch was enough to ignite sexual sparks...and his ability to do so was a blatant reminder of what was lacking between herself and Brent. The distinct contrast was one she couldn't deny, and one which made today's quest more important than ever.

Concern creased Jace's brows, and, luckily, the silk blouse she wore was loose enough that he couldn't see the way her nipples had puckered tight. And if he noticed the goose bumps that had risen on her arms from the soft scrape of his fingers, he didn't mention the telltale sign.

"Honey, whatever it is, you know I'm here for you," he said, reminding her of the reason why she was there. "All you have to do is tell me what you need."

She met Jace's gaze, gulped for air and courage and, remembering the *Sexcapades* invitation that had set her on this course, she took her second risk of the day. "I want you to show me what turns a man on, and how to satisfy him in bed."

JACE BLINKED at the woman standing in front of him, certain the words he'd just heard slip past those soft, full lips of hers were part of one of his deepest, most fondest dreams.

She was a far cry from what he'd consider a vixen, especially one who'd initiate such a sinful advance. No, Leah was more the traditional type, inside and out. The simple cream silk blouse and navy skirt she was wearing backed up his image of her, and also told him she'd just come from her job as a secretary for an engineering firm. But as conservatively as she dressed, he couldn't deny that he'd spent many pleasurable hours imagining her naked beneath all those buttoned-up outfits, wondering what it would be like to skim his hands over the firmness of her small breasts, the delicate curve of her waist and hips, the silky softness of her bared skin…

He shook his head, hard. Obviously, his imagination was spinning fantasies, because there was no way sweet, sensible, good-girl Leah Burton would ever issue him the tempting offer of being her tutor in the finer art of seduction, no matter how much he might have wished for such an opportunity.

When he'd first met her as the sister of his friend in middle school, Leah had been a young girl, and through the many years that he'd known her she'd become his good friend as well. He'd watched as she'd blossomed into a beautiful, desirable young woman with thick, shiny chestnut-brown hair that reached her shoulders, and a slender figure with just the right amount of curves to complement her petite frame. A woman completely and totally off-limits to him—in deference to his friendship with her brother, and in respect for her parents, who'd accepted him into their lives despite his questionable background.

His father had walked out on him when he was five and had never looked back, and he'd been raised by a mother who'd spent more of her time cruising bars for men and booze than with her son who'd needed her the most. The Burtons had fed him when he'd been hungry and had given him a safe place to sleep when he'd been too scared to stay the night alone in the ramshackle house his mother had rented. They'd bought him new shoes and clothes when his few pairs of secondhand jeans and shirts had been too threadbare to wear, expecting nothing in return. And when he'd gone through a rebellious stage, straying to the wrong side of the law and getting picked up for shoplifting, it had been Leah's father who'd met him at the police station, not his own mother. Jace had gotten a lecture on responsibility from Mr. Burton and a tour of the local prison, which had scared the hell out of him and straightened him out real quick.

He'd always be eternally grateful for their generosity and guidance, and for being a part of Leah's family, and he'd never jeopardize his relationship with the Burtons by getting involved with their daughter. As a product of a dysfunctional family, he didn't do intimate relationships, not the kind that included an emotional commitment, because he just didn't know how to give to another person that way. But that knowledge didn't stop him from thinking about Leah beyond the friendship they shared. Her warmth and unconditional affection drew him and appealed to the loner he'd become, and the confirmed bachelor he'd sworn to be.

At the moment, though, the only thing that mattered was clearing up the misunderstanding that was wreaking havoc with his head and hormones.

"Want to run that request by me again?" He grinned ruefully, stroked his palms down her arms to her wrists and brushed his thumb over the thrumming pulse there, just to keep the connection between them. "I think my brain is working overtime today and I'm sure I didn't hear you correctly."

"I'm sure you did," she said with a slow, deliberately sensual smile, more bold than she'd ever been with him before. Then she repeated the same proposition that had tied him up in knots the first time. "I want you to show me what turns a man on, and how to satisfy him in bed."

Oh, shit. His stomach clenched, and he immediately dropped her hands and took a huge step back, the bond between them no longer the gesture of comfort it had once been. Heated, rippling overtures of keen awareness surged between them, the kind of attraction he'd been fighting for too many years now. He wanted Leah, but he'd also taught himself to keep his desire and need for her buried deep down into his soul, so no one would ever know.

And in one breathy statement she'd made him feel defenseless to resist her, and all too eager to accommodate her invitation to show her the ways of pleasuring a man—and eager to please her in return.

He exhaled hard and searched for a logical explanation to this bizarre, and far-too-arousing situation. "Leah...tell me this is some kind of joke that your brother cooked up to get even with me for getting him toasted when we went out drinking last weekend."

"I swear this isn't a joke, Jace," she said softly, her big blue eyes searching his, hopeful and daring at the same time. "I'm completely serious. I want you to be the one to tell me what fantasies men find exciting, and show me what drives them crazy with lust."

Licking her lips, she closed the distance he'd put between them and placed her hand on his chest, right over his rapidly beating heart. "I want to learn how to touch and caress a man in the most effective, arousing way," she said huskily as her palm slid lower, along his ribs to his belly. "And I wouldn't mind discovering a thing or two about what *I* like, either."

She was doing a damn good job of inflaming him right now. His skin felt hot and feverish, the muscles in his stomach coiled tight. And lower, his penis lengthened and strained against the fly of his jeans. It took every ounce of strength he possessed not to grab her hand, cup her fingers against his erection, and give her ample proof of just how much she turned him on.

Leaning his backside against his desk, he crossed his arms over his chest, trying to take a more logical, reasonable approach. "Why do you need me to teach you these things?"

She shrugged a slender shoulder and opened the cap on her bottled water. "I want a better understanding of men and what they like sexually."

He watched her tip her head back and take a drink of the cool liquid. "And what about you and what you like sexually?"

She licked a droplet of water off the corner of her mouth, and a light blush swept across her cheeks. But his straightforward question didn't deter her at all. "I figure I'll discover that along the way," she said, playful and teasing.

A stunning thought slammed into him, and he abruptly straightened. "Good God, Leah, you're not a..." He couldn't even bring himself to say the word.

"A virgin?" she supplied for him, and laughed lightly. "No, I've been with two other men, neither of whom rocked my world in bed, or out of it even. So, that leads me to believe that I'm missing out on some crucial element when it comes to sexual pleasure and seduction."

He rubbed a hand across his forehead. He couldn't believe he was having such an intimate conversation with Leah. Sure, as friends they'd discussed a variety of topics, but nothing so personal as her sex life. Or his for that matter. But that hadn't stopped him from thinking about her and the men she dated, which brought to mind the executive-type guy she was currently seeing.

"Why not ask Brent to help you with your...research?"

For the first time since propositioning him, she glanced away, but only for a few seconds before her gaze meet his again, more determined than before. "Because, quite honestly, he doesn't always do it for me in that way, and he doesn't have the kind of reputation you do."

He lifted a brow. Her comment flashed him back to the scruffy, insecure teenager he'd once been, and possibly always would be deep down inside, though he'd managed to build a façade of confidence around himself over the years. "Ahh, so you'd rather get down-and-dirty hands-on training from a bad boy from the wrong side of the tracks?" She wouldn't be the first woman who'd considered a fling with him in those terms.

She looked startled by the bite in his tone, but quickly recovered. "That's not what I meant, and you know I've never thought of you that way," she said adamantly.

He couldn't argue her point, because she was one of the few people in his life who'd accepted him for who and what he was—before he'd become a successful business man.

"As for your reputation," she went on, "you've been with a lot of women, so I'd think you'd have a whole lot of experience in this area."

She flattered him, and he did his best to hold back a snort of derision. Lots of women, hardly. Maybe half a dozen that he'd actually slept with over the years, and with age he'd grown more discriminating and hadn't found anyone who'd interested him beyond a date or two. He'd hardly label himself a Don Juan who'd been with a slew of women.

Reaching out, he trailed the back of his hand along her smooth cheek, watched her eyes catch fire from his touch, and a part of him was gratified to know that while she might question her ability to respond to other men, it was obvious she was incredibly responsive to him.

"Honey," he murmured huskily, "I don't know what other men like, or what turns them on. I only know what *I* like."

"That's good enough for me." Her voice was breathless, her breasts rising and falling heavily. "I'm asking you to do this for me, with me, because I trust you to show me everything from the basics to the more erotic, and to keep everything between us discreet and private. All I want, all I need from you, is this one weekend."

She was offering him two nights of anything goes. Judging by everything he'd learned thus far, Brent wasn't giving her the attention she needed to satisfy her more feminine desires. Otherwise she wouldn't be here right now, asking him for lessons in foreplay and mating rituals.

She tempted him like no other, yet he managed, just barely, to remain chivalrous enough to try and dissuade her from this wild idea. "And if I say no?"

Her chin lifted a fraction, a defiance and rebellious spirit so contradictory to her normal agreeable personality. "Then I guess I'll have to find someone else who *is* willing."

He knew a direct challenge when he heard one, and she was blatantly provoking him to accept her dare. She seemed hell-bent on following through with her impulsive plan, and the thought of her finding another man to agree to her proposition sent a jolt of jealous heat shooting through his veins.

And considering how bold and brazen she was being with him, he didn't doubt she *would* sway another man into agreeing to give her a crash course in how to please a man in bed and out.

He struggled with doing the right thing, the *noble* thing that even her own brother would expect him to do, but he just couldn't bring himself to push her into the arms of another man for something he was all too willing and eager to give her. And then there was the possessive emotion twisting low in his gut that took him by surprise, as well.

Sure, he'd always been protective of Leah given they were friends and his situation with her brother and family, but this feeling was different—a completely physical and intimate need to take charge and show Leah everything she wanted to learn.

Yes, he'd be her weekend lover. This way, he'd be in control of the situation, whereas there was no telling how another man, a stranger possibly, might take advantage of her. If anyone was going to satisfy her erotic curiosity, it would be him, he decided. No one else.

He could have Leah for one weekend. His every fantasy fulfilled, and hers, too. A perfect secret arrangement with no entanglements or expectations—just a hot mutual affair that would remain completely private between the two of them.

It really was an ideal arrangement.

Anticipation pumped through him, and he pushed his fingers through his already mussed hair and gave her what she'd come there for. "Fine, I'll do it."

She released a sigh that was pure relief. "Thank you, Jace."

She was smiling up at him, looking extremely pleased with herself, her eyes sparkling with unabashed excitement. He wondered if she realized what she was really getting herself into, and decided to give her one last chance to change her mind about this crazy plan of hers before she did something she'd regret later. He owed her, and himself, that much.

Yes, she trusted him, and he'd never, ever do anything to hurt her, but if he showed her exactly what to expect and how demanding and aggressive he could be when it came to getting what *he* wanted, maybe she'd come to her senses and realize just how potent and dangerous her scheme could be to them both.

"Since we have an agreement, are you ready for your first lesson?" he asked.

Startled surprise etched her expression, and she

cast a quick glance out the window behind him, overlooking the building's parking lot. "Right here? Right now?"

She was shocked, possibly uncertain about getting caught. Good. He was about to shake her up even more.

He backed her up against the nearest wall and flattened his hands on either side of her head, trapping her in the cage of his body and allowing her no escape…not unless she asked to be set free.

His gaze dropped to her soft, pink, glossy lips, then slowly, lazily lifted once again. "Sure. Why not right here, right now?" he drawled impudently.

The thrill of the forbidden flashed in her eyes. "Whatever the first lesson may be, I'm game," she whispered, teasing him with her words, her eagerness to explore anything and everything with him. "Let's go for it."

"Yes, let's." He lowered his head, took her mouth with his, and finally kissed her as he'd been wanting to kiss her for what seemed like forever.

CHAPTER TWO

LEAH HAD DREAMED of this moment for years, but her fantasies didn't even come close to the reality of having Jace's mouth on hers, the pressure of his lips parting hers so that he could slip deep inside and taste and stroke and tangle his tongue with her own. The kiss was hot and greedy and wickedly aggressive, bypassing all the gentlemanly preliminaries she was used to with Brent.

Jace was no gentleman, not when it came to kissing her, and his response excited her as nothing else had in a very long time, if ever. This was exactly what she craved. To be possessed by a man, and to experience passion in its most raw, untamed form.

One kiss, and she felt alive as a woman and a sexual creature with feminine desires and needs. And it felt amazingly, gloriously wonderful to experience such an instantaneous surge of lust for a man.

But as much as kissing him thrilled her, it wasn't enough. She ached for a more intimate contact with him, but other than their clinging lips, he wasn't touching her anywhere else. His hands were still braced firmly on the wall next to her head, and six inches of space separated their bodies. Embracing the assertive woman she was determined to be this weekend with Jace, she sought to remedy that problem, to break any last threads of restraint in him and let him know that she wanted no reservations between them.

Dropping her hands to the waistband of his jeans, she hooked her fingers into the belt loops at his sides and slowly, inexorably, pulled him toward her, until her soft, female curves molded to his hard, masculine contours. Their hips met, and the impressively thick, solid erection nestling against her belly surprised her in a very good way.

Knowing she was responsible for his state of arousal boosted her confidence, made her burn for him, and she slid her hands around to his backside and cupped his taut buttocks in her palms. She instinctively arched into him, shamelessly rubbed her mound against that solid ridge of flesh, and reveled in the low groan of need that rumbled up from his chest.

He threaded his fingers through the strands of her hair and slanted her head to better fit their mouths together for a warm, wet, and wonderfully erotic kiss. His free hand caressed her jaw and trailed down the side of her neck, until his thumb found the erratic pulse at the base of her throat, though he didn't linger there long. Releasing the first button on her blouse, he slipped his splayed palm into the loose, open collar. His roughened fingertips abraded her smooth skin, and her breathing deepened as he slid lower and nestled her small breast in his hand. The material of her bra was thin and insubstantial, all sheer fabric and lace, and when he grazed her tight, sensitive nipple with his thumb, she shuddered and nearly came apart.

He seemed just as lost in the heady pleasure of the kiss, just as sexually charged. The long fingers wrapped in her hair tightened, and he pressed her more fully against the wall with the lean, powerful length of his frame. Grinding his hips hard against hers, he thrust his tongue deeper into her mouth. Aggressive male heat radiated off him in waves, and her body grew pliant and damp, aching for his touch in places too long denied.

The phone on his desk buzzed, and he jerked away and stumbled back, nearly falling on his ass in his haste to put distance between them. His breathing was shallow and quick, and she almost laughed at the incredulous look on his face. Too incredulous, as if he couldn't quite believe that she'd allowed him to go so far.

And then it dawned on her. Obviously, Jace had meant to change her mind with that explosive, dominant kiss, but his plan had backfired. She wanted him now more than ever. He was everything she'd ever desired, and their sizzling encounter proved just how much he wanted her, too.

Abruptly, he rounded his desk and punched the intercom button on his phone, all the while his gaze remaining riveted on her flushed face. "What is it, Lynn?"

"Mr. Dawson is here to drop off his Porsche for servicing," his secretary said, her voice filling the small office. "And he wanted to talk to you about the repairs he's having done."

"Offer him something to drink, and tell him I'll be there in a minute." He disconnected the line, but remained behind the barrier of his desk.

Leah lightly brushed her fingers along her mouth, and watched his eyes dilate with a renewed hunger. Her lips felt wet, swollen, deliciously ravished. After experiencing too many of Brent's quick, passionless kisses, the lush sensation felt so, so good, as did witnessing Jace's heated reaction to the seductive way she touched her mouth.

She lowered her hand and was the first to break the silence that had descended between them. "I think you just covered first, second and third base in that lesson." A smile quirked her lips and humor laced her voice.

"Close, but not quite. There's still a whole lot

more to learn,'' he returned with a slow, lazy grin of his own. ''That is, if you're still interested.''

Did he really think she'd refuse? ''More than ever. I'm looking forward to every single minute of your private lessons.''

''Then I'll be at your place tonight, 7:00 p.m. sharp, and I want you to wear something short and revealing.''

She lifted a brow curiously. ''Another lesson?''

''You could call it that, yes.'' He finally rounded his desk, his gaze glittering purposefully, his demeanor just as sinfully direct. ''If you want to know what men find sexy, then there's one thing you should keep in mind.''

''And what's that?'' she asked, wide-eyed and eager.

''Most men like visual stimulation when it comes to the opposite sex.'' Gathering the sides of her loose blouse in his fists, he gradually tightened the material across her chest. ''Initially, if you want to turn our heads and keep our attention, then you need to give us an incentive to look. Bait the hook, so to speak. And a more formfitting outfit will do that every time.''

The fabric was now taut in his hands and cool across her flesh, revealing her small, pert breasts crowned with pointed nipples and the indentation of her waist and hips. He looked his fill, his ravenous gaze causing a delicious heat to spread through her veins.

"You have a nice body, Leah," he murmured huskily. "Don't be afraid to put it on display every once in a while. And since this weekend is all about executing lessons, I want you to wear something enticing for me."

He released her blouse, but her breasts remained tight and aching. "I'll see what I can do," she managed to murmur. If he wanted enticing, she'd definitely deliver on his request.

Picking up her purse, she left his office, her stomach fluttering with the exciting knowledge that sexy bad-boy Jace Rutledge belonged to her for the next forty-eight hours. And she was all his.

She only hoped that was enough time to satisfy her longing for him, and finally get him out of her mind and heart, once and for all.

AT FIVE MINUTES to seven, Jace made his way up to Leah's apartment, the anticipation of what the night might hold kicking up his adrenaline a few notches.

This was it, he thought. Once he stepped into Leah's place there would be no turning back—because his presence was just as good as a promise. His arrival meant he had every intention of following through on the pact they'd made.

He'd given her one last chance to change her mind. Considering the uninhibited way she'd responded to the hot, combustible kiss they'd shared, and her sassy attitude afterward, it was safe to say that she knew exactly what she was getting herself into, and her mind was made up.

Well, so was his.

From his perspective, all bets were off, and from here on he wasn't holding back with Leah. He'd selfishly accept anything she offered, take her as far as she dared to go sexually, and do his best to boost her confidence along the way. This weekend was for him just as much as it was for her, and he intended to give her an affair to remember.

He knocked on her door to announce his presence and used the key she'd given him months ago to enter her apartment. "Hey, Leah, it's Jace," he said, and closed the door behind him.

"I'm in my bedroom," she called out. "Come on back."

For as many times as he'd been in her apartment over the years, he'd never been in her bedroom before. There had never been any reason to traverse into that feminine domain. And now she'd issued a personal invitation he wasn't about to refuse.

"Hey there," she said, greeting him with a smile as she slipped into a pair of strappy, high-heeled sandals. "I'm almost done getting ready."

Jace stared at the vision before him, his every fantasy come to life. Leah's transformation from conservative to knockout gorgeous made his mouth go dry and awareness surge through his bloodstream. He'd always known that beneath the sensible, practical clothing she normally wore, she had the potential to be a sexy siren, and the alluring outfit she'd changed into confirmed his hunch.

The dress was thigh-length short with a flirty, ruffled hem and a bodice that nipped in at her slender waist. A gathered, scooped neckline tied together with a small bow between her breasts, and it was all he could do to stop himself from reaching out and tugging on that string and baring all her luscious assets to his gaze.

"Wow, you look...*incredible*," he rasped as he took in the way she'd piled her hair on top of her head in a messy topknot, exposing the elegant line of her throat for the stroke of his fingers, the caress of his mouth. He shook himself mentally and cleared his throat. "How long have you been hiding *that* outfit?"

"For a few weeks now." She shrugged a shoulder and smiled tentatively as she picked up a pair of gold hoop earrings from her dresser and pushed them through her lobes. "It looked so cute on the mannequin in the store, and so I bought the dress, but I haven't had the opportunity to wear it."

He lifted a brow and felt compelled to ask about her boyfriend's opinion on the matter. "Not even for Brent?"

"I wasn't sure that Brent would like it since it's so...different," she said, shades of uncertainty creeping into her voice. "He's more on the conservative side, and he doesn't think it's appropriate to have so much skin showing in public."

Jace stared at her, feeling both stunned and disgusted. Did Brent have rocks in his head? Or, more appropriately, in his pants? He doubted that Leah wanted to hear his point of view on Brent's way of thinking, so he kept his sentiments to himself. He hoped the lessons she learned this weekend would knock some sense into Leah about her significant other.

"Anyway, the dress has been hanging in my closet, and tonight just became the perfect opportunity to put it to good use." She twirled around, giving him a 360-degree view of her new outfit. "So, what do you think? Do you like it?"

"What's not to like?" he said, his gaze drawn to her supple thighs where the swirling hemline ended.

Brent's unappreciative attitude made Jace want to pull out all the stops with Leah, to make her feel desirable and sexy in every way. "You're a beautiful woman in a hot dress, and I, for one, love how much of your skin is showing. It makes me want to touch you all over, just to feel how soft and smooth all that skin really is.''

Her cheeks flushed a becoming shade of pink that spread down to the small swells of her breasts, but her eyes shone with a come-hither dare. ''Then do it.''

Without hesitating, he crossed the bedroom, closing the short distance between them. The dresser was right behind her, and he grasped her waist and lifted her so she was sitting on the smooth surface. Pressing his hands against her knees, he widened her legs and moved in between.

He'd definitely surprised her with his aggressive move, but she didn't object to their intimate position, and he considered skipping all the preliminaries of seduction and getting right down to the raw, primal need of making love to her. She'd made him excruciatingly hard, and he ached to feel her liquid and lush around him, the soft cushion of her naked breasts pressing into his chest. He thought about pushing up her dress, pulling down her panties, and sinking into her slick body. He imagined how she'd wrap her legs high around his waist, urging him deeper, and how she'd scream his name when she came.

The thought made him shudder.

He fingered an errant strand of hair that had

fallen from her topknot, the silken texture teasing his senses, as did the soft, feminine scent emanating from her. "I like your hair up like this." Cupping her smooth cheek in his callused palm, he tipped her head and nuzzled the side of her throat, and felt her shiver in response. "It gives me access to some of the most sensitive spots on your body...like right here," he murmured. He skimmed his open mouth up to her ear and laved the spot just below her lobe with his tongue.

She gasped and curled her fingers around his upper arms for support. "I...I like that."

He did, too. "Mmm, and right here," he went on, and gently sank his teeth into a tendon at the base of her neck, branding her with a love bite.

Her breathing deepened. "Oh, Jace..."

He smiled knowingly and whispered in her ear, "I'm betting you felt that biting sensation in other places, too, didn't you?" Like the tips of her breasts, her belly, between her thighs.

She managed a jerky nod and clenched her knees against his hips. "Yes."

Satisfied with her answer and the slumberous heat of desire in her gaze, he continued to tempt her and himself. "As much as I like your hair up, I love it down even more."

Releasing the clasp holding the chestnut tresses atop her head, he watched as the thick mass spilled free, then buried his hands up to his wrists in the luxurious strands. "I love it tousled around your shoulders and pretty face, and how warm and silky it feels wrapping around my fingers and against my skin."

"I like your hands in my hair," she admitted, and groaned when he massaged her scalp, then glided his thumbs along her jawline. "It feels so sensual and arousing."

"I agree." He was equally seduced by her, and the moment he'd created.

She was staring at his lips, so he crushed his mouth to hers and gave her what she wanted, what he craved, knowing that, soon, kissing her would no longer be enough to satisfy him. They'd boldly stepped over a line they'd never before crossed with this provocative proposition of hers, and being with her in so many intimate ways was unearthing a slew of emotions and needs he'd kept deeply buried for years.

He kissed her, long and slow and deep, her mouth so hot and soft and sweet under his, just as he imagined her body would be as he moved over her, inside her. With that arousing thought dancing in his head, he swept a hand down her back and shifted her bottom closer to the edge of the dresser, until the only thing separating their bodies were her insubstantial panties, and his khaki trousers. She locked her ankles against the backs of his thighs, rocked her pelvis against his erection in a natural, unconscious invitation, and his shaft swelled to the point of bursting.

With every kiss, he was slowly, gradually becoming addicted to her, and he wondered in the back of his mind if after this weekend he'd be able to let her go and watch her be with another man. The practical side of his brain said he had no choice, but his body and heart struggled to convince him otherwise.

One last lingering taste and he lifted his mouth from hers. But he still held her close, his fingers tangled in her hair, disheveling the strands even more. Her beautiful blue eyes were heavy-lidded, and a dreamy smile curved her puffy, well-kissed lips.

The pleasure she gave him was immense, beyond physical, and more than he had ever dreamed possible. "If you were mine, and you wore this dress out with me, I'd make damn sure you looked just like this before we left the house, so that every man who glanced your way would know without a doubt that you were taken."

The pulse at the base of her throat fluttered wildly. "And how do I look?" she asked curiously, guilelessly.

He brushed the back of his knuckles over the

soft, heaving swells of her breasts. "With your hair down and rumpled, your lips pink and wet and parted, and your eyes soft and unfocused, you look like a woman who just came from my bed after a long, hot session of mindless sex."

Her brows rose, shock mingling with sexy overtones of confidence. "Except I'm far from satisfied."

He groaned. She was going to kill him before the weekend was through. "That was just a sample to whet your appetite for more," he promised. "It's called the slow, gradual buildup of sexual tension that leads to the main event, and we've got the whole night ahead of us, sweetheart."

She laughed, the sound filled with low, throaty affection. "I can't decide if you're very bad for teasing me like that, or very good, Jace."

He grinned and helped her scoot off the dresser. "How about a little of both?"

"I'll give you that." Bemusement and eager anticipation etched her expression. "So, where are you taking me tonight?"

"Out dancing," he said, and twirled her playfully in his arms. "Where you can put that racy outfit to good use and drive a few men crazy with lust."

Placing a hand on his chest, she lifted up onto the tips of her shoes and nipped gently at his bottom lip. "The only one I want to drive crazy tonight with lust is you." With a sassy smile, she turned and sashayed out of the bedroom.

Jace didn't think that was going to be a problem. He was already there.

LEAH HAD NEVER BEEN to a nightclub before, at least not one as upscale and dynamic as Chicago's Red No. Five. Wearing a fun, sexy dress, and having a gorgeous guy on her arm, she was determined to enjoy the new and unique experience to its fullest potential.

Jace held her hand securely in his as he cut a path through the crowd, while she took in the seductive ambience, complete with laser lights, a huge dance floor, and intimate seating areas with private, secluded booths and couches swathed in rich velvet. They passed a cluster of women who were undoubtedly on the make, and there was no mistaking the appreciative, interested looks they cast Jace's way. He merely smiled politely and continued toward the back of the lounge.

The place was packed, the music loud with a distinct techno beat she found sensual and exciting, and thrummed rhythmically through her body. The people out on the dance floor were loose-limbed and uninhibited in their movements, and she envied their ability to just let go and enjoy themselves and their undulating bodies, uncaring of who watched. Which made her think of that *Sexcapades* invitation she'd taken, and how she needed to learn to be just as daring so she could strip with the same unreserved ease.

Jace found a vacant booth and let Leah slide across the seat first before he settled himself beside her. While the spot he'd chosen was dimly lit, they had a perfect view of the bar area and the packed-to-capacity dance floor.

He leaned close and said loud enough for her to hear over the blaring music, "So, what do you think?"

"I like it." So far, she was fascinated by the sexually charged atmosphere, and wanted to be a part of it. "It's also a good place to watch men and women flirt and interact with one another. You know, the seduction thing?"

He grinned wryly. "I'm sure you'll get a good feel for the various kinds of mating rituals between couples."

A bar waitress came up to their table, set down napkins in front of them, and bent low to be heard. "What can I get the two of you to drink?"

Jace glanced at Leah, indicating that she should order first. If she were with Brent, she would have ordered a glass of chardonnay without hesitating.

But she wasn't with Brent, and she definitely wasn't in a wine mood tonight.

"I want the most outrageous drink your bartender can make," she decided. "Something fun and exotic and uncivilized."

The pretty blonde thought for a moment, then her eyes sparkled in female camaraderie as she extended her suggestions. "Well, you've got your choice between a Blow Job, an Orgasm, or a Deep Throat."

They all sounded perfect for her wild, liberating weekend with Jace, and Leah definitely wanted to experience all three. "I think I'll start with an Orgasm and go from there."

"Good choice." The woman jotted down her drink preference and glanced at Jace, who looked taken aback by Leah's bold pursuit of the ultimate festive cocktail. "And for you, sir?"

"Since I'm the designated driver for the evening, and my date here is going to be enjoying orgasms, I'll take a cola." He flashed the waitress a grin.

Laughter danced in the woman's eyes. "You got it."

Minutes later, their drinks were delivered, and Leah anxiously sampled the smooth concoction flavored with Amaretto, vodka and rich cream. The drink was delicious, unlike anything she'd ever indulged in, and a moan of appreciation and pleasure rolled up from her throat.

Jace watched her, arresting her with his hot stare and the wicked slant to his smile. "Better watch out, sweetheart. Those orgasms are potent stuff."

She didn't miss the double entendre woven into his playful warning, and tossed out a sexy innuendo of her own. "Mmm, but they sure do go down easy." Enjoying the sensation of being naughty, of feeling sensual and wanton, she swirled her finger into the sweetened cream and slowly licked it off. "Would you like to taste my orgasm?" she asked, not so innocently.

He choked on the drink of soda he was swallowing, and it took him a moment to recover. And when he did, he leaned in close, filling her vision with his bold, masculine features. "There's nothing I'd like more than to taste your orgasm," he said, his voice rough around the edges. "But *alcohol* is out of the question since I'm driving tonight."

The man's willpower and restraint amazed her. Undaunted, she dipped her finger into her drink once more, but this time she rubbed the creamy substance along *his* bottom lip. "Then let me taste it on you," she whispered, and grasping his jaw between her palms, she brought his mouth to hers and slowly lapped and nibbled away the heady flavors along with the pure male essence that was Jace.

She felt him shudder, felt that control of his slip a notch, and continued to tease him with her tongue and the arousing scrape of her teeth, relishing a feminine power that she had never before realized she possessed. Or maybe it was a matter of being with the right man, one who made her feel free to be assertive and confident.

In their dimly lit corner booth they were afforded a semblance of privacy, not that anyone would care if they were making out, because she'd seen a few couples doing just that when they'd entered the lounge. She was out with Jace tonight to test her sensuality, to seduce him, in a place where no one knew her. The exciting thought was more intoxicating than the drink she'd just consumed.

With one last leisurely lick, she lifted her mouth from his and slowly dragged her tongue across her own bottom lip. "Now *that* was potent."

Blazing heat flared in his gaze, so hot she felt scorched to her toes. The warmth of the liquor flowed through her limbs and unfurled in her belly, and the vibrating beat of the music pulsed within her, low and deep, adding to the sense of freedom she'd embraced for the weekend.

She glanced out at the other couples enjoying the lively music and wanted to be right in the middle of it all. "Let's dance," she said enthusiastically, and he didn't refuse her request.

Time passed quickly, and Leah couldn't ever remember having as good a time as she had flirting with Jace, dancing with him and teasing him. That luscious sexual tension between them built with every brush of their bodies, every heated look, every provocative comment that passed between them.

This, she realized, was the kind of seduction she'd craved.

Thirsty from dancing, she ordered the Deep Throat drink the waitress had mentioned earlier— this one a shot glass of vodka and Kahlua, topped with whipped cream. She downed the drink as the bartender instructed. Jace watched in amusement, and Leah fleetingly thought how appalled Brent would be to learn how well educated she was becoming when it came to cocktails. And she wasn't talking the dry martinis he preferred.

She finished off the exotic drink and kissed Jace on the lips, uncaring of anything but their time together. She refused to let thoughts of Brent ruin her short time with Jace.

An hour later, the ladies' room beckoned, and she excused herself to take care of personal business. When she returned minutes later, she couldn't find Jace where she'd left him at the bar. She searched the lounge, but no luck there, either.

Still curious about that last drink she'd yet to try, she made her way back to the bar and ordered a Blow Job, giggling as she did so because it felt so wonderfully wicked to say such an outrageous thing out loud. She felt just as naughty drinking the concoction in a quick shot, the liquid sliding down her throat in a rush of coffee-flavored brandy and more whipped cream.

When a friendly, nice-looking guy asked her to dance, she was flattered by the interest in his gaze and figured what could it hurt to enjoy another man's attention for a few minutes?

She followed him out into the crush of people gyrating to the beat rumbling through the speakers. The drinks she'd consumed relaxed her body and mind, allowing her to let go of any last inhibitions and move to the provocative tempo of the music.

JACE GLANCED toward the ladies' restroom one last time, fairly certain he'd missed Leah's exit while another woman had been diverting his attention with her numerous attempts to convince him to join her for a good time. He'd forgotten what ruthless pickup joints nightclubs could be, and that thought worried him for Leah, wherever she might have disappeared to.

Despite how she'd shamelessly flirted, touched and toyed with him the past few hours, she was inexperienced when it came to the kind of brazen games these singles played, and much too vulnerable to a sophisticated guy who could see past the eye-catching dress and vivacious attitude to the sexually naive woman beneath. Mix in a few potent drinks, and she was ripe for the picking, just waiting to be taken advantage of.

His stomach cramped, and he knew he'd never forgive himself if something happened to her. Neither would her brother, he thought with a grimace. Undoubtedly, if John ever discovered that he'd introduced his sister to such iniquity and left her unchaperoned, he'd not only be disappointed in Jace, but more than a little furious.

Jace continued his search through the club, and finally learned from the bartender that she'd enjoyed a Blow Job before heading out to the dance floor with another guy. While the bartender's statement held overtones of amusement, Jace couldn't bring himself to laugh at how sexual his comment sounded. And he certainly didn't like that she'd so easily gone off with another man.

Minutes later, as one song segued into another, he finally found Leah in the partying throng of people on the dance floor. Her face was flushed and her eyes were bright and sparkling. A light sheen of perspiration gathered on her throat and chest, damp tendrils of hair clung to her temples, and she was laughing and smiling at the good-looking guy she was with, who seemed completely smitten with her. Jace was unprepared for the sharp kick of jealousy that flared through him, but he welcomed the white-hot possessive streak as he made his way toward Leah and her temporary date. He stepped between them, and Leah's sultry grin widened when she saw him.

"Jace!" she said breathlessly. "I was wondering where you'd disappeared to."

"I think *you're* the one who disappeared, sweetheart," he drawled, then glanced back at the other man who didn't seem at all surprised that Jace had cut in. "Sorry, buddy, but she's with me tonight."

A wry grin tipped the man's mouth. "Yeah, she told me she was with someone else for the evening, but I was hoping maybe you'd forget about her and I'd get lucky."

Jace's jaw clenched, though he couldn't fault the guy for being so honest in his interest in Leah. "Not a chance. She's mine, and I don't share."

The man backed down gracefully and left the dance floor to find another willing partner. Leah continued to sway provocatively to the beat of the music, then leaned close and said into Jace's ear, "I like you being all macho like that."

He grunted in reply because he'd never, ever acted so territorially before with a woman, then he groaned when she turned around and shimmied her bottom against his groin with utter abandon. The wanton movement made him instantly hard, and before she could spin around again he wrapped an arm around her waist, splayed his hand on her belly, and pulled her close, until her sweet backside aligned with his chest, stomach, and thighs.

Submerged in the middle of the crowded dance floor, he followed Leah's lead and rolled his hips against hers, showing her exactly what she did to him, letting her feel every thick, powerful inch of him. Having his rigid erection nestled against her bottom was sheer torture and exquisite pleasure, all rolled into one.

She glanced over her shoulder at him, her gaze brimming with a sexual energy that was nearly palpable. With his arm secured around her waist, he could feel her rapid breaths, could sense the need building within her, as strong and undeniable as the tempo of the music pulsing through them. Boldly, she grabbed his free hand and slowly, daringly, skimmed his flattened palm up her bare thigh and beneath the short hem of her dress, until his fingers encountered the damp crotch of her panties.

Slick, wet heat scalded the tips of his fingers. She was just as aroused as he was, and he instinctively pressed deeper, sliding the silky fabric between the soft, swollen lips of her sex. Her head fell back against his chest, her lashes drifted closed, and her lips parted as her entire body shuddered along the length of his. Her orgasm was only a stroke or two away, he knew, and her gyrating hips beckoned for him to give her that release.

The insane madness of the moment struck him and brought him back to where they were with a jolt of reality. Apparently, those drinks she'd indulged in had stripped away her inhibitions, and while Jace wanted nothing more than to give her body what it craved, he wasn't about to allow her first climax with him to happen in such a public place.

That was a fantasy he didn't intend to share with anyone.

He swore, low and succinct, and grabbed her wrist. "Let's get the hell out of here," he growled, and pulled her through the nightclub to the exit, not giving her a chance to refuse his spontaneous decision.

Not that he believed a protest was forthcoming. One quick glance at the soft, expectant smile on her face, and he knew she was just as anxious to be alone with him, to finish the seduction flowing hot and illicit between them.

CHAPTER THREE

THE DRIVE BACK to Leah's apartment was as insane as their erotic encounter out on the dance floor at Red No. Five. Leah couldn't keep her mouth or her hands to herself and, while Jace kept his fingers wrapped tightly around the steering wheel, she leaned across the console and nuzzled, nipped, and licked the side of his neck in the most incredibly wicked way.

Her breath was warm and sweetly scented as she placed a damp kiss on the corner of his mouth and her fingers fumbled to unbutton his shirt. Once she managed the feat, she slipped her hand inside the parted material and caressed his chest, plucked at his stiff nipples with exploring fingers, and slid her palm lower, over his abdomen. His stomach muscles contracted in response, and he drew in a quick, harsh breath.

Her hand stilled. "Can I touch you?" she whispered, and he heard the threads of uncertainty in her voice.

His mouth lifted in a sinful grin he tossed her way. "Sweetheart, you *are* touching me."

"I want…" Her voice faded away, and she swallowed, then tried again, this time with more determination. "I want to touch you the way you touched me out on the dance floor."

His pulse raced, and his groin throbbed, recognizing the pleasurable ramifications inherent in her request. He'd agreed to show her how to satisfy a man, but he'd never expected her curiosity to emerge while he was attempting to drive a car. Yet he couldn't bring himself to refuse her request because he ached to feel her hands on him—all over.

Lifting her hand, he drew her palm down to the rock-hard bulge straining against the fly of his pants and curled her fingers tightly around his erection. "This is what you do to me," he said, wanting to make sure she was well aware of her effect on him.

She looked into his eyes with something akin to wonder and fascination before he had to return his attention to the road. But that glimpse of enchantment was nearly his undoing, as was the tentative way she squeezed and fondled him through his slacks. She seemed unsure at first, but all it took was a low, encouraging groan from him to persuade her to be more assertive—to stroke the hot, rigid length of his erection against her palm, and learn the size and shape of him with the slow, firm slide of her fingers along his confined shaft.

By the time they arrived at her place, his blood was running hot and thick in his veins, his breath was coming fast and shallow, and he was damn close to erupting into a scalding release. He shut down the engine, removed her hand from his lap, and glanced her way.

A full moon glowed in the night sky and illuminated the interior of the vehicle, tipping the ends of Leah's tousled hair in a silver halo effect. Except, at the moment, she didn't look at all angelic. Her lips were parted and damp, her eyes shone with unquenched lust, and her expectant expression was turning him inside out with wanting her.

The modest, conservative girl he'd known for years had seemingly overnight evolved into a woman on a mission to destroy his restraint, and she'd nearly done just that!

"Will you come upstairs with me?" she asked huskily.

He'd nearly come right there, he thought, but kept the remark to himself. He'd promised Leah a sensual, uninhibited weekend filled with passion and seduction, and while he wanted her to remember everything about the first time they made love, he wasn't about to take advantage of her inebriated state. However, there were many other pleasurable lessons to teach her that didn't include actual con-summation.

Besides, they had unfinished business to take care of that she'd started out on the dance floor right before they'd left. He could at least take the edge off all that suppressed desire stringing *her* tight. As for him, he'd have to take matters into his own hands later.

"Yeah, I'll come upstairs with you," he said, and buttoned up his shirt before they exited the vehicle.

Once they were inside her apartment with the door shut and locked behind them, she flicked on the living-room lamp and kicked off her strappy sandals. She leaned against the wall with a languid sigh and a naughty smile curving her lips, then reached for him. Grabbing him by the shirt, she pulled him close, giving him no choice but to brace his hands on the wall on either side of her head to keep from crushing her with his body.

She tipped her chin up so that her eyes met his and her delectable mouth was positioned inches be-low his. "I have to tell you, that last Blow Job I had was scrumptious."

The sexual insinuation in her comment was like a well-placed stroke along his shaft, instigating vivid and arousing images of her tending to him in such a carnal way. The woman was too adept at throwing him curves when he least expected them, but he most definitely liked this improper side to Leah and had no qualms about playing along.

He raised a brow curiously. "What do you know about blow jobs?"

"I know they taste good," she murmured, and licked her lips. "*Real* good. See for yourself."

Curling a hand around the nape of his neck, she drew his mouth down to hers. She kissed him, openmouthed, hot, and deep, sharing the delicious flavor of the rich, sweet, coffee liqueur still lingering on her tongue.

Minutes later, she finally let their lips drift apart, and he grinned down at her. "That did taste good," he agreed. "Now, what do you *really* know about blow jobs? The real thing and not the drink?" While his tone was teasing, he was extremely interested in hearing her answer.

She blinked at him, feigning confusion. "What do you mean?"

Oh, she knew exactly what he was referring to, and after her brazenness tonight, he wasn't about to let her evade the risqué topic or slip behind a shield of modesty. "I mean oral sex, sweetheart," he said, so there would be no misconstruing his meaning. "Pleasuring a man with your mouth, and vice versa. How much experience have you had?"

"Not much," she said, a flush of embarrassment

staining her cheeks, along with an endearing amount of vulnerability. She glanced away for a brief second before returning her gaze to his and lifting her chin to a rebellious slant. "All right, 'not much' is a lie. I don't have any experience in oral sex at all."

Chuckling at her indignation, he touched the pads of his fingers to her soft mouth. He skimmed his thumb across her plump bottom lip and was gratified to feel a tremor of response ripple through her. "Ahh, so you're a virgin, at least in that respect." He was amazed and ridiculously pleased by the notion.

"So I am," she admitted, more easily this time. "But I'd like to learn. Will you teach me?"

Her eager request nearly brought him to his knees, literally, which would put him in the perfect position to worship her body with his mouth and tongue and fingers and give her a mindless lesson in those provocative pleasures. But as much as that fantasy excited him, he wasn't sure she was in the right frame of mind to make that leap to such an intimate act so soon. So he decided to improvise.

"I promised to teach you whatever you want to know," he said, and led her to the couch in the living room. "So, if you're ready for a lesson in oral sex, and what a real blow job is like, then let's do it."

She sat down, an avid student, and he settled in close beside her, making sure she was relaxed against the soft sofa cushions. "We'll start with you first." Because there was no way in hell he'd last with her mouth and tongue on any part of his anatomy.

Picking up her hand, he skimmed his finger along the webbing of skin between her thumb and forefinger. "Imagine, for the sake of this lesson, that this crease right here is the lips of your sex."

His frank monologue didn't shock her, and she shivered as he stroked that spot again. "It's very sensitive."

"It should be," he said, and gently bit down on the pad of skin just below her thumb, making her gasp. "Imagine how sensitive you are between your legs, along your cleft, and when you add lots of wetness and lots of tongue, like a French kiss, it feels incredibly good." Fastening his mouth along that ridge of flesh between her fingers, he simulated the technique, licking slowly, sucking gently and using his tongue to stroke and lap softly.

Her arm went lax, and her eyes rolled back as a low, throaty moan escaped her. "Jace…"

The one word was filled with such aching need, matching the same hunger pulsing through his shaft. But he wasn't done with this particular lesson, not until she learned what it was like to give him the same kind of erotic attention.

Releasing her hand, he touched his index finger to her lips and exerted a gentle, persistent pressure. "Now it's my turn," he said huskily, and eased closer so he could kiss her cheek, her jaw. "Open your mouth and let me inside."

Her eyes smoldered with blue fire as she parted her lips and let him slip his finger into the warm, sleek, wetness of her mouth.

His stomach and thighs tightened reflexively, and he forced himself to concentrate on instructing her. "When it comes to pleasuring a man with your mouth, the best way to describe what you're going to do is pretend his erect penis is your favorite flavor of Popsicle. You're going to lick and suck and swirl your tongue along the length and over the tip."

Grasping his wrist, she pushed his finger deeper into her mouth, then slowly withdrew the length along the tantalizing stroke of her tongue. His cock stiffened painfully, all hot, thick sensation gathering between his legs.

"Mmm, cherry," she whispered, a sensual smile curving her lips as she immersed herself in the lesson.

He let her take over, let her experiment any way she wished, and imagined her mouth elsewhere,

where he was excruciatingly hard and throbbing for release. And what she lacked in experience, she more than made up for in eagerness. She teased him with her tongue and lightly grazed his taut skin with her teeth, then sucked him back into the silky depths of her mouth and flicked and swirled her tongue along the sides and tip of his finger. Her eyes fluttered closed, her rapturous expression reflecting her enjoyment of the act as she continued to increase his excitement and whittle away at his restraint.

She didn't think she had what it took to seduce a man, yet he was drowning in her innate sensuality, dying to rip off her panties and just take her right then and there, with little finesse. When she adopted an instinctive up and down rhythm while sucking him, his control completely shattered.

Pulling his finger from her mouth, he replaced it with the heat of his lips on hers and kissed her urgently, insistently. Deeply. She whimpered and speared her fingers into the hair at the nape of his neck as her mouth opened wider beneath his for the hot, sexual thrust of his tongue.

She was just as wild and feverish as he felt. Knowing what her body craved after all that mental and physical stimulation, he shifted closer, pressing his aroused body against hers, and eased her down so that she was stretched out on the couch beneath him. With his mouth still fastened to hers, he wedged his knee between her legs, opening them for him, and slid a hand beneath the hem of her dress and up the back of her thigh. He smoothed his palm over a rounded hip, followed the elastic band of her panties downward to the very heart of her femininity. Then he slipped his fingers beneath the thin barrier of silk so he could graze his thumb along the soft, swollen folds of her sex.

She was hot and wet, drenched with desire, and her low moan and the way she arched into his touch were all the permission he needed to finish what he'd started with her. Wrenching his mouth from hers, he stared down into her beautiful face, and her trusting expression caused his heart to punch hard in his chest.

With effort, he continued. "Imagine my mouth right here," he murmured, and caressed her slowly, spreading her wetness upward, over her clitoris. "My soft tongue teasing, then pressing deeper..."

She tossed her head back and rolled her hips sinuously against his fingers, and then she was unraveling, coming in soft pants that turned into a long, ragged groan as her body shook from the force of her orgasm. But instead of her climax sating her, it seemed to inflame her even more. Within moments of her release she was shifting beneath him on the couch, spreading her legs wider, urging him between.

Before he realized her intent, she reached for the waistband of his pants, unzipped his fly, and tugged his slacks over his hips to his thighs. She cupped his erection in her hand through his briefs and, amazingly, he grew longer and thicker with each stroke of her fingers.

His breath hissed out between his teeth and barely able to hold back his own needs any longer, he caught her wrist, then her other hand, and pinned them both above her head to keep him in control. He knew the drinks she'd had at the night club were partly responsible for loosening her inhibitions, and while he refused to make love to her without her being completely lucid, there was no denying what both of them wanted. He could at least give her, and himself, this bit of pleasure.

Capturing her mouth with his, he rubbed his shaft against her cleft, deeply and rhythmically. Instinctively, she wrapped her legs around his waist and arched up into him, causing wet silk to rasp against the soft cotton briefs confining his swollen penis. He imagined thrusting inside her without the barrier of clothing between them, imagined being surrounded by her slick heat and softness, and when she strained against him and cried out as she climaxed a second time, that's all it took to send him right over the edge with her.

His breath hissed out between his teeth, and he shuddered as he came, his own release pumping out hard and fast and scalding hot, draining him, more than just physically. He buried his face against her neck with a groan, and it took a few minutes for him to regain his bearings. When he finally lifted his head and met her gaze, she smiled up at him, her features replete and content.

"Thank you for that very enlightening and enjoyable lesson," she said softly, her lashes falling slumberously.

"It was my pleasure." He kissed her on the lips and eased up off her. "I'll be right back," he said, and made a quick trip to the bathroom.

When he returned, she was right where he'd left her, with her hands still above her head, the hem of her dress bunched around her hips, and her thighs splayed. She looked deliciously rumpled, and if it wasn't for the fact that she'd fallen asleep, he wouldn't have had the willpower to resist her a second time.

But the night's events had finally caught up to her, and it was time for him to go, no matter how much he wanted to stay.

"Come on, Sleeping Beauty," he murmured as he scooped her up from the couch and adjusted her in his arms. "Let's get you into bed where you belong."

With a soft sigh, she snuggled against his chest as he carried her into her bedroom, and damn if she didn't feel as though she belonged in his arms, and in his solitary life, as more than just a friend. As more than just a temporary, weekend lover.

He helped her remove her dress and bra, and smiled when he realized that he hadn't spent much time on those small, perfectly shaped breasts. But there was still tomorrow and more lessons to teach her, and he'd be sure to give those sweet mounds of flesh the attention they deserved.

By the time he pulled the covers up around Leah and tucked her in, she was already fast asleep, her breathing deep and even. He stood there and watched her for a few minutes longer, aching to crawl into that bed beside her and hold her close instead of heading back to his own quiet, lonely house and equally empty, lonely bed.

He was in way over his head, deeper than he'd ever allowed himself to admit to before. And he was no longer sure what to do about those growing feelings that made him wish for the impossible with her.

LEAH WALKED into Jace's Auto Repair the following afternoon with a light bounce to her step and a sensual confidence she'd lacked the day before when she'd come to proposition him. In the span of twenty-four hours, she'd gone from a woman who hadn't had the nerve to seduce a man with a *Sexcapades* invitation, to an impetuous female who was going after what she wanted, without guilt or regrets, and was reaping the pleasurable benefits of being so spontaneous and unreserved.

Last night with Jace, at the nightclub and then later at her apartment, she'd been daring and adventurous and willing to experiment, in a way she'd never been able to with any other man. Jace had brought out the wanton in her, and it had felt amazingly wonderful to be so fearlessly sexual, to openly enjoy his attention and his tutoring—and to know that she had the ability to tie him up in knots, as well.

She strolled through the quiet, empty reception area and into the back garages, a smile on her lips as she recalled how she'd touched and stroked Jace through his briefs, and that's all it had taken for him to lose control with her. She'd been awed by that feat. Watching him let go of his precious restraint, and feeling the extent of his need for her, had brought her to climax—a second glorious time in a row.

Tonight, she wanted to feel every inch of his shaft inside her, wanted to experience being filled

to overflowing with the heat and strength and scent
of him, with nothing between them. She wanted
that intimacy, needed that unforgettable memory,
before she had to let him go.

Since closing time on Saturday for Jace's shop
was in a half an hour, at one o'clock, there were
only a few mechanics on duty who were finishing
up basic vehicle services, such as rotating tires and
oil changes.

"Hey, Gavin," Leah said, approaching the garage manager from behind as he tightened the lug
nuts on a tire. "Do you know where I can find
Jace? He's not in his office."

Gavin cast a quick glance over his shoulder at
her, then did a double take—obviously stunned by
the difference from yesterday's conservative sec-
retarial outfit to the formfitting jeans that laced up
at the front, and the peach-colored top that crossed
snugly over her breasts and nipped in at the waist—
revealing that she did, indeed, have a bit of cleavage when the right kind of push-up bra was worn.
Gavin abruptly lifted his gaze from her chest to her
face, his expression suddenly sheepish. "I'm sorry,
what did you ask me?"

Leah bit back a grin. The other man's reaction
definitely backed up Jace's claim that men were
visual creatures. For her, dressing this way was
about self-assurance and presentation. There was a

certain satisfaction in knowing that she did have what it took to capture more than a passing glance from those of the male gender.

She'd applied Jace's advice about "baiting the hook" when it came to turning a man's head, and she was prepared to show him that she was a quick learner. Last night she'd worn a dress that had garnered its fair share of attention at Red No. Five, and this morning she'd gone shopping and bought a few fun weekend outfits. And it appeared that other men weren't immune to her transformation, either, though she was certain that Brent would be less than thrilled with her new selection of playwear, since he preferred her to dress more on the subdued side.

She knew she ought to feel a twinge of guilt about that, but this weekend wasn't about Brent, she reminded herself. It was strictly about *her* and what she wanted, and she intended to enjoy her newfound sensuality to its maximum potential.

Geared up even more now by her thoughts, she was anxious to find her weekend lover. "Do you know where I can find Jace?" she asked again, and lifted the white deli bag she held in her hand. "I brought him lunch."

Gavin cleared his throat, recomposed himself, and hooked his finger toward the back of the establishment. "Uh, yeah, he's out in his private garage."

"Thanks." She sauntered past the other man, and feeling his eyes on her as she walked away, she put an extra feminine sway into her hips.

Jace's private garage was located at the far end of the shop, separate from the other bays. Normally, he stored his Chevy Blazer there during the day while he worked. But she'd seen the vehicle parked out front, which was odd, since Jace was so finicky about his meticulously detailed SUV, and liked to keep it covered as much as possible.

As soon as she entered the last adjoining building, she realized why his Blazer hadn't been parked in the garage. Another vehicle had taken its place. And just like yesterday, she found Jace bent over the hood of a car as he worked on the engine—this one an old sporty classic Chevy Camaro that had been restored to its former beauty.

"Time for a break," she said lightly, announcing her presence. "And I hope you're hungry."

Jace ducked his head out from beneath the hood, straightened, and turned around. "I'm starved, actually..." His cheerful voice trailed off as his surprised gaze took in her new and improved outfit. His smile faded into a frown. "Jesus, Leah, you can't come through here looking like *that*."

She lifted a brow, amused by his disconcerted

attitude. "Like what?" she prompted, curious to know what he found so objectionable about her fashionable jeans and top.

"Like…like…" Frustration edged his tone, and he waved his hand in the air between them and shook his head, clearly at a loss for words.

She set the deli bag on a nearby workbench, refusing to let him off the hook so easily. "What happened to your lecture about giving men an incentive to look? I was just applying what you taught me, and I thought you'd be impressed by the results."

"I am," he said, his reluctance to admit as much obvious. Heading to the sink at the back of the garage, he vigorously scrubbed his hands and arms up to the elbows with cleaning solvent, and glanced back at her. "It's just that…that my guys aren't used to women traipsing through the garage wearing something so…so provocative and tempting."

She smiled, undaunted by Jace's forthright remark. On the contrary, it delighted her. "Yeah, Gavin's jaw did drop a little bit when he saw me."

"And you seem pleased by that."

She shrugged unapologetically. "It was flattering."

Jace grumbled something beneath his breath as he ripped off a roll of paper towels and dried his hands.

She batted her lashes playfully at him. "Why, Jace, I do believe you're acting jealous, and a bit possessive." And it seemed much more like a lover's jealousy than brotherly protectiveness; she liked that change.

He drew a long, slow breath and pitched the wadded paper towel into a nearby trash can. "I just don't think you want to give guys the wrong impression, especially by wearing a pair of jeans that look like with one tug of that leather tie, they'd slide right off your hips and drop to your knees, and a top that makes your breasts look like they're going to spill out of that bra you're wearing."

So, he'd noticed, which made the bra well worth the astronomical price she'd paid for it. "It's amazing what underwire and a bit of push-up support can do for a woman's figure, don't you think?"

He grunted in response and came to a stop in front of her, bringing with him the clean, delicious scent of orange-citrus.

She sought to understand why he seemed so piqued with her, when he'd been the one to suggest a more visually appealing package to tantalize a guy's senses. "So, are you trying to say in that roundabout way of yours that you just want me to look sexy for you, and no other man?"

He lifted a finger between them, and his lips pursed. "I didn't say that."

No, he hadn't, but she would have been thrilled if he had.

"I just don't want you to take these lessons to the extreme, because there are men out there who'll misinterpret your signals." His tone gentled, and he brushed tousled strands of hair off her cheek. "You come across sensual and confident, and guys see that as a huge turn-on and a green light to proceed."

She relished his touch, and felt his caress all the way down to the tips of her breasts. "All I care about is whether I'm turning *you* on. I'm not out to deliberately impress anyone else, but I'd be lying if I didn't say that the attention doesn't feel good for a change. I just want to enjoy it for a little while with you."

With a sigh of defeat, he pressed his forehead to hers and hooked a finger into the front waistband of her jeans, drawing her hips closer to his. "Fair enough, but I have to warn you, if anyone is going to be pulling these ties of yours open, it's going to be me. At least for this weekend."

She laughed at his low, possessive growl, even as that qualifier, *at least for this weekend,* became a vivid reminder of where she stood with Jace— that he was hers for a very short time, for an exciting, forbidden fling that would inevitably end and become nothing more than a sensual memory, one she'd always treasure. And she hoped she'd become a fond recollection for him, too.

Her initial goal for this weekend had been to indulge her desires for Jace, to fulfill the fantasies that crowded her head at night, and ultimately to shake him from her mind and her heart. Unfortunately, with every lesson they engaged in, with every touch and kiss and illicit caress they shared, she wanted him even more, not less.

Refusing to let those tangled emotions encroach on her time with Jace, she rerouted her thoughts back to his sexy threat. "Since I don't think it would be too appropriate having my pants drop to my knees with your mechanics still on duty, let's eat lunch."

Jace let Leah slip from his embrace and watched as she cleared a spot on the workbench to make room for their meal. She set tools aside and spread out paper towels over the wooden surface, seemingly unaffected by the less-than-sterile environment.

He came up beside her and stopped her before she could set out their lunch. "You know, we can eat in my office where it's fairly clean."

"I kind of like it back here." Brushing his hand aside, she continued with her task, placing a wrapped sandwich on his place setting, then hers. "It's quiet and private and I feel like I'm inside some secret male domain.'' Her eyes sparkled with fun-loving amusement.

"You are,'' he admitted, and accepting that she was truly okay with eating in his garage, he retrieved a soda and water from his stock of drinks in the fridge beneath the workbench. "Not many people, other than my mechanics, come in here.''

She slanted him a curious look that caused her hair to tumble temptingly over her shoulder. "And why is that?''

"Because this garage is mine, and it's quiet and private,'' he said, using her own words as he dragged a padded stool over for her to sit on. "It's a sanctuary for me in here, a place where I can escape to immerse myself in what I love the most.''

A knowing smile tipped the corners of her glossy lips. "Tinkering with cars?''

"Yep.'' He unwrapped his sandwich, not at all surprised to discover that it was pastrami with mustard and pickles, his favorite. "This private garage also reminds me of who and what I am, and all that I've accomplished.''

"And you've definitely come a long way,'' she said, then took a bite of her own turkey and cheese sandwich.

"I'm constantly amazed how taking on a job at a gas station as a grease monkey at the age of sixteen led to owning my own car repair business.''

It was a venture he hadn't been able to accomplish alone, though, and he was well aware of the people who'd made such a difference in his young, undisciplined life. "I was fortunate I had a lot of mentors along the way who saw potential in me, and kept me on the straight and narrow. Teachers, employers and your family, too."

"I've always been very proud of you, Jace," she said softly. "And my parents have, too."

He met her gaze and held it. "I owe them a lot." He certainly owed them much more than fooling around with their daughter, yet no matter how selfish, he knew there was no way he could have refused Leah, or himself, this weekend together.

"You owe them nothing." She rewrapped her half-eaten sandwich, and stuffed it back in the deli bag. "They love you as if you were their own son. Don't ever doubt that."

Yet despite the Burtons' unconditional acceptance, he'd always been plagued with deeper uncertainties instilled by a mother who'd never been there for him when he was growing up. Jace had wanted her love first and foremost, and it had never been forthcoming. If anything, she'd resented his presence, especially after his father had walked out on them. According to Lisa Rutledge, Jace looked just like his father, and that had been enough for her to ignore his existence and drown her bitterness with alcohol and faceless, nameless men.

Now, she was dead and gone, and he was left with the deep-rooted inability to sustain a long-term commitment with a woman, an inability to love strongly enough, because a part of him feared the same kind of rejection. Over the years, it had been easier and less painful to keep women at a distance and remain a bachelor than to take that emotional leap.

Yet sitting beside him was the one person who made him ache for that intimate emotional bond, who tempted him to take those risks. But Leah deserved more than he could ever give her and, regardless of their sensual weekend together, she had Brent—a polished, sophisticated executive type who was more suited to Leah than the simple, ordinary kind of guy Jace would always be.

"If it wasn't for your brother's friendship so early on in my life, and your family's unconditional support and guidance, God only knows where I'd be right now," he said, and shook his head. "I'd probably be some hoodlum evading the law."

"But you're not," she said, and rested her palm against his jaw. The tender gesture told him how much she'd always believed in him—possibly more than he'd ever believed in himself. "You're a talented mechanic and a successful businessman, Jace.''

Still, insecurities lingered. ''What I am is a man who is usually covered from wrist to elbow in grease.'' That was his daily reality, and one that turned most women off when they realized what his work entailed.

She smiled at him, a lilting, flirtatious grin that caused a rush of heated awareness to surge through him. ''And when you wash it all off, you smell like a big, juicy orange that I want to take a big bite out of.''

Finished with his sandwich, he crumpled up the wrapper, tossed it into the trash, and slanted her a searching glance. ''And what would you do if I missed a spot of grease and smudged some on you?''

She looked at him oddly. ''I'd wash it off,'' she said, as if the answer to his question was a simple one.

He downed a long drink of his soda, then said, ''Grease doesn't wash off silk at all. It stains permanently.''

Brows raised inquisitively, Leah crossed her arms over her chest, which served to prominently display the upper swells of her small, firm breasts. ''And how would you know that?''

The tips of his fingers itched to caress the soft,

plump upper curves spilling from the neckline of
her blouse, but instead he crushed the empty aluminum can in his hand and pitched it into a recycle
bin. "Experience, unfortunately."

"Hmm," she replied thoughtfully. "Do tell."

He hadn't meant to share details of that humili-
ating ordeal, but even now it served as a reminder
that he was and always would be a blue-collar mechanic. "A woman I was dating a while back was
impressed to learn that I owned my own business,
until she unexpectedly stopped by one day and realized that I actually work on the cars in my shop,"
he said wryly. "When I accidentally brushed
against her arm, you'd think I'd committed murder
by the way she shrieked and carried on about her
designer silk blouse being streaked and ruined by
grease." His tone was harsher than he'd expected,
and he cleared his throat. "Pretty nice, huh?"

"Pretty shallow," she countered, and gave a
snort of disgust.

He smiled, appreciating the way she so vehemently defended him. "Women are initially impressed that I run my own business, but once they
learn I repair cars for a living and maintain a modest lifestyle, they tend to become completely dis-
enchanted. The fact that I work in the garages turns
them off, and they move on to someone more exciting."

"They obviously weren't in the relationship for *you*." With a sexy glimmer in her eyes, Leah closed the short distance between them, her chin lifting sassily. "Unlike myself, who wouldn't mind having a handprint or two on my person as a sign of your possession...right here," she grasped his wrist and placed his big palm on her jeans-clad bottom, "and here," she said, and curled his long fingers around the lush softness of her breast.

He skimmed his thumb over the tight nipple beading against his hand, and kneaded the luscious curve of her ass, thrilled by her brazen and arousing advances. Luckily, he didn't have any grease left on his hands, but a part of him wished he did, just to be able to mark her as his in a very elemental, territorial way. But, since permanent handprints weren't possible, he'd just have to claim her in the only other way available.

Squeezing her bottom, he drew her hips to his and bent his head for the deep, hungry kiss he'd been craving since she'd first walked into his private garage. But before their lips could so much as touch, the intercom on the wall buzzed, interrupting the moment and causing Leah to jump out of his embrace, her eyes wide and startled.

"Jace, it's after one, and we're closing up the shop," Gavin announced. "Do you need anything else before we leave?"

Jace pressed the connect button as Leah moved away toward the Camaro parked in the garage. "Just make sure the bays are secure, and lock up the front on your way out."

"Will do," his manager said. "Have a good weekend, and I'll see you early Monday morning."

Jace disconnected the call and returned his attention to Leah, more than a little disappointed that the sensual mood between them had been shattered. So, instead, he watched as she caressed her hand lovingly over the smooth, glossy hood of the vintage vehicle, painted a bright red with two white racing stripes down the center.

"When did your auto shop start working on classics?" she asked curiously.

"We don't. This is mine. I just got it." He came up beside her, wishing those hands of hers were on his body instead of the car. "I've wanted a '67 Chevy Camaro since I was a teenager, and this muscle car was too good a deal to pass up. What do you think?"

"I think it's hot, and a total chick magnet," she said teasingly. "Do you mind if I test it out?"

"Not at all." He opened the driver's side door for her, but instead of sliding behind the wheel, she pushed the front seat forward and crawled into the back. "There's not a whole lot to see and do back there," he said, ducking low to see her.

She reclined against the upholstered seat and shook her head in disagreement. "Don't you think, as a teenager, you would have found plenty of things to do back here with a girl who was hot for you?"

Excitement pumped through him, and he grinned like a fool. "Ahh, so, are you offering to fulfill a teenage boy's fantasy?"

"Absolutely." She crooked her finger at him, a come-hither dare etching her features. "Care to join me?"

Unable to resist such a tempting overture, he slid into the back seat and shut the door behind him, enveloping him in the warmth inside the car, the heady scent of Leah, and the promise of seduction glimmering in her bright-blue eyes.

CHAPTER FOUR

LEAH HAD Jace right where she wanted him. Okay, so maybe the small, cramped back seat of his classic Camaro wasn't as comfortable as a bed but, for the moment, it was absolutely perfect for what she had in mind.

Pressing her hand in the center of his chest, she pushed him back, so that he was reclining against the side of the car. Then she boldly straddled his waist and sat her bottom on his muscular thighs.

"I've never made out in the back of a car before," she said huskily, and scooted closer so that the hard bulge behind the fly of his jeans pressed firmly against the crux of her thighs. "Care to broaden my lessons a little bit?"

He settled his hands at her waist, and ever so slowly tugged the hem of her top out of the waistband of her jeans, his irises turning dark and hot. "Honestly, this is a first for me, too, but I'm sure I can still offer some guidance."

Leah shivered as his fingers strummed across her ribs, and decided if this was his first time making out in the back seat of a car, too—and his newly restored Camaro at that—then she wanted the encounter to be exciting and memorable for him. A treasured recollection that would bring a smile to his face whenever he happened to glance in his rearview mirror.

"Actually, would you mind if *I* took the lead this time, and you just followed along?" she asked.

He grinned indulgently, causing that disarming dimple of his to make an appearance. "God, Leah, that's a request few men could resist."

She pushed his shirt up his torso, and he helped her pull it over his head. "You included?" A hint of insecurity crept into her voice—not many men, if any, had found her sexually irresistible.

He suddenly grew as serious as the question she'd just asked, and it amazed her just how in tune to her feelings he was.

"Especially me, sweetheart," he murmured, and trailed a finger down the low-cut V of her blouse, leaving a tingling sensation in the wake of his heated touch. "Resisting you is becoming damn near impossible."

And for her final day and night with him, that's all she cared about. "Good."

Splaying her hands on his bare chest, she leaned forward and kissed him. Their lips met and meshed damply, and she slipped her tongue inside his mouth to lazily tease and explore and chase his tongue with her own.

His warm palms tunneled beneath her top again, this time to move restlessly up and down her back, then around to her breasts. With her bra still on, he fondled the small, taut mounds of flesh with his hands and lightly pinched her nipples through the material—pleasuring her, yet still allowing her to be the one to dictate the direction of the unfolding seduction.

The rigid length of his erection pressed hard against her sex, and she rocked her hips, creating a pleasurable friction that made him growl deep in his throat and deepen the kiss even more.

Knowing what he wanted, what he craved, she moved her mouth to his jaw, nuzzled his neck, and let her lips and tongue traverse their way lower. She laved his nipples, and his fingers threaded through her hair as her teeth grazed his belly and her tongue dipped into his navel. With his body angled across the back seat, she found a relatively comfortable position between his legs and fumbled with the button on his jeans until she managed to unfasten them. Then, with utmost care, she slowly lowered his zipper, relishing the anticipation of touching him so intimately, of learning his shape and texture and taste without any barriers of clothing between her hands and his flesh.

He caught her wrist before she could go any further, and when she looked up into his face, his expression was taut with restraint, dark with desire and need. "Are you absolutely sure about this?"

"Absolutely, positively." She nipped at him though his cotton briefs, and watched in fascination as his impressive erection twitched. "I want to apply what you taught me last night about a blow job. Not the drink, but the real thing."

His answer was a full-body shudder, and he released her, allowing her to proceed. She grasped the waistband of his jeans and briefs, and he lifted his hips so she could pull them down to his thighs, freeing his shaft. Dampening her lips with her tongue, she touched her fingers to the engorged head of his penis and marveled at how smooth and velvety soft the tip was—a contrast to the hot, hard length of the thick stem.

The sight of him—all virile, aroused male—made her equally hot, and wet too, but this afternoon tryst was solely for him, and she'd get hers later, tonight. Wrapping her fingers tightly around him, she gently fondled the swollen sacs between his legs with her other hand. His breathing quickened and the muscles in his thighs tensed as she parted her lips and enveloped him in the wet heat of her mouth, deeply, eagerly, all the way down to the base of his shaft.

There was something powerfully invigorating about holding the most masculine part of Jace in her mouth and being in complete control of his pleasure. And something wonderfully provocative about him trusting her so unconditionally with the most vulnerable part of his anatomy.

She felt incredibly sexual, so wicked and uninhibited, and her own pulse raced in growing excitement. She wanted desperately to make him come, just like this.

Remembering the techniques he'd taught her the night before, her lips and tongue joined in on the foray, licking and swirling, stroking rhythmically, then finally she added a slick, steady suction that made his hips buck upward and a raw expletive escape his throat.

His fingers tangled in the strands of her hair, alternately pulling her close, then trying to push her away as his climax neared. *"Leah,"* he whispered gruffly, her name a husky warning.

She ignored him and continued resolutely, drawing him deeper and sliding her mouth and tongue wetly down the length of him, then sucking strongly. With a primal groan that rumbled up from his chest, he came, his body taut, his hips arching, as he gave himself over to his release. She stayed with him all the way, until the last tremors ebbed and he slumped back, his head resting against the back of his seat. His eyes were closed, and he was breathing hard, as if he'd just completed a two-mile sprint.

He looked totally, deliciously wasted, and that satisfied Leah more than an orgasm of her own, because she'd been the one to put that dazed look on his face. She moved up beside him and noticed that the windows were steamed from the heat they'd generated. She experienced the girlish impulse to write an intimate note in that fog, an I Love Jace message that would claim him as her own.

Her stomach took a deep free-fall, then her heart followed with erratic pounding as the truth shook her to the core. As a teenager, she'd been infatuated with Jace and had cloaked her attraction to him in friendship. As a woman who was learning about intimacy and passion and experiencing an emotional connection with a man for the very first time, she knew she was falling deeply, irrevocably in love with Jace.

She swallowed hard, knowing she'd never reveal her feelings to him—the last thing she ever wanted was for him to feel forced or obligated to return the sentiment. Their time together was about sex, not love, and she wasn't about to throw him such an unexpected, and likely unwanted, curve halfway through their weekend.

"Well?" she prompted, and nestled against his

neck, determined to keep things light and playful and fun. "Did I pass?"

He laughed, the sound low and rough, as if expressing his amusement took effort. "You're a quick learner." He pried open his eyes to look at her. "You definitely earned an A-plus."

She couldn't stop the silly grin that lifted her lips. "You're a great teacher," she said, returning the compliment. "You do realize, don't you, that we're going to have to make sure that stellar grade-point average doesn't falter."

"Then let's go for some extra credit by letting me return the favor." He fingered the leather ties securing the front placket of her jeans.

Before he could tug open the fly of her pants and make her melt with his deft, skillful touch, she reluctantly moved back, just out of his reach. "As tempting as that sounds, I've got to go."

A frown marred his brow and added to his perplexed expression. "Go where?"

"Shopping."

He pulled his pants back up and fastened them. "Shopping?" he repeated, sounding dumbfounded.

"Yes, shopping." Finding his T-shirt on the seat beside her, she handed it back to him to put on. "I still need to buy a few things for tonight, especially something to wear."

His gaze drifted lazily, hotly, down the length of

her as he undressed her with his eyes. "What if I don't want you wearing anything at all?"

Heat sizzled along her nerve endings, rousing her libido all over again, enticing her to stay and take him up on his offer to return the favor. "Now what fun would that be?" she said with effort. "I want to buy something that teases and tantalizes, and drives you crazy with lust."

He groaned like a dying man. "Ahh, we're back to that again, are we?"

She planted a quick kiss on his lips. "Yep." She was looking forward to finding an outfit that would turn him inside out with burning desire. "If it makes you feel any better, I promise you can have your wicked way with me tonight."

A slow, sinful grin eased up the corner of his mouth, and his green eyes gleamed with anticipation. "You can count on that, sweetheart, because tonight, *I'm* calling the shots."

LATER THAT EVENING, Jace reclined against the sofa in Leah's apartment, watching as she slipped a CD into the stereo player. Within moments, the soft strains of Enya filled the living room and added to the romantic, provocative atmosphere Leah had created for the two of them.

True to her word, Leah had found herself an outfit that had made him instantly hard the moment she'd opened the door and greeted him. The vivid purple silk, lace-edged camisole molded to her breasts, and the matching drawstring pants shimmered along her hips and slender thighs whenever she moved and walked. She'd called the two-piece set a casual lounging outfit, and he countered that the sexy lingerie was downright illegal for any viewing purposes outside of the house.

Not that they were going anywhere tonight, thank God, because he wasn't in the mood to share Leah with anyone.

She lit the half-dozen pillar candles scattered on the nearby tables, wall unit, and shelves, then switched off the lights except for a lamp in the corner. She turned toward him, and the luminescent glow of the candlelight made all her bare skin shimmer with warmth. She'd worn her hair down, and the chestnut strands fell in soft waves to her shoulders. Her eyes held the self-assurance of a woman who knew how the night was going to end.

It was a heady thought to know that the confidence in this exciting woman in front of him was partly a result of their weekend together. Jace suspected she'd always harbored those sensual tendencies; they were just waiting to break free under the right circumstances. With the right man. One who'd take the time and care and allow her to embrace her uninhibited side and indulge in erotic whims and fantasies.

She'd chosen him to be the lucky man to take her on this journey of discovery, and while he accepted that their agreement had included no entanglements or expectations beyond their brief weekend affair, he never would have guessed that he'd become so addicted to everything about her. Like her sweet smiles and infectious laughter. The soft, feminine way she smelled, and how she so effortlessly seduced him in spite of her mistaken impression that she needed lessons to tempt a man. Then there was the way she understood him as had no other woman he'd ever known, and most especially the way she accepted him.

She sat on the cushion next to his, facing him, and curled her legs beneath her. "So, what's on tonight's agenda?" she asked eagerly.

You. Me. Together. Finally, he thought. "Foreplay," he drawled.

A naughty smile canted the corners of her full, glossy lips. "It seems like this weekend has been one long session of foreplay. Not that I'm complaining, mind you."

"Then consider tonight an overview, an enticing and final seduction leading up to the main event." Stretching his arm along the top of the sofa, he rubbed soft strands of her hair between his fingers, which brought back memories of their afternoon together, and how he'd wrapped his hand in those silken tresses while she'd pleasured him with her mouth.

"You have my full attention," she said, prompting him to go on.

He inhaled a slow breath, and focused on the lesson at hand. "Foreplay is the most important part of making love. It's all about taking the time to learn what excites your partner, what makes them hot and bothered, what turns them on. It's all the touching, fondling and kissing that gets your juices flowing and leads up to the actual act of sex."

Placing his free hand on her silk-clad knee, he feathered his thumb along the inside of her leg, demonstrating the arousing effect of an illicit caress. Her breath caught, desire darkened her eyes, and the tips of her breasts tightened against the thin silk of her camisole.

Satisfied with that reaction, he continued. "Foreplay is all about that tickle you feel in your belly when you're excited, and the way your nipples pull tight and ache for the wet heat of my mouth, the soft stroke of my tongue," he murmured, aching to do just that. "It's about you getting wet, and me getting hard."

His blatant description caused her to shiver, but

he wasn't done stimulating her mind and body with his monologue just yet.

"Foreplay is about pushing each other to the absolute limit and sharing mutual pleasure before letting your partner come," he said, and slowly glided his hand higher up her thigh, watching as her lashes fell to half mast and the pulse in her throat quickened. "And there are dozens of different ways to do that."

A lazy smile tipped her lips. "Which begs the question burning in my mind. What excites *you*, Jace?" she asked brazenly.

"Anything that excites *you*," he returned, refusing to let her turn the tables on him. After her generosity with him that afternoon, tonight was all about her sensual gratification, first and foremost, and he meant what he'd said about him being in charge this time.

Deciding it was time to move on to the next phase of their lesson, he slid off the couch and knelt on the plush carpet in front of her. "There's nothing sexier to me than a woman who enjoys the pleasure her own body has to offer, and doesn't hold back in what she wants or needs."

"Right now, I need you to touch me," she whispered. "All over."

"I will," he promised, and pushed her knees wide apart so he could fit in between her spread thighs. "But first, I want you to scoot your bottom to the edge of the couch."

She obeyed, the intimate position forcing her to straddle his waist until the most feminine part of her pressed against his belly and he was eye level with her luscious breasts. Their clothing separated them, but not for long.

He stripped off his shirt and tossed it aside, but left his jeans on for now. She placed her cool palms on his shoulders and let her fingers drift down to his nipples to tease the erect disks. Knowing he'd never last with her touching him so enthusiastically, he gently removed her hands and flattened them on either side of her legs on the couch.

She looked confused, and he sought to reassure her. "Keep your hands to yourself for a little while, and just *feel*."

An adorable pout puffed out her lower lip. "But I want you to enjoy this, too."

"Trust me, I will." Smiling, he leaned forward and gently, softly, kissed her mouth. "Just watching and feeling the way your body responds to me makes me hard, so don't hold back. And don't hesitate to let me know that what I'm doing to you feels good, or to tell me what you want."

He skimmed his damp, open mouth along the side of her neck, and she moaned in encouragement and tipped her chin back to give him better access to her throat.

"Yeah, just like that," he praised and marked her with a love bite right at the sensitive curve of her shoulder, making her gasp in delight. Slipping his fingers beneath the thin straps of her camisole, he pushed them down her arms, causing the silky fabric to pool around her waist. Aching to see her naked, he lifted his head, awed by the beauty of the small but firm rose-tipped breasts that strained toward him, so lush and ripe.

His mouth watered for a taste, and this time when she delved her fingers through his hair and pulled him forward, he didn't have it in him to chastise her for not keeping her hands to herself. She brushed a peaked nipple against his parted lips, and he teased her with a leisurely lick of his tongue over the swollen crest, and the warmth of his breath along her damp skin.

She moved restlessly against him and her thighs clenched at his hips. "Take me in your mouth, all the way," she begged.

He kneaded her breasts, closed his lips over the engorged flesh and all but devoured her with his hot, hungry mouth. And still, it wasn't enough for either of them. He sucked her deeply, strongly, using his teeth and tongue to heighten the sensations rippling through her and increasing the heat burning him up inside.

She arched into him, breathless and impatient, and tried to pull him on top of her.

Instead, he pressed her back against the sofa, let his mouth move down to her stomach, and rasped, "I'm not done with you yet."

He dipped his tongue into her navel for a leisurely taste, and she squirmed and groaned restlessly. He pulled at the ties of her silky pants, loosening the waistband. Then he tugged the bottoms down her long legs and off. He removed her camisole as well, leaving her scantily clad in a pair of insubstantial lace panties. The deep shade of purple was an erotic contrast to her pale skin.

He looked up and met her drowsy gaze, glittering from the candlelight. He took in her flushed face, waiting to find a trace of modesty, possibly even a bit of reserve, but finding none.

"Take them off," she said, granting him her consent, her ultimate acquiescence, and letting him know she was in this all the way.

Relief surged through him, and he hooked his thumbs into the elastic leg bands of her panties and peeled the scrap of damp fabric off. He splayed his hand on her belly and slowly dragged his palm downward, until his thumb grazed across her tight clit, then burrowed between her slick folds. She was hot and wet, and so incredibly sexy, her delectable body all his for the taking.

Soon.

She closed her eyes, clutched at the edge of the

sofa cushion, and gyrated her hips against his hand. He stroked her rhythmically, watching as she let every one of her inhibitions slip away, watching as she tried to grasp that illusive orgasm he deliberately kept just out of her reach.

"Jace...*please*."

He eased one finger, then two, deep inside her, and her inner muscles instantly contracted around him. "*This* is foreplay, sweetheart."

She made a low, raw sound of need. "This is sheer torture."

His cock throbbed painfully against the confines of the denim, echoing her sentiment, but he'd ignore his own discomfort until he'd satisfied her. "Tell me what you want, and I'll give it to you."

"Let me come." She bit her bottom lip, then revealed more tentatively, "I want to feel your mouth on me."

There was no denying Leah anything, and this was something he wanted just as badly. Withdrawing his fingers, and ignoring her moan of protest, he grasped her bottom and pulled her closer to the edge of the sofa. He draped her legs over his shoulders and lowered his head, rubbed his stubbled cheek against the inside of her smooth thigh, and let his open mouth drift upward as he licked and kissed and gently bit her flesh along the way.

By the time he reached her core, her hands were tangled in his hair and she was panting in anticipation. He inhaled the heady, rich scent of her, all aroused woman, then closed his mouth over her sex and pressed his tongue deep, swirling and teasing and suckling greedily on her hot, sweet flesh.

Her back bowed and she released a ragged moan as she erupted into a shattering climax. Sheer primal lust reared through Jace, along with the desperate urgency to possess her in the most elemental, physical way possible. He wanted Leah so much that he shook with the force of his need. He couldn't wait another minute to have her—as hard and fast and deep as she'd allow.

Leah gasped for breath, still trembling from the aftershocks of her orgasm as the sensual haze clouding her mind dissipated and her surroundings, and Jace, gradually came back into focus. He was still kneeling in front of her, and she watched as he dug a condom from the front pocket of his pants, then unfastened his jeans and shoved them down to his thighs, freeing his thick erection. Ripping open the foil packet, he gritted his teeth as he rolled the snug latex over his shaft, then glanced back up at her, his eyes hot and hungry and demanding.

Leah fully expected him to take her on the couch, but instead he pulled her down to the floor with him and gently turned her around so that she was facing the sofa and her arms were braced on the cushions. He kneed her legs apart and pressed his groin against her bottom. She swallowed hard as she felt the head of his penis nudge along the wet, swollen tissues of her sex, and knew he was going to take her in this untamed, primitive way. It was what she wanted, too—to be thoroughly possessed by Jace and be the recipient of his wild passion. It was a heady thought to realize that she'd driven him to this extreme.

The thrill of the forbidden beckoned, and she glanced over her shoulder at him, letting him know that she trusted him, with her body, her heart, her soul. She was all his for the taking.

With a low, rumbling growl, he gripped her waist and entered her in one long, driving stroke that made Leah toss her head back and gasp as he filled her to the hilt. Then there was only pleasure and friction and heat as he pumped harder, faster, deeper, and she undulated her hips sinuously and instinctively pushed back against him, matching the frenzied rhythm of his thrusts.

He leaned more fully into her, covering her from behind. He grazed his mouth across her shoulder and sank his teeth into the taut tendons along her neck, adding to the erotic sensations spiraling within her. His movements became more frantic, more urgent. His hands slipped around to her breasts, fondling them, rolling her nipples between his fingers, then he stroked her belly and lower, where they were joined.

Another firm stroke, another sleek caress, and she arched against his hips as her climax hit and she contracted and convulsed around his shaft. Her breath came out on a low, earthy moan that seemingly obliterated the last thin thread of his restraint. Jace's entire body stiffened then shuddered as he rode out the pulsating waves of his own orgasm.

He slumped against her, a quivering mass of spent energy. Remaining inside her, he nuzzled her neck, placed a sweet kiss on her cheek, and murmured, "I can't believe I took you like an animal."

She glanced over her shoulder and met his contrite gaze. Knowing he was about to plead for her forgiveness, she refused to allow him the opportunity to dilute what they'd just shared. "Don't you dare apologize for the best sex I've ever had," she said adamantly.

Jace chuckled, grateful that Leah was open to a bit of sexual adventure. "All right, I won't apologize because that was the best sex I can remember ever having, too."

Which said a helluva lot for the woman he was with. He'd had good sex before, but he'd never lost control as he had with Leah. And even though he'd just had her, he was far from sated. He feared it would take him a lifetime to get his fill of her.

Unfortunately, he only had this one night left to satisfy any and all cravings he had for Leah. And he planned to take full advantage of that fact.

Despite her assurance that she didn't mind his more aggressive side when it came to sex, he didn't want to leave her with that unrefined impression of him. "At least let me make love to you properly on a soft, warm mattress instead of both of us kneeling on your living-room floor.''

She sighed, her smile as intimate as a kiss. ''Now that's an offer I'm not about to refuse. My knees do feel a bit rug-burned.''

He laughed in agreement and, minutes later, after she'd blown out all the candles and he'd made a quick trip to the bathroom, he met Leah in her bedroom. She was already lying on the bed waiting for him, beautifully naked and temptingly tousled. With a sultry look in her eyes, she feathered the tips of her fingers along her flat belly and strummed them up to her breasts, arousing herself with that lazy caress.

Mesmerized, he strolled to the foot of the mattress. The lamp on the nightstand allowed him to view every intimate dip, curve, and feminine swell of her body. And just looking at her made him so damn hard he hurt—from his chest all the way down to his groin.

''It appears you're very happy to see me,'' she teased, her gaze riveted to the erection nearly parallel to his stomach.

''You're beautiful,'' he said huskily, branding this moment in his mind for those long, lonely nights ahead.

''So are you,'' she replied just as reverently.

He'd brought with him the other prophylactics he'd had in his jeans pocket, and he tossed all but one of them on the vacant pillow next to Leah, knowing he'd likely use every single condom before the night was through.

He sheathed his shaft and crawled up onto the mattress. Starting at Leah's ankles, he leisurely worked his way upward, worshiping every inch of her body with his mouth and his hands, intending to make this time around a long, slow buildup of pleasure. Easing her legs apart, he grazed her inner thigh with his lips, his warm breath, and let his tongue stroke and gently explore her tender flesh before moving on. His palms caressed her hips, he kissed her quivering belly, and paid homage to both breasts, then suckled Leah's jutting nipples until she writhed restlessly beneath him and he knew she was more than ready for him.

He moved over her, positioned himself between her spread thighs, and groaned when she wrapped her legs around his waist and pulled him forward. He was poised at her hot, wet center, a thrust away from being inside her liquid heat. He wanted her so desperately, far beyond this physical joining, and the depth of his need made him feel stripped down to his soul, for the first time in his entire life.

Oh, God he loved her.

Bracing his arms at the sides of her head, he stared deep into her eyes, his heart pounding relentlessly in his chest as he let the realization settle over him. Out of all the lessons he'd taught Leah this weekend, this joining was by far the most profound, and he wanted to be sure she knew it, too.

"*This* is the way it's supposed to be between a man and a woman," he murmured. *Magical. Sublime. Emotional.*

He slowly pressed deep into the tight heat of her body, and she clenched around him, so soft and giving, and so incredibly, perfectly right.

"Oh, Jace," she whispered, and he could have sworn he saw tears gather in her eyes before she pulled his mouth down to hers for a searing, tongue-tangling kiss.

This time around, he took her on a slow, sweet journey, the intensity of it rising steadily, leisurely. She climaxed first, and only then did he let go and lose himself in the ecstasy and pure emotion of being such an intrinsic part of her.

CHAPTER FIVE

LEAH KNEW the moment she awoke the following morning that there was no way she'd be able to accept Brent's proposal. Not when she'd spent the most glorious night of her life with another man. Jace had shown her how hot passion could burn between a man and woman, had spent the weekend teaching her that she was irresistible and desirable. Just thinking of how thoroughly Jace had made love to her last night, and again earlier this morning, made her body tingle with renewed heat.

She rolled over in her bed and discovered she was alone, but the muted sounds coming from the kitchen and the scent of freshly percolated coffee assured her that Jace was still there. She was comforted by the fact that he hadn't skipped out on her, even as she dreaded facing him this morning, knowing that their affair was over.

Just as her relationship with Brent was over. As soon as he returned from his business trip this afternoon, she'd not only tell him that she could not marry him, but she'd also explain that their relationship was lacking all the important elements she now knew were necessary to sustain a lasting marriage. Not just fantastic sex, but the kind of emotional bond that had been missing between them— the kind of intimate connection she'd experienced with Jace last night, when he'd been buried deep inside her, and when he'd held her so securely while she'd slept.

She cared for Brent, and in hindsight she knew he'd done her a huge favor by putting off a physical relationship with her. If they had slept together, she never would have pursued Jace, and she never would have known how amazing and unforgettable their time together would be. And, quite possibly, she would have accepted Brent's proposal for all the wrong reasons, mostly because he was offering her all the things she wanted in her life.

Yes, she wanted to get married. Yes, she wanted kids and a family of her own. None of those dreams had changed, but she, as a person, had evolved because of Jace's belief in her, and she liked the sensual, self-assured woman she'd become. One determined not to settle for anything less than honesty, mutual attraction and unconditional love. Which was everything she felt for Jace.

The realization made her heart hurt, because he was the one man she wanted for a lifetime but would never have. He'd given her exactly what she'd asked for—lessons on how to arouse a man and two nights of incredible passion. He'd made her no promises beyond this weekend, and she'd known from the beginning that he had no interest in being involved in a committed relationship. She wasn't about to break the rules they'd established and pressure him for anything more than what they'd agreed to. Their friendship was too important to her to risk, and she'd make the transition from lovers back to friends as smooth as possible for both of them.

With an aching sigh, she drew his pillow to her chest, buried her face in the softness, and inhaled the purely masculine scent of Jace. She closed her eyes, trying to squelch the misery working its way to the surface, and instead focused on gathering the fortitude to face him after last night and not give away how much she loved him.

Oh, Lord, getting Jace out of her system had been a good idea at the time, but never would she have guessed her plan would backfire and leave her so heartsick and emotionally devastated. And feeling more alone than she'd ever felt before.

Knowing she couldn't stall the inevitable forever, she got out of bed, slipped into her favorite chenille robe, then brushed her teeth and attempted to restore some order to her wild, disheveled hair. Heading down the hall, she entered her small kitchen and found Jace sitting at the table, drinking a cup of coffee and perusing a piece of paper in his hand. A slight frown marred his dark brows.

She was disappointed to discover that he was already dressed in his jeans, shirt and shoes, as if last night had never happened. As if he didn't plan on sticking around for long. It was obvious there would be no morning-after intimacy between them, and she berated herself for wanting a few more moments with him when she had no right to expect anything more than he'd already given her.

"Good morning," she said softly, and padded the rest of the way into the kitchen.

He glanced up and smiled. "Hi."

She thought she saw a glimmer of yearning in his eyes, but it was quickly masked by a reserve that made Leah's stomach twist with dread. She hated that a part of him had withdrawn from her, but she couldn't blame him for being cautious, for making the end to their affair as cut-and-dried as possible.

She ought to do the same, mostly to preserve their friendship, and that meant holding her emotions in check until he left.

"What's this?" he asked curiously, and turned the paper in his hand around for her to see.

Ahh, she thought, recognizing the *Sexcapades* invitation she'd taken from Divine Events two days ago that had prompted her to proposition Jace. She'd left the paper on the table, on top of a pile of magazines and mail, never thinking that he might find it or question her about it.

She bit her bottom lip as the words "The Dance of the Seven Veils" mocked her, forcing her to remember her inability to test out her feminine wiles on Brent. All for good reason, she realized now, and was grateful she hadn't attempted to try and seduce him when he wasn't the right man for her. On the other hand, she would have been more than willing to perform the dance for Jace, given the chance. He'd given her that confidence, had coaxed her to embrace her uninhibited side and enjoy the pleasures her body had to offer.

"*That* is a provocative invitation I took from a book I found at the wedding planner's boutique last Friday," she replied, and headed over to the counter to pour herself a cup of coffee.

"What were you doing at a wedding planner's?" he asked with tension in his voice as she filled his mug with the steaming brew, too, then returned the carafe back to the burner.

With her back facing him, she stirred cream and sugar into her coffee and drew a deep breath, knowing Jace deserved to hear the truth. All of it. About her and Brent. About the invitation that had played on her insecurities, and Jace's part in it all. She owed him that much.

Cradling the warmth of the mug in her hands, she turned back around. "I was at a wedding planners because Brent asked me to marry him."

Jace stared at her in incredulous shock. "He did?"

She nodded and took a sip of her coffee, unable to look Jace in the eyes, afraid to see condemnation in them for the weekend she'd spent with him now that he knew the truth. "I asked him to give me some time to think about his proposal, and he gave it to me. He's been out of town, and I thought maybe going to see a wedding planner might help with my decision." She left out the part about her experiencing a bout of anxiety the moment she'd walked into Divine Events, opting to keep those uncertainties to herself. "But, instead, I found an erotic book of invitations titled *Sexcapades,* and I took one of the pages inside."

Finally, she glanced at him and wanted to weep with relief when she saw no signs of censure or criticism in his expression. He sat there patiently, waiting for her to continue.

"When I read the invitation, my first thought was that I couldn't imagine performing that intimate dance for Brent." She let Jace come to his own conclusions about those reasons. "So, I enlisted your help to teach me how to please and arouse a man, and to show me what they find exciting and—"

"—what drives them crazy with lust," he finished for her, a wry grin tipping the corners of his mouth.

"Yes, that too," she said quietly.

He stood and strolled across the kitchen, bringing his mug with him and setting it in the sink. "You're a natural, Leah. Don't ever doubt what a sensual, desirable woman you are."

Maybe we're just great together, and you bring out the best in me, she thought, but kept the comment to herself.

Jace moved in front of Leah and brushed his knuckles across her warm, soft cheek, unable to resist touching her any longer. He felt so torn up inside, aching to take Leah back to bed and keep her there forever, yet knowing he didn't have that right.

"Tell me something," he murmured, following the lapels of her robe down to where it crisscrossed over her breasts. Jace had to forcibly hold back the urge to strip her bare and take her right there on the kitchen counter one last time. "After this weekend, do you have the confidence to perform that Dance of the Seven Veils?"

"Yeah," she whispered huskily. "Yeah, I do.

You gave me the confidence, and I appreciate everything you taught me this weekend, most especially to believe in myself and to embrace my sensual side.''

And now he was going to send her back to Brent, armed with all the seductive knowledge he'd taught her, and he wanted to roar with the injustice of it all. Except he'd gotten exactly what he'd agreed to, and she'd gotten precisely what she'd asked for.

Good God, when had the arrangement gone so emotionally awry?

"I have to go," he said abruptly. His chest felt tight, and he desperately needed air and space. He had to get the hell out of there.

He turned to leave, but made it only as far as the living room before Leah chased after him. She clutched his arm, giving him no choice but to stop. He caught the hopeful look in her eyes and his heart leapt up into his throat, nearly strangling him.

"Jace…" Her voice trailed off, but there was no mistaking the uncertainty in her tone, as if she were afraid to speak what was truly on her mind.

"Yes?" he asked, his voice rough and gravely like never before.

"I…"

He held his breath, waiting, a part of him praying for the impossible.

"Thank you," she finally said instead, and followed that up with what appeared to be a forced, and very brave, smile. "For everything."

"You're welcome...for everything," he replied, and gently kissed her temple one last time before heading out the door.

JACE GAVE the wrench another forceful push and ended up stripping the bolt, causing his knuckles to scrape along the edge of the exhaust manifold.

"Shit," he cursed, and tossed the tool onto the bench with a loud clatter. He glanced down at his hand and winced at the two knuckles he'd skinned, now bleeding. Stalking to the first-aid kit on the wall next to the back sink, he opened it and withdrew the medicinal aids he needed to disinfect the cuts.

After leaving Leah's several hours ago, he'd come directly to his shop to do more engine repairs on his Camaro. Normally, working on cars proved soothing to him, a way to calm his nerves when he was feeling uptight, but nothing could shake the agitation riding him hard.

No matter what he did, Jace couldn't keep his mind off Leah. Couldn't stop thinking about her going back to Brent, accepting his proposal, and doing that veil striptease for him—a preppy executive who didn't seem to appreciate Leah for the woman she was. And, mostly, he couldn't stop be-rating himself for being such an idiot and walking out on her earlier. He'd left because of the promise he'd made before their weekend together, and because he believed it was the right thing to do.

He wasn't so sure anymore.

Taking out the small bottle of antiseptic, he clenched his jaw as he scrubbed his wounds with the astringent, wondering when he, someone who'd always been a fighter, had become such a coward. He was so hung up on the fact that Leah deserved better than a kid who'd grown up on the wrong side of the tracks, a mechanic who spent his days elbow-deep in grease, that he couldn't get past the possibility that maybe, just maybe, she'd take him, as is…. Yet he'd done nothing, absolutely nothing, to sway her to take a chance on him.

His heart thudded hard in his chest as he cast a quick glance around his private garage, seeing all that he'd accomplished over the years, and realized that *he* was the one with the hang-ups. And that meant he was going to have to step up to the plate and get over the insecurities he'd lived with since childhood. He might not be some fancy-schmancy executive, but he owned his own business and supported himself with plenty left over. It was about damn time he had more faith in himself, and if there was going to be a man in Leah's life, it was going to be him.

Because that man certainly wasn't Brent.

He patched up his knuckles with a few Band-Aids, now mentally prepared to fight for Leah, and to hell with the consequences he might have to suffer with her family and her brother—his best friend. He'd deal with them later, and make sure they knew he'd never, ever hurt Leah. That she was incredibly precious to him, and he'd do whatever it took to make her happy.

But first, he had to stop her from making the biggest mistake of her life—and his. As he locked up the shop, he prayed he wasn't too late.

IT WAS OVER with Brent, and Leah was more relieved than she'd ever thought possible. She was also grateful that he'd taken the breakup so well, but his lack of anger or hurt feelings just reinforced the fact that he hadn't had a whole lot invested in their relationship—emotionally or physically.

Yes, he'd been disappointed, but he'd wished her well and seemed to mean it. The whole encounter had been disturbing because she'd seen so clearly that she would have been nothing more than a convenient wife and social hostess for him had she accepted his proposal. Ending their relationship had, undoubtedly, been the right thing to do.

And she had Jace to thank for that. For making her realize she didn't have to settle for less than the real thing. Now, as she stared at her reflection in her dresser mirror, scantily clad in a sexy bra and panties and sheer, colorful scarves, she was a nervous wreck. More so than she'd been breaking off her relationship with Brent. Her stomach was in knots, her heart was a tangled mess. So much was riding on this, because she intended to seduce Jace back into her life on a permanent basis. He'd been the one to teach her all about the power and sensuality of being a woman, and it was only fitting that she return the favor by showing him what an avid student she'd been—by performing the Dance of the Seven Veils for his eyes only.

Tonight, she'd not only give him her body, but her heart and soul, as well.

A knock on the door startled her, since she wasn't expecting company. She quickly grabbed a knee-length coat from the coat closet to cover her skimpy, barely-there outfit, and tightened the sash. One quick glance through the peephole revealed Jace standing on the other side of the threshold.

Surprised by his unexpected visit, she opened the door, taking in his fierce expression. His thick hair was mussed as though he'd repeatedly finger-combed it. Restless energy seemed to radiate off him.

"Jace," she said breathlessly, and with more

than a little uncertainty. "I was just coming to see you."

"Good, then I saved you a trip," he replied, all dominant male, and moved past her to enter without an invitation. As if she'd ever deny him entrance into any part of her life.

"You certainly did." Closing the door, she leaned against the hard slab of wood, trying like mad to figure out why he'd returned and failing to come up with any answer that made sense.

So, she asked outright. "What are you doing here?"

He jammed his hands on his lean hips, his stance uncompromising. "You can't marry Brent."

His order was the last thing she'd expected to hear pop out of his mouth, but his possessive demand made her feel giddy and kicked up her pulse an optimistic notch. But before she relieved Jace of his mistaken assumption, she needed to hear the reasons behind his adamant request.

"Why not?" she asked.

"Because for as long as I can remember, I've wanted you, and after this weekend, I can't let you go off and marry another man, especially one who doesn't appreciate you in all the ways that matter."

Her breath caught and held in her throat, cutting off her ability to speak. But he seemed to have plenty to say, so she remained where she was against the door and just listened.

"I've been running from any kind of emotional commitment since I was a kid, first because of my father's abandonment, then my mother's rejection, and I just didn't believe I had what it took to give to another person in that way. It was so much easier, and simpler, to remain single and alone than to let anyone close." He took a step toward her, closing the distance separating them, filling the air she breathed with the intoxicating scent of orange. "Except you always had a way of being there for me," he murmured gently, "even when I didn't realize how much I needed you in my life."

She melted inside, his words touching her deeply, profoundly. "That's what a friend is for."

"Yes, you're a friend, but you've always tempted me, Leah, and I've fought my attraction to you for years."

Her eyes widened. "You have?"

"More than you'll ever know." Bracing an arm on the door behind her, he lowered his head and skimmed his lips along her throat, making her shiver from the delicious, intimate contact. "You understand who I am and where I've come from, and you accept me for the person I've become— you did that even before I did. I want to learn to give in return, to be the kind of man you want and need in your life. Just give me that chance.''

''It's yours, Jace,'' she said huskily, and, framing his face in her hands, she pulled him back so she could look into his eyes. ''*I'm* yours.''

He pressed his forehead against hers. ''Then tell Brent no.'' His tone was ragged, desperate.

She smiled and kissed his lips. ''I already have. I had doubts before our weekend together, but after being with you, I knew I couldn't marry Brent.''

He shuddered, his relief palpable. ''Thank God.'' Then another round of doubts darkened his gaze. ''Your family has been so good to me, and I don't want to disappoint your parents or your brother by getting involved with you.''

''Oh, Jace…disappointing them is impossible. They love you as much as I do, and you're already a part of the family.''

He reared back, caught her under the chin with his fingers, and stared deeply into her eyes, watching her face carefully. ''You love me?''

She nodded jerkily, her heart swelling with the emotion. ''For longer than I can remember.''

''I love you, too,'' he said and flashed her a dimpled grin as he tugged on the ties of her coat, loosening them. ''And I think we've wasted way too much time being friends, and have a helluva lot of loving to make up for.''

Desire rippled through her, warm and exciting. "I couldn't agree with you more." Cool air washed over Leah's bare skin as he opened the lapels of her coat and pushed them wide apart.

He gaped at the sheer outfit she wore, and his brows snapped into a protective frown. "Jesus, Leah, where in the hell were you going dressed like this?"

"To see you. To dance and strip for you. To be your every fantasy. To tempt you to enjoy an invitation to seduction and put to good use everything you've taught me this weekend." Grabbing his hand, she led him into the living room and pushed him down onto the easy chair, then she dimmed the lights and switched on the stereo, which still held the Enya CD. "But since you came to me, I'll just have to improvise."

The soft strains of music filled the room, and she let the sensual beat infuse her mind and soul and stimulate the confidence Jace had instilled in her. Then, to an avid audience of one, she began moving slowly, gyrating gracefully, her body picking up on the evocative rhythm and making it her own.

As she lost herself in the music and the hot look in Jace's eyes as he watched her, she pulled away one of the scarves she'd tucked into her lacy bra and let it flow over her curves, across her belly, and along her thighs before dropping the silky fabric to the floor at her feet. Then she started the process again, gracefully twisting and turning—methodically, temptingly, stripping away the veils and creating an aura of sexual excitement with each scarf she removed.

She shimmied out of her bra and panties too, and smiled as he tugged off his shirt and skinned out of his jeans so he was just as naked as she was. His need for her was visible, and she went to him without hesitation. She straddled his hips and sank down on his shaft, taking him all the way. They moaned simultaneously, letting the pleasure of the moment gradually, leisurely sweep them away. Wonderful minutes later, Leah slumped against Jace's chest and rested her cheek against his shoulder, replete and happy, their heartbeats mingling.

"That was nice," Jace murmured as he caressed a hand along her spine, holding her close. "Very nice. I taught you well."

She laughed. "Yes, you did."

His fingers slid into the hair at the nape of her neck and gently drew her head back so that she was looking into his eyes, which had grown serious and searching.

"What is it?" she asked.

He exhaled a deep breath. "Being friends and all, I think we know just about everything we could possibly know about each other, don't you?"

She thought about all the years between them. "Pretty close, but I'm sure there're a few surprises that will crop up along the way." She grinned. "Luckily, I like surprises."

"Me, too." And then he gave her the biggest surprise of all. "Marry me, Leah. I love you and I swear I'll do everything in my power to make you happy. And I want babies with you, a family—"

She covered his mouth with her hand to cut off his rambling so she could get a word in edgewise. "Yes, Jace," she said, amazed at how an erotic invitation had changed the course of her future and had given her her heart's desire. "Yes, I'll marry you."

And as he kissed her again, long and slow and deep, Leah knew their lessons weren't over, that they'd only just begun. She was certain it was going to take a lifetime for them to teach one another all the pleasures of satisfying one another…in bed, in life and in love. And she was more than up for the adventure.

* * * * *

1

"I WANT YOU."

"Oh, you do, do you?" Michaela asked, her eyebrow arched. "And just how much are you willing to give to get me?"

For an instant, Bas had thought Michaela Carmichael would be shocked by his admission. Maybe even intimidated. Scared. He was, after all, Sebastian Stone, the mysterious millionaire venture capitalist who lived on his airplane and regularly circled the globe in search of the ultimate deal. But Michaela, Micki to her street friends, didn't give two flips about who he was.

However, *what he wanted* intrigued her quite a bit. He'd misjudged her. It wouldn't happen again. And yet, his error verified a dark, enthralling suspicion—his need for this sassy sprite of a woman had pushed him into new territory. He'd made his millions by thinking one step ahead of both his business partners and his corporate rivals. He knew the content of their next thoughts before the ideas formed in their minds.

But with Michaela, he had no idea what to expect, what to anticipate. Luckily for both of them, he rather liked the novel sensation. Not nearly as much as he enjoyed the soft flutter of her skin against his, but he'd adjust.

"Tell me what *you* want," he said, certain he could fulfill any request.

She leaned back against the seat and crossed one leather-encased leg over the other. "That's a tall order. You see, I want a lot. And interestingly, you're bound by your promise to give me my heart's desire."

Bas cleared his throat and sat forward, his elbows on his knees. In the tight confines of the limousine, the warmth from her skin seemed to seep between the seams of his tailored wool suit, injecting him with her musky, scented body heat. A rim of perspiration formed just beneath his mustache and when he licked his lips, he could taste the salty flavor. Only he didn't want to taste his own sweat—he wanted to taste hers. Her sweat, her skin, her mouth. Her sweet center.

The memory of her, naked, crept into his mind. Flesh pink and ripe from the heat of the shower, nipples puckered and pointed. With her heavy-handed makeup swirling down the drain, he'd caught a quick glimpse of Michaela's natural beauty, making him ache for her in a way he'd never experienced.

And what Bas wanted, he got. End of story. If he managed to fulfill her wishes at the same time, that would be the icing on the proverbial cake.

"Let's get one thing straight," he said. "I promised Danielle that I would make your fantasies come true, yes. I intend to keep that promise. But if I didn't want you for myself, I would have found a loophole in my vow. I don't do anything I don't want to do."

She narrowed her gaze, skewering him with glints of sapphire blue. "Aren't you a man of your word?"

"No man's word is more solid than mine. Trust me. But you need to know that I want you because *I* want you, not because my sister asked me to fulfill some matchmaking fantasy of hers."

"Matchmaking?" she asked, disbelief in her humorless smile. "Danielle didn't say you had to fulfill my *sexual* fantasies."

He chuckled. "Are there any other kinds?"

Bas may have been a notorious shark in the business world, but he always played on the up-and-up with women. He'd continue with Michaela, even if the truth rankled. The more successful his business became, the less often he had time for lovers. When he did pursue a woman, the attraction usually boiled down to his coveting the pleasure her body would give him while she coveted the luxury provided by his cash. And even though most of the women he dallied with had bank accounts that didn't exactly rival his, none had been strapped for capital. They'd wanted sex with a multi-millionaire. He'd simply wanted sex.

From Michaela, he knew he wanted more. The sex was a given. No man could possibly resist her compelling combination of strength and sass. But beneath her street-tough exterior, she possessed a latent sensuality, a vulnerability that a less observant, less in-tune man might have missed. Yet, something more niggled at the edges of his consciousness—something subtle, unnamed. Something he knew he wouldn't identify until he had Micki with him in the sky, en route to whatever destination she chose.

Fascinating.

"Sexual fantasies are the most interesting, aren't they?" she asked.

"They can be."

He saw an idea flash in her eyes. A potential for risk. Before he could ask her what she was thinking, she bent forward and retrieved her backpack.

"I can't believe I'm going to do this…" she muttered, unzipping the largest compartment and tossing random clothes aside. She shoved the pack back onto the floor of the limousine when she had what she wanted.

A big red book.

Aha! The big red book she'd shoved under the covers just this morning.

"Is this a diary?" he asked, knowing it wasn't.

"Yeah, do I look like the journal-keeping type?"

"Your look defies your type, Michaela."

Her eyes widened, but she ignored his assessment. No matter. They had plenty of time for conversation later.

"This was a present from my sister."

"Aurora?"

"Rory," she corrected. Bas couldn't understand why either twin would shorten such beautiful, musical names, but for the sister, he'd concede to the nickname. For Michaela, he would not.

Michaela handed him the book, which bore no title on the faux leather cover. He flipped to the first page. As practiced as he was in hiding his reactions, he couldn't contain a shocked chuckle at the title.

"Sexcapades?" he read, eyeing her with an arched brow. Amazingly, he'd heard of the book. A collection of sealed sexual fantasies, intended for use by lovers requiring challenge to spice up their love lives. He'd never imagined he'd need help or instruction in sensual matters—but what the hell.

With Michaela, even the most ignominious activity could prove incredible.

"Intrigued?" she asked.

He flipped the page, then ran his finger down the gap inside the spine, where dozens of pages had been torn from their perforations. He wondered if Michaela had availed herself of the sexual suggestions, or if her sister had used them. Not that he cared one way or the other.

He ran through a few pages, reading the fancy scripted titles aloud. "'Feed Me', 'World Series Workout', 'Gypsy Magic.' Intriguing doesn't begin to describe it."

She grabbed the book from his hands, shuffled through the remaining pages with keen familiarity, and then, after taking a deep breath, tugged one fantasy free. She slid the book off her lap and held the chosen sexcapade flush against her chest—as flush as a woman could with such curvaceous breasts.

"This one," she said simply, decisive energy dancing in her eyes.

He held out his hand. "May I see?"

"Not until you agree," she insisted, clutching the page tighter to her blouse.

Bas sat back, narrowing his gaze, surveying the way she trembled with wicked anticipation. He glanced at the wrinkled page hugging her breasts and knew he'd do just about anything to be right where the paper was at this very moment.

"Fine. I **agree**. Now show me what I have to do."

Is your man too good to be true?

Hot, gorgeous AND romantic?
If so, he could be a Harlequin® Blaze™ series cover model!

Our grand-prize winners will receive a trip for two to New York City to
shoot the cover of a Blaze novel, and will stay at the luxurious Plaza Hotel.
Plus, they'll receive $500 U.S. spending money!
The runner-up winners will receive $200 U.S.
to spend on a romantic dinner for two.

It's easy to enter!

In 100 words or less, tell us what makes your boyfriend or spouse a true romantic
and the perfect candidate for the cover of a Blaze novel, and include in your submission
two photos of this potential cover model.

All entries must include the written submission of the contest entrant, two photographs of the model
candidate and the Official Entry Form and Publicity Release forms completed in full and signed by
both the model candidate and the contest entrant. Harlequin, along with the experts at
Elite Model Management, will select a winner.

For photo and complete Contest details, please refer to the Official Rules on the next page. All entries
will become the property of Harlequin Enterprises Ltd. and are not returnable.

Please visit www.blazecovermodel.com to download a copy of the Official Entry Form and
Publicity Release Form or send a request to one of the addresses below.

Please mail your entry to: **Harlequin Blaze Cover Model Search**

In U.S.A.	In Canada
P.O. Box 9069	P.O. Box 637
Buffalo, NY	Fort Erie, ON
14269-9069	L2A 5X3

No purchase necessary. Contest open to Canadian and U.S. residents who are 18 and over.
Void where prohibited. Contest closes September 30, 2003.

HBCVRMODEL1

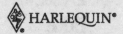

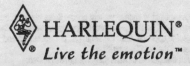

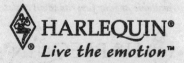

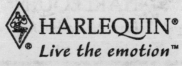